THE SUMMER RESORT

A SEASON OF CHANGE

2015

This is a work of fiction. Names, characters, events, and incidents are products of the author's imagination, or used in a fictitious way. Any resemblance to actual persons, living or dead, or actual events is purely coincidental.

While the Resort is a fictitious place, much of the geographic layout comes from Lumina Resort, located on the beautiful Lake of Bays.

Cover design by Damonza.com

Layout by Chrissy @ Indie Publishing Group

ISBN 978-1-7752965-0-8

Davidsinclairbooks@gmail.com

No one saves us but ourselves.
No one can and no one may.
We ourselves must walk the path.

– Buddha

Character List

THE GUESTS

THE LAPOINTE FAMILY

- *Stéphane LaPointe* – 60 years old (born 1955), from Montreal, owns a Law firm, divorced from wife Marion five years ago, now married to his former legal assistant Annette, stays in 'Pigeon'.
- *Marion LaPointe* (also Meme, Maman) – 55 years old (born 1960), first wife of Stéphane, divorced 5 years, has a dog named Bijou, stays in 'Cardinal'.
- *Annette Link* – 32 years old (born 1984), second wife to Stéphane, was a legal assistant at his law firm, having an affair with Stéphane two or three years prior to divorce, originally from Ottawa.
- ***Sarah Murray** (née LaPointe)* – 30 years old (born 1985), eldest daughter of LaPointe family, got her law degree but did not become a lawyer, now does legal counselling, married to Chris Murray 3 years.

- ***Chris Murray*** – 33 years old (born 1982), architect, married to Sarah 3 years, coming to the Resort for 5 years, stays in 'Blue Jay' with Sarah.

- *Daniel LaPointe* – 28 years old (born 1987), finished law school and joined the family business, single, enjoys a good party, stays in 'Pigeon' with Stéphane and Annette.

- ***Craig LaPointe*** – 26 years old (born 1989), chose not to study law like the rest of the family, became a mechanic, dating Terry for about a year, stays in 'Whistling Duck' with Terry.

- *Terry Duschene* – 26 years old (born 1989), studying to be a teacher, girlfriend of Craig.

- *Chantelle LaPointe* – 19 years old (born 1995), youngest daughter of family, moved out of the house at 16.

THE WATSON FAMILY

- *Walter Watson* – 55 years old (born 1960), businessman and investor, very wealth, brother named Gerry, stays in 'Crane' with family.

- *Selina Watson* – 53 years old (born 1963), has a dog named Buddy.

- *Michelle Edwards (née Watson)* – 27 years old (born 1988), architect, married one year to Brad Edwards.

- *Emma Watson* – 25 years old (born 1990), studying psychology at McGill University.

THE WEBERS

- *Hugo Weber* – 74 years old (born 1941), from Buffalo, NY, coming to the Resort for 48 years.
- *Beryl Weber* – 73 years old (born 1942), stays in 'Hummingbird' with Hugo.

THE BENNETTS

- *Gene Bennett* – retired real estate agent, stays in 'Sparrow' with Maxine.
- *Maxine Bennett* – retired teacher.

THE HARRIS FAMILY

- *Carl Harris* – retired factory foreman, stays in 'Plover'.
- *Eclipse* – granddaughter of Carl.
- *Nova* – granddaughter of Carl.

THE WALSH FAMILY

- *Carrie and Marc Walsh* - Couple from Toronto with 2 young kids (Caleb & Noelle), enjoy a good party, stay in 'Stork'.

THE HOFFMAN FAMILY

- *Max Hoffman* – Doctor, father of Ariel, coming to the Resort since before her birth.
- *Celeste Hoffman* – Mother of Ariel, stays in 'Grouse'.

DARRYL AND CHARLIE

- *Darryl* – From Toronto, first year at the Resort with wife and young child, owns a roofing business, stays in 'Grebe'.
- *Charlie* – From Toronto, first year at the Resort with wife and young child, investor, stays in 'Puffin'.

THE ABIDI FAMILY

- *Tariq Abidi, his wife and 4 kids* – Stay in 'Albatross'.

THE LOPES FAMILY

- *Serena Lopes, her husband, and son Dylan (aged 4)* – Stay in 'White Dove'.

THE HOLDEN FAMILY

- *Randy Holden* – Principal from Toronto, stays in 'Loon'.
- *Reilly Holden* – Principal from Toronto.
- *Robby, Reese, Ricky* – Children of Randy and Reilly.

THE STAFF

- ***Stanley Henderson*** – 54 years old (born 1961), took over the Resort from his dad in 1988, no children, sister named Linda, nephew named Spencer.
- *Melissa Henderson (née Olmstead)* – 55 years old (born 1960), wife of Stanley, married since they were 20, father named Peter Olmstead.

- *Walter Henderson* (1929-1988) - Stanley's father, ran the Resort for 20 years, took over from his father, died of a heart attack at the Resort in 1988.

- *Bill Henderson* (1904-1968) – Stanley's grandfather, bought the Resort in 1940.

- ***Blaine*** – 26 years old (born 1989), fourth year as the Bartender, likes to party.

- ***Dave*** – 36 years old (born 1979), perfectionist, tenth year as chef, suffers from anxiety.

- ***Michelle*** – 31 years old (born 1983), head waitress, worked at the Resort for 7 years, daughter named Scarlett (8 years old) and an ex-husband named Phil.

- *Courtney* – 21 years old (born 1994), third year waitress at the Resort.

- *Christine* – 20 years old (born 1994), second year waitress at the Resort.

- *Ariel* – 19 years old (born 1995), first year at the Resort, daughter of Max and Celeste Walsh.

- *Greg* – 20 years old (born 1996), works in kitchen doing dishes and prep work, first year.

- ***Pascal*** – 18 years old (born 1997), only child, works in kitchen doing dishes and prep work, first year.

- *Rob* – 20 years old (born 1995), second year at Resort, waiter this year.

- *Zack* – 23 years old (born 1992), second year as social director at the Resort.
- *Wei* – 18 years old (born 1997), first year chamber maid at the Resort.
- *Maria* – 18 years old (born 1996), first year chamber maid at the Resort.
- *Stacey* – 18 years old (born 1996), joins the Resort as a waitress this week, comes from a large family.
- *Marcus* – Part of the band playing at the Resort for 13 years.
- *Vince* – Part of the band playing at the Resort for 13 years.
- *Trevor* – Part of the band playing at the Resort for 13 years, had lung cancer 3 years earlier.

Chapters

THE SUMMER RESORT

A SEASON OF CHANGE

2015

DAVID SINCLAIR

Chapter One

CHRIS

I CAN'T BELIEVE I have to sit here with my mother-in-law's dog breathing on the back of my neck as sweat trickles down my balls. As always, French music is blaring. And of course, there's no air conditioning. Those are the conditions of Sarah's mom; a recipe for disaster if you ask me, but she never asks. She says the dog can't handle the smell from the stale air, and it sneezes in any air conditioned environment. Can't say I've ever heard the damn dog sneeze.

The drive from Montreal should take about four hours. In this traffic, it'll be more like six. I wouldn't have minded had I been able to sit back and listen to my IPod; but Marion, or Meme, as I'm supposed to call her, insists that we plan for the upcoming week. 'Meme' is usually what little French children call their grandma. No pressure there!

For the past five years, since the divorce from Stéphane, the interactions with family have had to be strategically organized. Time spent at the Resort has been a series of well-planned days, rather than the relaxing unfolding of events a vacation should be. Meme insists that everything be planned before we arrive, so as to avoid any conflict once we're there.

"How about fifteen minutes of air-conditioning Meme? Bijou and I are getting a bit hot back here."

"Once this traffic gets moving the air will flow," Marion states matter-of-factly. This is usually the way with Marion, a complete disdain for the feelings of others, apart from her beloved Bijou.

I turn away, kicking myself, knowing it's always futile fighting with Meme.

Sarah, sensing my irritation, says, "We're only two kilometers from the exit. After that, we should be able to get moving."

"So, what I was saying, dear, was that you *and* your brothers must sit with me for the final dinner this year. Last year your father and that ….."

"Yes Maman, we know," Sarah sighs.

"I'd like if we *all* tried sitting together this year," I say, letting the humid, dog-breath air of the back seat get the best of me. I am fully aware that I am poking the bear. It's been five years since the divorce. Had it not been for Stéphane getting remarried to Annette, who is only two years older than Sarah, we may have all been able to be together for longer than thirty seconds at a time. That was five years ago. Marion is still furious. A wealthy older man can find a fit, young legal assistant to marry much easier than it is for a middle aged divorcee to snag a young buck.

"As long as he is bringing his little sex toy, I will not share a meal with him," replies Marion, not bothering to make eye contact with me.

"Let's settle down. It's been a long drive," Sarah adds, trying as always to be the voice of calm.

We make it to the exit and the road begins to open up.

The air roars through the car. Without officially committing to anything, Sarah reassures Marion that the seating arrangements for the final dinner should be fine. With Bijou distracted by the air whizzing by her window, I am able to find a few minutes of peace before we arrive and the shit hits the fan.

Chapter Two

CRAIG

IT'S WELL PAST lunch time as I start to put the lug nuts back on the 2007 Camry that I've been working on all morning. I know I could have finished a couple of hours sooner; but that would have meant leaving for the Resort earlier. By now, Terry knows how much I dread the time we spend there.

This will be Terry's second year coming with the family on vacation. Last year, we had only been dating for a couple of months when my family's Resort week came around. It was a difficult decision then as to whether to let her in on our yearly retreat. We were together enough that I couldn't have just disappeared for a week without telling her. If I had told her and not invited her, I know it would have sent a message that I wasn't all that serious about things. So I had to invite her. Of course, I was secretly hoping that she had some other plans that would have prevented her from being able to go. The perfect scenario would have been for her to drive up one morning, spend the day on the boat, eat dinner with the family, stay the night for some vacation sex, then take off in the morning. But she had absolutely beamed when I invited her. I was instantly torn between being happy that the woman I was falling in love with was excited to go away with me for a week, and dreading every second of the crazy show that had become my family summer vacation.

As I waste a few more minutes tidying up the shop, Terry phones.

"Hi Babe," I answer.

"You know you can't hide at the shop forever," she says in a half-joking, half-irritated way.

"I was just leaving. Honestly. My keys are in my hands."

"OK. Don't forget to bring the cooler home." There's a pause for a second, but I know she's not done. "I'm sure this year will be better Craig. We'll make sure we find lots of time to get away together."

"I'm sure you're right," I reply, not believing a word of it.

The best way to describe last year's vacation is to say that it was interesting. The family tensions were flaring right from the moment we arrived. Mom and dad showed up within ten minutes of each other. Dad was just loading his stuff on the golf cart that he always borrows to get to the cabin, when Mom, Sarah and Chris pulled up. Stanley, the Resort owner, usually so jovial and friendly, who never misses a chance to shoot the shit, knew exactly what was about to happen. He looked at his watch and disappeared into the main lodge. Terry had only experienced one dinner with my dad by this point. Her introduction to my mom was hearing her calling Annette a 'little whore'. The week only got better.

I turn off the lights, lock up the shop and drive home. The midsummer sun is beaming down as I pull out of the shop. It looks like it will be a perfect weather week.

Being a mechanic, you come to learn a lot about cars. Most mechanics don't drive around in luxury Lexuses. I've always been partial to sporty cars. A few months ago, a customer was looking to sell his Mustang. It became my little pet project. Any slow days at the shop were spent tinkering. It's perfect now, but if Terry and I ever want a family, this is not the car.

I became a mechanic after my second year of university. I always knew that I was interested in cars, and in taking things apart. When I was ten, I took apart Daniel's Walkman. He wasn't pleased. I could have put it back together just fine, but he was always such an asshole that I decided to leave a couple of screws loose so that the volume would cut in and out sporadically. I know it was petty, but that was the gist of our relationship. Despite being only two years apart, we were never really all that close.

When I arrive home, Terry has all our stuff on the porch. I try to argue that I need a shower before we go, but I know it's a losing battle. Terry never minds when I come home a little dirty from work. She's always there to greet me with a hug and a kiss. I hope my family doesn't fuck things up for us. We pack up the cooler with some food and head off.

It only takes about ten minutes to get out of the city. The roads are not too congested, and the sky is a clear blue, dotted with those wispy cotton-candy clouds that look like they're in no hurry to do much of anything. Listening to some CSN&Y with Terry seated next to me, I feel a sense of peace that I wish could last forever.

Chapter Three

BLAINE

"THANKS FOR A great week Blaine; as always!"

"No worries Mrs. P. Have a safe drive and an awesome year." I can't say I really give a shit about seeing Mrs. Parsons next year, but I sure as hell want to see her daughter again. Kerri just turned seventeen. Since last year, she changed dramatically, from a slightly chubby, brace-faced, sixteen-year-old to a considerably thinner, little hottie. By next year, at eighteen, she will be primed for a summer hook up with an older man!

The rest of the guests are packing up. I say all my yearly goodbyes. For most of these people, I couldn't give a squirt of piss if I ever see them again. Part of my job here is to smile, crack jokes, and ask about how their years went. I hear about school successes and failures, marriages and divorces, and all other sorts of boring shit. The interesting stuff comes at night after I serve a few beverages. That's when all the juicy stories come out. This year, after a night of chugging gin and tonics, one middle-aged guest told me all about an affair she was having with her son's sixth grade teacher. Hilarious!

I've been bartending at the Resort for four years now. The pay isn't amazing, but the perks make it worth it. Every year, there are a couple of new chamber maids and waitresses spending a first summer away from mommy and daddy, looking for independence. It's almost my duty to show them a good time. Then there are the tips. After three years, I know where to invest my time. With some families, you'll get a decent tip regardless of how much attention you give them. Others are seriously high maintenance; you have to check in on them at least three times each meal or you offend them.

I'm on my way back from the storeroom with a last load of liquor when Michelle walks in. She is *not* one of those fresh, young waitresses. Michelle has worked at the Resort for seven years now. When I first started, I tried to hit on her. Probably because she initially showed no interest in me at all, I spent a good month pulling out all my moves. I love a good challenge. Now I don't even bother; not just because I think she might be a lesbian, but in three years, she looks like she's aged six. I never actually asked her age, but she's at the point where things are starting to become less perky. There's plenty of other girls here to entertain myself with over the summer.

"What's up Mich?" I ask, knowing full well that nobody ever calls her that.

"Looking for Wei. You haven't seen her have you?" There's clearly a tone of irritation in her voice, mixed with accusation. Wei's one of those new chamber maids. Nice girl, but a bit flighty.

"Yup. We were just bangin', back in the storeroom. She needed a moment to get herself together. Really gave it to her good."

"Funny," she says without expression. "If you see her, tell her she's behind on her cabins. The Walsh family has arrived. It's their first year here, and right now their cabin looks like crap."

"Will do babe," I respond. Joking around with Michelle is rarely met with any good humour; but on turn around day, it's a particularly bad idea.

Everyone is stressed today. Guests leave somewhere between nine and eleven. The next week's batch arrive somewhere after two. My job is pretty easy; stock all the booze, clean the bar and settle any leftover bar tabs from the week. I plan on sneaking out on the boat for a couple of hours before it all begins again.

This year is a bit of a special year here at the Resort. It's the 75th anniversary. Stanley has been running the place for 27 years. His grandfather, Bill, built the first cabin on the land back in 1940. He made a bunch of money in the booze business back in the twenties and bought up the land around where the Resort now stands. Over the course of the next ten years, he built fifteen cabins and had established a nice, little, family retreat. His children, Stanley's dad and his brothers and sisters, grew up here in the summertime. Most of them moved on to other things; but Stanley's dad, Walter, took over the Resort when Bill died. Bill had a vision and Walter took over that vision. He fought hard to keep things exactly the way they had been, resisting expansion and improvements. While his intentions were honourable, the Resort was stuck in a rut. All Stanley ever wanted was to take over the Resort and make it what he wanted. When Walter had a heart attack right there on the dock, Stanley's time had come.

For the first ten years, I guess Stanley lost money every season. He renovated cabins, improved the infrastructure and built a new main lodge. He talked to all guests and made them feel at home. Guests who came, came back every year. The Resort became a special place where people got together once a year, shared stories of successes and failures, and basically grew up together.

One area that does not look like it's been renovated in a while is the plot of land that holds the staff cabins. When you come to work at the Resort, the rooms are definitely not the main attraction. There are two big cabins, a bit like army barracks. One is meant for the girls and the other for the boys. Stanley and his wife Melissa give a talk every year about responsibility and expectations for staff behaviour. We listen and nod, then ignore most of it. There's never anything too bad going down, just your average adolescent partying. I've noticed that Stanley, usually prompted by his wife Melissa, starts the summer off by being strict for the first week, even sending home a couple of staff on occasion. But by July, we never see Stanley or Mellissa in 'The Favela'.

I walk in the boy's cabin to the smell of beer, sweat and pot. This year, we have Rob, a waiter; Greg and Pascal, the dish pigs (although they like to call themselves sous-chefs); Zack the social director, and myself. There are at least 8 girls in their cabin. We also have a few other staff members who don't spend the nights at the Resort. Most live in the small towns around it. Doesn't mean they don't spend the occasional night here.

The staff cabins themselves are uniquely designed. They're pretty much one big room with some partitions, plus a bathroom. It's a bit of a shock to the rookies. There's no TV, no Wi-Fi, and no mint on your pillow in the morning. On one wall, the staff members over the past thirty-odd years have engraved their names, along with some interesting messages. There's kind of an unwritten rule about who can carve into the wall and how much they should contribute. It took me two full years before I felt I had earned the privilege.

The place is empty as I walk to the back where the bunks

are. There's almost an army feel to it, with a footlocker at the base of each bunk where all your personal possessions are kept. I open up my locker, grab a joint out of an old sock, and head for the boathouse.

Chapter Four

SARAH

ARRIVAL IS RELATIVELY smooth. Maman hugs Stanley and Melissa. They chat for a while and we move her into her cabin. Since the divorce, cabin arrangements have changed quite a bit. Maman has held on to Cardinal, the two-bedroom cabin that she and dad had been in the year they separated. By then, the kids had mostly grown up and made the move to smaller cabins with partners. Growing up, our family had the biggest cabin at the Resort, Loon. As I pass by, a vivid memory from my youth hits me; sitting on the front step where Daniel had chipped a tooth, threading hooks onto fishing line and dreading having to put the wriggling, slimy worm on that hook once we were out on the boat. Even after all these years, it's still strange to see other families staying in the cabin where I spent one week every summer. In many ways, Daniel, Craig, and I grew up in that cabin.

Chris and I are staying in the cabin right next door to Maman, Blue Jay; a quaint, little one bedroom cabin with a nice balcony. The location is ideal for spending some quality time together; however, we rarely get the chance for the two of us to be alone.

Family vacations are a tradition in our family. Maman and dad first came to the Resort the year Craig was born. I was four and Daniel was two. They needed a family-friendly place to take the kids, and the Resort was reasonably priced and perfect for a young family. They used to hire a babysitter to watch us at night while they went to the bar and played cards with the other guests. It only took a couple of years for them to develop some lifelong friendships.

We've been coming here for twenty-six years. I remember the great times and forget most of the bad ones; but there are still moments every year now where I ask myself if Chris and I wouldn't be happier flying to some tropical island one year, not even telling the family where we were; just not showing up at the Resort one summer. One of these years, it might happen. More and more, it's starting to feel like I need a week off to recover from our vacation week here.

By mid-afternoon, we've settled in and Chris is offering me a beer.

"Probably a good idea to have a drink or two before the rest of your gang gets here," he adds.

"Thanks. I just hope Daniel and Craig get here before dad shows up."

"What? And take some responsibility for dealing with your parents?" he says sarcastically.

"Craig isn't that bad," I respond. Craig at least deals with the situation. Daniel's way of handling the tension between our parents is to disappear; sometimes to go play golf, other times to sneak off with some girl.

"I guess. I just don't see why we have to be right next door to your mom while your brothers are way over on the other side of the Resort."

"That's just how it worked out. I guess I could talk to Craig and see if he's interested in switching with us and staying here with Terry," I suggest, knowing full well that Chris would hate having to stay in the cabin right next to Daniel.

"No thanks. But if something else opens up, I'd totally be up for switching. Wouldn't it be nice to have a bit more privacy?" he asks as he comes over to give me a hug. "Maybe that little place up the hill? What is it, Sparrow?"

"I think the Bennett's would have to die before they give that place up," I answer.

Cabin rights follow a very strict code of ethics at the Resort. People who stay in a cabin have the right to reserve that cabin the following year, during the same week of the summer. If you miss a year, then you forfeit your claim on that cabin. There are a couple of exceptions though; medical issues usually give you a year exemption. Chris first came with us the same year mom and dad separated. We stayed in the cabin with mom that year. Talk about weird. It's always a challenge for us to get some alone time at the Resort, but there was definitely no sex happening that first year. The following summer, Blue Jay opened up right next door to Cardinal. We were newly engaged. We moved in, and have stayed there since.

"Maybe we could slip something into their coffee this evening," Chris jokes as he kisses my neck, "then we could swoop right in and take over their cabin."

"That is really horrible," I say, giving him a smack on the chest. "The Bennett's are a lovely couple. I remember when I was a kid, Maxine would make s'mores for all the kids at the big bonfire."

"We wouldn't have to kill them. Maybe just make them sick enough to have to miss the week," he says playfully.

He pulls me up against him and kisses my lips. I'm just starting to let myself enjoy the moment when my father's laughter snaps me back to reality.

"I didn't hear anything," Chris says as we make eye contact.

"Let's go!" I answer, not terribly enthusiastically.

*

"Papa, how was the drive?" I ask.

"Excellent dear. How about you?" my father responds, kissing both cheeks and giving me a hug.

"Long. Traffic was terrible. I swear it gets worse every year."

"You should wait a while and leave later. We were pretty clear the whole way," adds Annette. She approaches to give me a hug.

Our relationship has always been a bit awkward. Having a step-mother only two years older than me makes for a bizarre dynamic. To her credit, she has never really tried to be a step-mother. At first, she tried to act like my friend, but that didn't last too long. I was a bit chilly towards her when she and dad first made their relationship public; now we just kind of chat in a superficial way.

"Maman likes to arrive pretty early," I respond, a bit passive-aggressively I suppose.

"Of course. It's so good to see you Sarah." Again, a kiss on each cheek. This is a habit she has passed on to my dad. She considers herself very European.

"Do you need any help getting stuff moved in Stéphane?" Chris asks, coming around the corner.

"That would be great, son." My dad has always called Chris 'son', and it has always made Chris feel a little uncomfortable;

as do the new cheek kisses that follow. "How have you been? Taking care of my little girl?"

"Always."

Chris grabs some bags and starts off up the hill towards my dad and Annette's cabin. Maman does not even come out to acknowledge their arrival; and that's the best case scenario. Next obstacle: The first dinner.

Chapter Five

MICHELLE

"STANLEY, HOW THE fuck am I supposed to work with those two never taking anything seriously?"

"Ok. Slow down. What's the problem?"

"Blaine is getting worse every year. You know it. He's lazy, unprofessional, obnoxious, self-absorbed,.."

"Ok. Calm down Michelle. Tell me what *actually* happened." Stanley says, trying to settle me down. He's very calm in everything he does. It can be extremely frustrating when I am feeling far from calm myself. But I settle a little and try to plead my case. I take a seat on the old, plastic, off-white deck chair across from his relic of a desk. That desk must weigh three hundred pounds. It's the original one Stanley's grandfather used when he first started the Resort. Stanley never tries to jazz up his little office; he's rarely in there. The pages on the wall are yellowing, the wood panelling gives off a slight mildew odour, and the chairs are old, hard, and uncomfortable.

"Blaine is more concerned with hitting on every girl he sees than actually doing his job. I saw him go out on the boat a couple of hours ago and he's still not back."

"Well, as long as he's stocked the bars ready for the week, he doesn't really need to be here."

"I know he doesn't *need* to be, but it would be nice if a few more people would do more than the bare minimum. Ariel is useless. If she's not on her phone, she's standing around talking to Greg and Pascal in the kitchen. Last week, two of her tables pulled me aside and basically told me how terrible she was."

"I know," Stanley responds, "a couple of them spoke to me too. She's new. Give her a chance. Maybe you could coach her a little. You know, you catch more bees with honey than vinegar."

"Flies."

"What?"

"Flies Stanley. You catch more flies with honey."

"You get the point. Take her under your wing. She's never been a waitress before. I gave her the job as a favour to Max and Celeste; they've been coming here since before she was born."

In the past seven years, we've had at least four waitresses who got the job because their parents have been coming to the Resort for years. In three of those cases, the girl didn't make it back the following year. Ariel is probably the worst.

"I doubt she would respond to that. She's too busy becoming one of Courtney's little tag-alongs."

"Easy Michelle. Courtney is a very good waitress."

"True; but she's also a snotty, little bitch."

This is Courtney's third year at the Resort. She's one of *those* girls; super full of herself, entitled, and always thinking she's God's gift to… well… everyone. She's the type of girl who thinks everyone is watching every little thing she does; when in reality, people are just watching how full of herself she is, thinking that she's absolutely ridiculous. Yet, some people still follow her. That has always mystified me.

"Listen. It's the third week of the summer. There's a long way to go. Just keep doing what you're doing. Your tables love you and you do a great job," Stanley says; then he looks down at his books.

"Don't patronize me Stanley. This isn't about me. Ariel follows Courtney around and laughs at every little thing she does. And she sucks at her job. Blaine is going to get himself into serious trouble if he doesn't watch it. You have to come down a little harder or they will get out of hand."

"I'll talk to them both. I can't do anything about your feelings against Courtney. That's your business."

As I leave Stanley's office, I run into Sarah Murray. This will be the fourth year that I am in charge of her mom's table. You never know what you're going to get with their family.

"Michelle, how are you?" Sarah asks.

"Great Sarah. When did you get in? Good trip?"

"A bit longer than we would have liked. Hot too. I hope we have you for dinner again this year?"

"You bet. I gotta run now to start getting set up. We have a few staff members this year that are new; still not quite up to speed." I probably shouldn't have said anything. Things at the Resort tend to get discussed, then over discussed, then discussed some more. But Sarah has always been pretty good. The rest of her family though, is something else.

"Alright. Make sure my mom and dad are far enough away from each other," Sarah adds with a half-laugh.

The dining room is nothing fancy, but seated in the right spots, it does provide a gorgeous view of the lake. Families like the LaPointe family have established themselves in the best spots. When they all used to sit together, they were right in the middle, against the huge bay window. When Sarah's parents split up, there was some upheaval. Both parents wanted to keep the family seat. Stanley, ever the peacemaker, decided that neither would keep the spot. He set the parents up along the opposite sides of the dining room. Both areas provide a view of the lake, and both are central enough that they feel like the most important spot in the room. Nice job Stanley. A few other families were shuffled around; but none really kicked up too big of a stink.

I plug in my earbuds and get to work setting up my tables.

Chapter Six

CRAIG

WE PULL INTO the Resort just as several guests are making their way to dinner. The Watsons, a wealthy family from Ottawa, are meandering along together as we pull up next to the main lodge. Emma, the youngest daughter, waves and comes over. There was a bit of tension last year with Emma and Terry; more from Terry's side. She was convinced that there was a history with me and Emma, who is only a year younger than me. Terry is not usually the jealous type, but I can tell sometimes that she's protective of me. She always says that I'm blind to how women look at me. It irritates me when this causes unnecessary arguments between us; but it also feels kind of good to know that she cares so much that she gets jealous.

"Craig, Terry, how are you? You're getting here late this year," Emma says as she comes to give us both a hug. I can tell from Terry's body language that the memories of last year have come back; at least momentarily.

"Yeah, we left a bit late. Had some work to finish," I

respond, trying hard to give her a hug that sends the message clearly to Terry that there's nothing more there, while still hugging enough to reflect the fact that Emma and I haven't seen each other in a year. Little shit like this makes this vacation more work than it should be.

"Are you guys coming straight to dinner?" Emma asks Terry.

"Not too sure. I think we'll dump some stuff off at the cabin first and then head over," Terry replies.

"Ok. See you there. Hope you've been practicing your euchre. It's *on* this year," Emma challenges as she returns to her family. Several other Watsons wave as we start to unpack the car.

The final euchre tournament is kind of a big deal. Emma's family and mine have battled for years for the title. The winners from each week's tournament get their names on a large plaque in the main lodge; right next to the trophy for the biggest fish caught on the lake each summer, and a big, grainy photo of the owner's grandfather with a huge bass hanging from his fishing rod. Last year, a first-year couple won the euchre title, beating my brother and his partner in the finals. Terry and I beat Emma and her sister in the quarter-finals.

"You alright?" I ask Terry as we reach the cabin with our first load of things.

"Yeah, why?" she asks.

"Well, I know you kind of had issues with Emma last year."

"Craig. She totally loves you."

"She does not. We're like siblings Terry," I respond, trying not to sound like I'm starting an argument. I regret saying anything.

"You just don't see it. But I know you love me. And you know I'd kick your ass if you ever cheated on me," Terry threatens playfully.

"Oh, I know!" I lean over and give her a kiss. "I really do love you!"

"I know." Terry smiles and heads back towards the car, giving her gorgeous ass an extra little shake as she walks away.

*

After we drop off all our stuff at the cabin and freshen up a bit, we walk down to dinner. We stop to chat with Beryl and Hugo Weber, a couple from Buffalo, NY, who have been coming to the Resort for something like 48 years. It sounds morbid, but I hope that when their time is up, they go together because I can't imagine one existing without the other. They stay in a cabin that feels like it was built specifically for them. Both of them have had issues with their knees in recent years, but they still battle the little hill that leads down to their 'honeymoon suite' as Hugo always describes it with a wink; holding on to each other's arms and helping each other along.

Our conversation is broken by an AUDI R8 pulling into the laneway leading up to the lodge. My brain automatically thinks: "What kind of asshole needs to spend that much money on a car to impress other assholes with fancy cars and suits; pulling in here with music blaring and dust flying?" I already know the answer. Daniel steps out of the car.

"What's up, *buddy*?" Daniel asks, as if we were two best buds in a beer commercial. "Terry, you hottie, how's my brother treating you?" he asks Terry

"Fancy car," I state, without any real intonation in my voice. I somehow manage to make it not really a statement, and not really a question.

"Thanks. Fuckin' flies down the highway. Can't even feel it going 160," Daniel brags, clearly interpreting my comment as a compliment. That's kind of how he is. Let's say he's '*confident*'.

"How's things with mom and dad?" Daniel asks, turning to walk towards the dining room and expecting us to follow. It's this type of behaviour that makes it very hard to be with my brother. There's very little actual concern for others.

"Not sure yet. We just got here."

"Well, I hope there's no drama this year. I really need to relax," Daniel adds.

Daniel has been working with dad for a couple of years now. He's always talking about the stresses of his job, yet he always seems to have time to get up to all kinds of fun. Daniel is never at a loss for a story of some debauchery.

"Just make sure you spend some time with mom this year. You know how she gets," I say.

"For sure," Daniel responds absent mindedly.

Walking through the front doors, the familiar feel of the main lodge hits me. The sun is shining through the few windows where the blinds are up. There are couches, chairs and tables arranged throughout the big, open sitting space. To the right, there's a little area that's a bit like a front desk; although there's rarely anyone sitting there. Just behind that is a little hallway leading to Stanley's office. To the left, the double doors to the dining room are propped open.

We walk into the dining room together. It's a hustle and bustle of activity with wait staff zipping around, and a girl chasing another little guy, presumably her little brother, around a couple of tables. The room is large and open, with only a couple of pillars interrupting the space. The tables are standard square tables that are easily rearranged based on what size the groups are each week. As always, there are a few new faces mixed in with familiar ones. We greet many people with hugs and handshakes. Dad hasn't arrived yet, so we go over to see mom, Sarah, and Chris, who are just finishing up some dessert.

"Nice of you both to make it," Sarah states with clear irritation in her voice.

"Yeah, made great time on the highway," Daniel responds, either choosing to ignore Sarah's tone, or completely oblivious to it.

"Sorry Sarah. I had a few things to finish up before we came," I add.

"Will you sit with us?" Mom asks, directing her question mostly at Terry, giving her the best chance to get us to join her.

"I think we'll head over to the other table; but we will all have breakfast in the morning," I reply before Terry has a chance to. I also give a long look in Daniel's direction.

"For sure," Daniel replies before moving away to chat with Blaine, the bartender. I think Daniel sees in Blaine the younger brother he should have had. For the past couple of years, one of the first things Daniel has done has been to seek out Blaine to scope out all the females for the week; each staking his claim to a variety of staff and guests. I never really shared Daniel's view of women. When we were younger, Daniel tried to include me in his escapades. One summer, at the Resort, he convinced me to help him drill a hole in the wall of the staff shower, so that he could spy on the waitresses. Once I reached about twelve, he realized I was not fun to do those things with. That's when he started the rumour that I was gay. Those were a couple of fun years!

As Terry and I make our way to my dad's side of the dining room, we watch my brother smile and chat with several guests, mostly women of course. We do a friendly 'smile and wave' ourselves to a few familiar faces. Terry and I take a seat. I take advantage of the time to see how she's doing.

"You OK?" I ask.

"You know you don't have to ask me that every hour," she responds.

"I know. My brother just makes me antsy and I can tell you get irritated."

At that moment, we both look up and watch Daniel chat with Blaine and three waitresses. Daniel is standing next to Courtney; who has worked at the Resort for a few years now, and Daniel seems to be working on her already. He leans in and whispers something in her ear, gently placing his hand on the small of her back. She gives a giggle and flips her hair. Terry and I exchange a glance and can't stifle our laughs.

"Are we the only ones to find that a bit absurd?" I ask.

"I seriously hope not," Terry responds. "Your brother is something else, but it's got nothing to do with you and me," she reassures me.

We are able to share about three minutes of hand-holding, staring-into-each-others-eyes-time before my father enters the dining room with one arm around Stanley, the owner, and the other arm linked with Annette; who is, as always, dressed like she's on her way to dinner with a movie star.

Watching my dad cross the dining room, moments after seeing Daniel do it, strikes me as such a contrast. While Daniel just seems superficial and a bit creepy, my dad makes it look smooth. He stops to chat with several guests, taking the time to look everyone in the eye and make them feel like they are the most important thing in the world to him at that moment. I am relieved to see that Sarah, Chris, and my mom have already left their table. So far, it's a fairly smooth start to the trip. Seven days to go!

Chapter Seven

DAVE

I BUTT OUT MY joint after taking a few last tokes. A few too many to be honest; I have a couple of those 'cough-out-your-nose-while-trying-to-hold-in-the-toke' coughs. I've been smoking quite a bit of pot so far this summer because I haven't gotten my coke yet. Should be coming this week.

I take a few moments to sit and enjoy my high before getting back to work. This job isn't exactly hard, but it's definitely getting to me. This is my moment of peace and joy; sitting on an upside-down bucket, just outside the door in the basement of the main kitchen. It's not like there's even a view. Instead of a view of the lake, I get to look out at the road and the parking lot.

It's all I deserve.

The Resort is my summer gig. It's regular, pays fairly well, and is comfortable. I know it will also slowly kill me if I stay here much longer. When I finished my two years of college, I had big plans to start a restaurant. Then all of a sudden, everything started to feel too big. Getting to work on time seemed like a big enough chore most days. My parents finally got me to go and see a therapist, who pulled the old, 'How does that make you feel?' shit after whatever I said. The next day, I took everything out of my bank account, hopped on a bus, and toured around for a couple of years; working in kitchens all over the country.

Parents probably threw a fucking party when they got rid of me.

I met Stanley in a diner in town. He came in with his wife during the winter to have breakfast every Sunday. I guess he liked the food because he asked to meet me. He offered me the job right there. He even helped work out a deal so that I could keep my job at the diner in the winter and work the Resort in the summer. That was ten years ago.

I'm certain Stanley knows about the drugs, but he never says anything directly. As long as it doesn't fuck up my ability to get the work done, I think he'd prefer to just ignore it. Last week was the closest to that fuck up happening so far; too close. If Greg and Pascal hadn't noticed that the gas had not been shut off on the old stove, I might have burned the whole place down.

The night before, a friend had come by with a bag of mushrooms. I ended up eating some after dinner, and I was never able to get to sleep. The next day, I was a walking zombie. I'm not a young guy anymore. New rule: Save mushrooms for days off.

Walking back into the kitchen, I do a lap around before returning to my station; clockwise of course. One thing my brief time with the shrink revealed is that I have some pretty clear OCD tendencies. I looked it all up online and there sure are some fucked up things that people do. I can still function pretty well, and people mostly get used to my tendencies; however, I do have some pretty clear triggers. I've lost a ton of jobs along the way because I need my space to be a certain way and some assholes just can't resist touching my shit. Here, it's kind of nice because this is pretty much my kitchen.

Nobody talks to me for the first minute or so after I come back in. That's kind of the way it is. Everyone notices my behaviour, but it's easier not to talk about it. That's kind of how society is these days. God forbid you should have a conversation about something real. People don't know how to communicate anymore. Want to know how to shut a room up? Tell people you have a mental disorder. Or Cancer. Lots of things are called 'silent killers', but that shit is the killer of conversation; silence creators.

"Everything going OK?" I ask Greg once I've had the chance to settle in.

"Looking good boss; other than a couple of waitresses dumping their dishes without scraping them first."

"Still? I'll have a word with them after dinner." I reassure Greg. He and Pascal are a couple of good kids; even though they are kind of dumbasses. Every year we get a crop of new waitresses that have never really worked in a kitchen before. A part time job at Subway is great, but it doesn't teach you the etiquette of how to deal with six tables during a dinner rush. Working the dish pit is not a glamorous job, but it doesn't mean they should be shat on by a couple of spoiled waitresses.

"Thanks Dave," Greg replies.

*

After dinner, I call a meeting for all kitchen staff. It's something I was planning on doing anyway.

"This'll only take a minute or two. Thanks for staying," I start.

"Are we in trouble dad?" Blaine jokes. If I didn't know him, I'd probably take more offense to that; but I know he's just a guy who always needs to break the tension with a joke.

One of these days though, I'd feel great to bash that pretty boy face in.

"Yeah, you're grounded." I don't want to start the meeting off negatively, so I make nothing of it. That's probably related to the joint from earlier. Another time, I might have blown up. In other kitchens, I have.

"Just a few things. We've been here a couple of weeks now and there are some items to review. If you know all this already, I'm sorry."

After mentioning the dish dumping and reviewing some other general clean-up issues, there's clear tension from some of the wait staff. Courtney has brought some serious attitude now that she's got a couple of years under her belt.

"I think we should also talk about how half the time we come to collect food, we have to wait," Courtney snips, looking at Greg and Pascal.

Courtney's little princess attitude leaves me dumbstruck. Thankfully I'm not the first one to talk; Michelle, who's a solid, hard-working waitress, pipes up.

"We are not going to start getting into any political shit here. Dave's just trying to get things running right," Michelle says, trying to avoid a blow up. She's been here for seven or eight years now and while we aren't best buddies, we respect each other. She's also seen me freak out on one or two occasions.

"If there's anyone else who has something to discuss about the way my kitchen is running, *please* say it now," I challenge, looking each and every person in the eye. Most look away. I end with Courtney. She holds my stare for a couple of seconds, then adds: "There have been a couple of times that I have had to wait for my orders; usually salads and that kind of thing." Once again, she gives Pascal and Greg a look.

"That was a super crazy dinner!" Pascal responds. "There

were like three extra families visiting, and we ran out of spinach cuz the one box was bad, and …"

"And this morning at breakfast, I had to wait for like five minutes for my French toast," Ariel adds, looking at Courtney for approval.

"Don't even start," Michelle snaps. "I have covered your ass numerous times since you started. *You* need to focus on your own shit."

Ariel looks around nervously, unsure of what to do. There's no way she's bold enough to challenge Michelle outright, and she knows it. She looks to Courtney, hoping she'll stick up for her, but the support doesn't come. Courtney looks at her nails. The tension sits in the air as nobody speaks.

"OK. Good therapy shit guys. Dave, don't worry. We'll tighten up the ship. As for now, I got an idea. Let's open up a bottle of Jack Daniels, turn up some tunes and get this place set up for tomorrow," Blaine says, leading Courtney, Ariel and Christine out to the dining room.

Michelle puts her hand on my shoulder as she starts to leave. "You OK?" she asks.

"Yeah, no problem. You know I got no issue with you Michelle."

"I know. Ditto." She gives me a half-hug, then grabs some linens to start setting up her tables.

I think I more or less controlled my anger. It's probably mostly because of the pot, and the fact that I'm tired as hell recently. Michelle helped too. I think I need to have a chat with G to see about some Xanax or something to mellow me out a little.

Chapter Eight

STANLEY

IT'S WELL AFTER midnight before I make it home. Turnaround day is always crazy; but the issues in the kitchen made today even longer. Trying not to wake Melissa, I grab a beer out of the fridge and head out on the balcony. This balcony is the one special place on this Resort that's just ours. Melissa and I will often sit out here and look out over the lake; me with a beer and her with a glass of red wine. Our house is built just up a hill from the main lodge. The balcony is on the back of the house, on the second floor, overlooking the lake and blocked from view of the main lodge. There are six candles positioned perfectly to keep the bugs away. The recliner chairs that we splurged on a few years ago glide up and down so fluidly that I swear they must have been designed by NASA. The retractable awning is old and spotted with mildew; but it still provides us with enough shade and rain protection. On that balcony, we've watched countless sunsets, seen shooting stars slash across the sky, and played thousands of games of backgammon.

I slide the screen door closed and settle in to my chair. It's one of those early summer nights where the temperature is right between needing a sweater and not. I usually go with 'not'. Melissa must have heard me come in because she slides the screen door open and joins me; wearing a sweater.

"What was all that about with Dave and the kitchen staff?" Melissa asks.

She has a way of knowing exactly what's going on.

"I'm hoping it's just some normal restaurant crap and that it'll blow over."

"I'm getting a bit worried about him, Stanley." Melissa has always been the observant one when it comes to people. I notice when a light bulb needs to be changed, or when a tire is a little flat. She notices what's going on with people; when someone needs a hug, or just to talk.

"He's always been a bit of a live wire. Remember three years ago when he kicked a hole in the wall after an argument with that delivery guy?"

"That was six years ago dear."

"Golly," is all I can say.

"I know he's always been edgy, but he's changed Stanley. You can see it in his eyes. He looks troubled." Melissa says, taking the beer from my hand and having a sip.

"Maybe he's just tired. It's been a busy start. We're booked solid this week."

"I know that dear; I do the books. Just keep an eye on him. Maybe have a chat and see if he's alright."

We sit in silence for a while and listen to the frogs. Only someone who has grown up outside the city can understand the comfort that comes from certain sounds and smells. Frogs at night might be the most beautiful sound I've ever heard.

"Has it really been six years?" I ask, still not believing how quickly time has started to move.

"Yes dear."

"Like a stitch in time."

"Not quite, dear," she says.

After another minute of enjoying the peace, Melissa asks, "Have you given any more thought to the offer from that business man?"

Last fall, we had a visit from a man who wanted to buy the Resort. He was well dressed and smelled of cologne. His hand shake was firm and his teeth were really darn white. I hated him right from the minute his fancy shoes crunched across the gravel to introduce himself. Despite everything about him making me squirm, his offer was generous. Of course I've been thinking about it. Every day!

"I told you that I'm not selling to that guy," I say with irritation in my voice. I just can't help it.

"I know Stanley, but maybe we should think about selling to *someone*."

"I can't think about it now." This is my standard response.

"You always say that dear, but I know you've at least *thought* about it. You always get so defensive. You know we'll have to make some decision soon. We're not getting any younger."

"I feel great dear. We have many years left," I respond, only half convincing myself. Time sometimes feels like it's flying by; but at the same time, it's crawling along like a pregnant snail. Years are starting to blend together. I guess I have been starting to wonder if it's all still worth it. I just can't imagine selling this place to some rich city boy who will never appreciate the sound of frogs. Melissa and I never had any kids of our own, so there's no little prince or princess to inherit the kingdom. I have a couple of nephews and nieces who could take over, but none of them have expressed too much interest.

"I know now isn't the time," Melissa says getting up to go inside, "but you have to start thinking about it soon. Your dad dropped dead right on that dock at the age of fifty-nine, and your grandfather died here at sixty-four. We are not far off from that now, and I don't want to see you work yourself to death." She manages to say all this without it sounding like nagging. She kisses my forehead and goes in to bed; leaving me alone with my personal symphony of frogs.

Chapter Nine

CHRIS

THE FIRST MORNING starts out absolutely perfectly. I know the expression is probably a bit overused, but the lake is like glass as I push out the kayak. Last night was fairly typical for the first night here; most people unwind with family. Sarah talked with her mom while I sat on the deck. After a couple of beers, I was ready for bed. I'm never really one for staying up too late here; to me the best part of the day is the peaceful morning. An hour or so on the kayak does wonders for the soul.

Besides the calmness of the water, there are also no motorboats on the lake at this hour. I like to go out on Stéphane's fancy boat - I even tried waterskiing for the first time last year - but I've always found it hard to reconcile the peaceful beauty of a lake like this, with the loud speed boats and jet skis that most people love.

I'm just about to turn around and head back when I see a fairly large boat heading my way. I slowly paddle back towards the Resort, occasionally glancing behind me. I eventually realize it's a provincial police boat. They cut their engines, and I wait for them to glide close.

"Morning," one officer calls.

"Good morning. Everything alright?" I ask.

"Yes sir. Just finishing up a lap of the lake. We've had a few people complain about some boats driving very recklessly, in the early mornings this summer."

"I haven't seen anyone other than a couple of canoers."

"Yeah, it all seems quiet. I see you have a lifejacket. Do you also have a safety kit with you today?" The second officer asks. He's younger than the first officer; seems very much like he's training.

"Yup," I answer, pulling out the orange bucket.

"Excellent. Enjoy the rest of your morning," the first officer replies.

"Thanks."

*

It's 7:45 when I get back to the boathouse. A tired looking father is fishing off the dock with his son. There's a brief moment where the dad and I catch each other's eye. I know that as a tired father of a five year old, he looks at my kayak and sees freedom; a chance to have some time to himself. I'm pretty certain he recognizes in my eyes, the look of a young man ready to start a family, wanting one of those special father-son moments myself. We smile and nod, each reminded to enjoy what we have.

I walk back to the cabin to find Sarah standing at the coffee maker, talking on her phone.

"It doesn't make sense for you to get a room in the lodge. I'll talk to Maman. You can stay with her, Telle. She'd love it."

Sarah's younger sister, Chantelle, is the baby of the family.

She's also a handful. She moved out when she was sixteen years old, just a year after Marion and Stéphane split.

"Just be careful driving. How much sleep did you get last night? You sound tired," Sarah asks with that concerned voice she gets when she speaks to Telle.

"I'm not nagging. Just concerned," she adds. Their relationship has always been volatile. Sarah tries her best to take care of her baby sister, and Telle resists and pulls farther away.

"Ok. See you later. Love you," she says with some exasperation.

"Chantelle coming up today?" I ask after she's hung up.

"Yeah! By herself," Sarah responds.

"Is she actually going to stay with your mother?"

"I doubt it. She might have to though. It seems pretty full this week. I didn't notice any empty tables in the dining room last night."

"It might be good. She can help out a bit with keeping your mom happy. Maybe you can have a bit more *relaxation* time," I say, raising one eyebrow and trying to look sexy. It either works, or Sarah feels pity for me, because she gives me a little smile.

"It's still pretty early. We could have some *relaxation* time before breakfast," she says playfully.

Slowly backing away towards the bedroom, I take off my shirt. Sarah watches me, looking me up and down. She takes off her own shirt and follows me in, shutting the door behind her. Not a bad start to the first day; a kayak and morning sex!

*

We manage to be ready for breakfast by 9:00, both with some colour in our cheeks and smiles on our faces. Resort sex is not anywhere near as frequent as I would like it to be. Family vacations just present too many obstacles; especially with Sarah's family. But when we do find the time, it's really fucking hot.

This morning was no exception. Sarah had ripped my shorts off almost before the bedroom door had completely closed.

We stop by Meme's cabin before crossing the back lawn to the dining room. There's no sign of the rest of her family. It's become accepted that the first breakfast belongs to Marion. Stéphane usually takes Annette to a nice restaurant for breakfast to avoid any scene.

"Have you talked to your brothers this morning Sarah?" Marion asks once we sit down.

"Craig texted me earlier; he should be here any minute. I got no response from Daniel," Sarah responds with some irritation.

"I'm sure he'll be here," I add.

"So Maman, I talked to Chantelle this morning and she's coming at some point today."

"Is she bringing that boy with her?" Marion asks. The guy she's talking about is the last man Chantelle was with; a man that most mothers would cringe at, if their daughters brought him home. He had piercings in about every place one can have them; at least in all the visible places. I only met him once, but I can imagine if I were a parent, he would be my worst nightmare.

"She's coming by herself. I didn't ask for details," Sarah says. "She was planning on getting a room in the lodge, but I told her I was sure you would be happy to have her."

"Of course dear. Melissa told me the Resort is completely booked this week anyway."

Craig and Terry walk in just then, hand in hand. Of all the members of Sarah's family, Craig has always been the most reasonable and responsible; and Terry is great – very down to earth and kind.

"Hey all," Craig greets as he and Terry give hugs all around.

"Did you happen to see Daniel on your way down?" Sarah asks.

Craig gives her a look of understanding. "He shouldn't be long," is all he says.

Once everyone is seated, there's one of those moments of silence where nobody says anything, but everyone is clearly thinking something. Terry breaks the tension.

"What are your plans for today, Marion?"

"I'm playing bridge with Maxine and Gene Bennett, and Carl Harris," she responds.

"Is he the one who brings his grandchildren every year?" I ask, turning to Sarah.

"Yeah. So nice of him to do that," she responds.

"Those poor children. This week is probably the highlight of their year," Marion says. Turning to me, she adds, "You know their father left them and their mother is a drug addict."

Most people come to the Resort to spend time either next to, in, or on the water. I swear Marion comes for the gossip. Since her split from Stéphane, most of her days at the Resort are spent positioned in a big, old arm chair in the lodge, chatting to anyone who passes by.

"Well, they seem like pretty descend kids considering," Terry adds.

Meme takes full advantage of having us all with her for breakfast. She tells us about some staff gossip, asks about our years, and complains about last winter's weather. When she's not confronted with Stéphane, Marion is pretty good company. Craig and Terry are also very genuine. We talk and enjoy a nice, hearty breakfast.

Breakfasts are always amazing at the Resort. Whoever is working in the kitchen knows how to prepare the perfect poached egg with crispy bacon, seasoned home fries, and fresh fruit. It always sets me up for whatever the day brings.

Almost an hour after we had planned to meet for breakfast, Sarah's brother, Daniel comes in.

"Mom, how are you?" Daniel asks, coming over to give his mom a kiss. "Sorry I'm late; had a hell of a time getting organized this morning."

"I think it was about an hour ago when you said you'd be right down," Craig adds without any real emotion.

"Got busy. How is breakfast this morning?" Daniel responds.

I still can't quite figure out the relationship between Craig and Daniel. Every once in a while, Craig will make a comment that seems to include some sarcasm, while also possibly being merely an observation. It's a certain tonelessness that he uses. Daniel usually either ignores it or doesn't notice. Sarah has told me stories of both antagonism and seemingly genuine brotherly love.

We have some coffee, and Daniel orders his breakfast. As he waits for his food, he takes out his dad's boat key. Stéphane loves his boat, but Daniel LOVES Stéphane's boat!

"Looks like an amazing day today. Who wants to do some skiing?" he asks.

There are a few seconds where I'm caught speechless. Marion usually blows up whenever anything about Stéphane is brought up. I'm clearly not the only person with this feeling because seconds pass before anyone speaks. I look at Sarah, who looks at me, then Craig, then Daniel. Everyone ends up looking at Marion; which is pretty much the worst thing to do.

She simply looks at Daniel and says, "I will not be going on that boat today, dear."

I think the nice, relaxed morning meal has calmed her. She's happy she had the chance to spend time with all of us together, and that she's got her day all planned. Sarah looks at me and gives a little exhale of relief.

Sarah gets up from the table and says, “We should go Maman. I’m going to talk to Stanley about Telle coming.”

“Ok dear, come and let me know when she’s here,” Marion responds.

As we say our goodbyes, Daniel places his hand on my shoulder and adds, “We’ll head out around lunch and get you up on the skis again, Chris.”

“Yeah, we’ll see,” I answer.

Chapter Ten

BLAINE

I HAVE A FEELING this is going to be a crazy week! The place is packed, several of the guests are pretty cool, and there's some tension boiling up with the staff. Dave was trying to set a few ground rules for the wait staff and Courtney and Ariel got a bit snarky. I seriously thought the top of Dave's head was going to blow off; that dude has some shit going on. Sometimes his eyes look like they're about to shoot lasers out. I know he smokes herb, but I think he's dabbling in some more serious shit too.

The bar was pretty calm last night; the first night here is usually pretty mellow. There was one couple from Toronto who took advantage of their first night here to let loose. Couples can recruit some of the chamber maids to babysit at night so that they can go out. It lets the adults get out and have some fun while allowing the workers to earn a little extra cash on the side. These two, Carrie and Marc, were pretty ripped by the end of the night. She was grabbing his ass and calling him Hercules at one point. As long as she didn't puke before they made it back to their cabin, I bet they had some good old drunk sex. I'll make a point of checking in on them at dinner; remind them who helped them let loose and have some fun. Set up a nice tip for the end of the week!

Tonight will be different though; it's trivia night. It sounds pretty geeky, but the guests have a blast. In teams, they have to answer questions from a bunch of categories. There are breaks in between; lots of time to drink. After spending a day with family, most people are ready to get down to partying. The staff usually has a trivia team going too. Might be a good night to send a few free drinks Christine's way. Last year, at the end of the summer, we screwed around a bit one night, but never sealed the deal. This year, she seems more adventurous. All I need is someone to occupy Courtney and Ariel for a while; give me a chance to work the charm. Those three girls are joined at the hip.

Daniel's another reason this week is especially entertaining. That guy knows how to party. I saw him heading out on his dad's boat earlier; a beautiful 24-foot Yamaha that looks like it absolutely flies. The Resort boat wouldn't be able to keep up for pure speed, but I bet I could make a trip around the lake faster in Stanley's little, 19-foot Tahoe. It would definitely handle better. We'll have to get them out one night after everyone has turned in. Nothing beats tearing around the lake under a clear, moonlit sky.

I set up the last bit of stuff for the evening and shut off the lights in the bar, ready to open up again at around nine. As I'm heading out of the lodge towards the staff cabin, I see a girl getting out of her car. She's average height, thin, with the darkest hair I've ever seen. She takes out a duffel bag and heads towards the main lodge.

As she walks towards me, she doesn't even make eye contact. I can tell a lot about a chick based on how she acts when she's walking towards me. Some girls will give a shy smile and look away; the girl-next-door type. Others will hold your eye for as long as you look at them, not really smiling, but inviting you to try to say something; the 'I'm too sexy' type. Then there are girls like this one; she's not avoiding my gaze in a shy way. She knows I'm looking at her and she doesn't give a fuck about it. Nothing turns me on more than a super-hot chick with attitude. As we get closer, I think to myself: *She will have my dick in her mouth before the end of the week.*

I alter my path just a little so that we're on a collision course and ask, "Checking in today?"

"Yeah, very astute of you, what with the big bag and all," she responds.

"Sure," I say, blanking on what 'astute' means. "I'm *very* astute. And helpful. So if you need any help with *anything*; or finding anything, you just let me know. I'm Blaine."

"Charmed, Blaine, but I know my way around. Thanks."

I'm certain that I detect a hint of playful flirtation in her sarcasm. Or I could be imagining it. Either way, she's hot.

"You've been here before?" I ask. "Must have been a while ago, cuz I'm sure I'd have noticed you."

"Yeah, many times. But not in three or four years," she responds.

"You must be meeting someone here," I state.

"Why do you say that?" She asks.

I finally remember what 'astute' means and reply, in a voice like a detective from an old movie; "Well, I astutely conclude that because you've been here *many times* before, and this isn't really the type of place that people our age come alone, and I'm pretty sure we aren't hiring any new staff; you must be meeting someone here."

A hint of a smile appears on her thin lips; very subtle, but definitely there.

"Nice job Nancy Drew. My family has been coming here since before I was born," she adds.

Just then I notice a familiarity in her face.

"Are you related to Daniel LaPointe?"

"*That's* my brother!" She responds.

"I didn't know that he had another sister. You look a lot like Craig," I add.

"Yeah, I get that a lot."

We stand for a second and look at each other. Her eyes are big and dark. "So are you going to tell me your name?" I ask.

"You never asked. It's Chantelle. And what do *you* do here, Blaine?"

"Your friendly bartender!" I answer with my best smile.

"Good to know. Always handy to know the bartender," she adds as she heads towards the lodge. She doesn't look back.

As I watch her walk away and wonder what she looks like under those sweatpants and T-shirt, I think, *I probably should let that one go.* I've gotten to know the LaPointe family pretty well over the past four years.

*

I reach my cabin and change into some beach shorts. The mid-afternoon sun is out, and has probably warmed up the water nicely. Time to check out the hotties on the beach; tanned, tight waitresses and MILFs out soaking up the sun on their one week of vacation. More importantly, it's time to let them check *me* out.

Chapter Eleven

SARAH

I'M AWAKENED BY the sound of kids playing outside our cabin. A moment of disorientation comes over me. At first I think it's morning and I have somehow missed a full day, but the stream of light coming through where the blinds curl away from the window confuses me. It takes a couple of seconds to remember that I decided to take a nap while Chris went out on the boat with Daniel, Craig, and Terry.

I'm sure I feel this way every year when we finally make it to our Resort week - it's a long stretch from our last vacation at Christmas; but it seems like I'm exhausted these days. I drag myself out of bed and have a quick, cold shower. Hoping to take advantage of some time alone, I grab my book and sit on the balcony. I'm a sucker for a crime drama.

I'm two chapters in when I see Chantelle come over the hill towards our cabins. She's dressed in sweats, with her hair tied back. My initial feeling is that she looks good. When I saw her at Christmas, she was pale and very dark around the eyes. Her boyfriend, Dimitri, is about as sketchy as anyone can be.

Hopefully she's come to her senses, and that's why she's here on her own.

"How are you Telle?" I ask, moving to give her a hug. She places her bag on the ground and hugs me back; which is nice. She hasn't always greeted me like that.

"Good. You? Where is everyone?" she asks.

"Craig, Daniel, Chris and Terry went out on Dad's boat. I actually haven't seen Dad all day though; I don't know where he is. And Mom's in the lodge playing bridge. You didn't see her on your way by?"

"I went around," she answers.

"Well she's excited to have you stay with her. I guess everything else is booked up," I say, trying to judge how she's feeling about staying with Maman.

"Mind if I drop my stuff off, then come sit for a bit?" she asks.

"Not at all," I respond, trying my best not to sound too surprised. "Want a coffee?" I add.

"I'd prefer a beer," she answers.

"Sure. Sorry. I just woke up from a nap; forgot it's afternoon."

*

When Chantelle arrives, she's changed into some yoga shorts and a tank top. She's always been thin, but a couple of years ago, she got *really* thin. Maman and I were pretty worried about her. Looking at her now, at nineteen, she seems to have grown into her body a bit more. She's still thin, but it looks more like a healthy thin, than an 'eating disorder' kind of thin.

"So what's up Telle?" I ask, getting straight to the point.

"What do you mean?" she replies, taking a sip of her beer and not looking over.

"I mean, you haven't been up here in years and now you call and say you're coming the next day. And here you are."

"I just felt like I had to get out of the city," she answers.

"How's Dimitri?" I ask, knowing that there *has* to be something up with him.

"Done," is her only reply.

"What happened?" I ask, having no idea whether she's going to want to talk to me about it.

"Just got a bit out of hand," is all she says at first.

I look over and stay silent for a few moments. She senses my gaze and turns to face me. For a split second, I see eight-year-old Chantelle in her face. Her pet rat has died and she's looking at me with hurt, angry eyes. I've always wanted to protect Chantelle from the world. When she was younger, I was able to do that. But when she got a bit older, she resisted any help from me. Despite being pushed away so many times, I can't help feeling that need to protect her again.

"What happened, Telle? Are you alright?"

She looks away again. "Yeah, I'm good," she says without too much conviction. "We've been fighting a lot recently and I just decided it's not worth it."

"Fighting about what?"

"Everything."

"Did he move out?" I ask.

"I did."

"But that was *your* apartment!"

"I need a change anyway. It's a shit place."

Chantelle moved out when she was sixteen. She had an older boyfriend and they moved to Toronto together. When that ended, she just stayed there. It's almost impossible to get her to talk about what's going on in her life, so I don't really know exactly how she got by for a couple of years. She slept on friend's couches, moved in with a couple of boys, and I think she even stayed in a cheap motel for a couple of months. She'd found a decent little apartment that she shared with a girlfriend. Telle met Dimitri and the friend moved out.

"What are you going to do?" I ask, trying my best to sound concerned, but not judgemental. If I were in her place, I would be freaking out; but this is how she lives.

"I'll be fine. I can stay with a friend until I find a place."

Before I even think it through, I reply, "You know you can always stay with us if you want."

I regret it before I'm even finished saying it.

"Sarah. That's so *you*; way too kind. You take too much shit for this family."

The tone of her voice isn't pity. Nor is it confrontational in any way. She's just stating a fact.

"It's what family does. Besides, someone has to be the voice of reason," I reply, trying to sound casual. "You know you can stay with us if you need to though. That goes for here too; if there's a problem with you and mom."

"I'll be fine."

Not wanting to push too much for details, I sit with her in silence for a while. We see dad's boat heading back. It disappears behind the boathouse to dock. A couple of minutes later, Chris, Craig, and Terry come up the hill towards us. Craig spots Chantelle and comes up the steps to give her a hug.

"How are you Telly?"

Only Craig still gets away with calling her 'Telly'. It was cute when she was five and we were all so much older; but now she'd probably kill Daniel or me if we called her that. For some reason, Craig was just allowed to continue.

"Good. You?"

"Great. You staying all week?" he asks, giving her a hug.

"Not sure," she answers. "Hi Terry. Hey Chris," she adds, giving Terry a hug too.

Chris and Chantelle just give a little nod to each other; and they're both fine with that because neither is really a 'huggy' person.

"Have you seen mom?" Craig asks.

"Not yet."

"Do you want to walk up and see if she's in the lodge? I know she was excited to see you."

"Sure," she answers, turning to walk away. She stops to add, "Thanks Sarah."

I feel a surge of emotion that prevents me from saying anything, so I just smile. I'm sure the next few days will not be all rainbows and lollipops, but I'm hopeful that Chantelle and I can have some more time like this.

"That was nice," says Chris, "a bit weird, but nice."

"Yeah, I know," I say with clear surprise. "How was your boat trip?" I ask Chris and Terry, who has stayed behind with us.

"Good. I actually stayed up for, like 30 seconds!" Chris says with some pride.

"More like 15 seconds actually," Terry adds.

"Really? Felt longer," Chris says, a bit disappointed.

It's a perfect early summer afternoon. The three of us sit on the little porch of our cabin and chat. There are families taking advantage of the nice day to play on the beach. In a way, it seems like only yesterday when Daniel, Craig and I were building sand castles there, while mom and dad sat in their lawn chairs. I wonder how much of our coming here is really just about remembering the past. There have been some difficult years recently, but this year has started well. Despite all the positivity, I can't help but feel a certain ominous sensation; the calm before the storm.

Chapter Twelve

PASCAL

I didn't know if it was day or night
I started kissing everything in sight
But when I kissed a cop down on Thirty-Fourth and Vine
He broke my little bottle of, Love potion number nine…

MY ALARM IS on. It's light out. Shit, I'm late for my exam. Gotta hurry!

I jump up and smash my toe on the footlocker at the end of my bed. I grab my foot and hop around for a few seconds; the pain helping me realize where I am. My alarm is going off; that oldies channel is the only station we can get on the piece of shit little alarm clock. I'm at the Resort. I had a nap.

I sit back down on the edge of the bed and check out my toe. It's already starting to bruise. That's never a good sign.

I've had a nap here pretty much every day this summer. We have to get up so bloody early to get everything ready for breakfast; and the nights are the best part, so I have to sleep in the day. When I told mom that I slept most afternoons, she was shocked. She told me I should be, '*out enjoying the fresh, lake air*'. I had called her at the end of the first week to let her know how things were going because she was so worried when she dropped me off. How embarrassing is it to have your mom bawling as she drops you off at your summer job? I can tell you: It sucks! It certainly isn't going to help my chances of hooking up with any of the waitresses here.

I'm glad there's nobody else in the cabin as I head to the washroom. I hate taking a shit when people are around. That's one thing that's been hard to get used to here: No privacy. Some people don't mind it as much. Last week, Greg and I came home from being out one night and we found Blaine and some girl in the cabin. There's not really anywhere to hide, so when we walked in, we got a great shot of him doing her from behind. Unfortunately, they were facing the other way and all we got to see was Blaine's ass. We shut the door, sat outside and lit a fire in the fire pit. Ten minutes later, they came out and had a smoke by the fire, like nothing happened. I don't know if I'll ever completely get used to that kind of stuff.

When I'm done, I change quickly and head outside. I can't be bothered to shower right now; I'll get cleaned up after dinner, before going down to the bar later.

It's pretty hot outside. Greg and Rob are sitting in the chairs, across the fire pit, throwing a tennis ball back and forth.

"Hey there sleeping beauty," Greg says as I grab a seat.

"I could sleep another six hours," I respond.

"Dave's been working you too hard in the kitchen?" Rob asks.

This is Rob's second year here. Last year, he started in the kitchen doing what Greg and I are doing now; basically all the shit jobs. He also waited on a few tables when one of the waitresses quit towards the end of the summer. Obviously he did OK; cuz Stanley hired him as a full-time waiter this year. In the first two weeks, he's made like $500 in tips. I gotta get me some of that.

"He's not that bad. Just not used to getting up so fucking early. I swear, on Thursday, for my day off, I'm sleeping all day."

"No you won't," Rob says.

"You could just turn in early tonight," Greg jokes.

Greg knows I've been trying to hook up with Maria, one of the chamber maids, since last week. She's kind of shy and doesn't go out much; but last week, she was out on trivia night and we talked for a while. If I had any skill with women, I might have some idea whether she's actually interested. But I suck at talking to girls.

"No way! Tonight's the night," I brag. We all know how full of shit I am.

"Good luck with that, Romeo," Rob adds.

We chuck the ball around for a while and talk about useless crap; my odds of actually scoring with Maria, whether the Leafs should trade their fourth overall pick in the draft, and some of the more unusual guests from the past two weeks. At around 4:00, we get ready to head to the dining room to set up for dinner.

Rob and Greg hop on the golf cart and peel off, leaving me to walk. Nice. The staff cabins are set back a bit from the rest of the Resort. They aren't really the places that Stanley would want to be on display for all the guests. It's your typical student housing; nobody really gives a shit about a few empty beer cans and broken chairs lying around. We tidy up a little most days, but it was probably a good idea to hide the staff cabins across the road and behind a row of thick evergreens.

I walk down the driveway towards the road. As I turn the corner, I see Dave and some guy standing by a car. Dave's back is to me, as he takes something from the other guy. I can't see for sure what it is; it looks like a bag of something, but I can tell it's not a bag of weed. He shakes the guy's hand and turns around. As he does, I see the pills he stuffs into the side pocket of his army shorts. He looks up and our eyes meet for a second before I whip out my phone and look down. The car pulls away and I can see that Dave is waiting for me as I walk across the street.

"Ready to get to work?" he asks.

"Oh, yeah. Had a nap this afternoon, so I'm feeling good," I respond. I try to act like I didn't see anything, while trying not to act like I'm hiding the fact that I saw something. I'm pretty sure I'm not succeeding, but there's no way I'm saying anything unless he does.

"Alright. Tell Greg to start de-boning the fish and you can get going on the marinade for the beef. I'll be there in a bit," he adds and turns away.

None of my business, I think to myself.

*

The first voice I hear when I get to the kitchen is Courtney's.

"Isn't it your job to have the dishes ready for us when we need to set up for dinner?" she asks Greg in a super snotty tone.

"It's also my job to do the prep work that Dave asks me to do," he answers.

Courtney sees me coming. "Where the fuck have you been?"

"I was just talking to Dave about what we need to be doing," I answer, a bit too timidly. Girls like Courtney scare me. I had a girl a lot like her in my high school. Once she didn't like someone, she made it her mission to bring them down. I don't want any part of that.

"What you both need to be doing is getting those dishes ready for us to set up our tables," Courtney orders.

"That's right," adds Ariel, standing, of course just behind Courtney. They both turn and storm off.

"We forgot to wash those this morning didn't we?" I ask Greg.

"Totally," he responds with a half laugh.

"Dave wants you to start the fish and me to marinade steaks," I tell him.

"Alright. We can knock these dishes off in ten minutes then do that other shit," he states.

I plug my phone into the speaker and hit shuffle on my '*Pumpin'* playlist. Pitbull and Ke$ha get us going.

Ten minutes later, we have everything ready for the wait staff to finish setting all their tables. We shut the music off and head to the walk-in to grab what we need. Just as we are starting to get set up for prep work, Dave comes in. He's got this weird habit of walking around the kitchen once before saying anything. He touches a couple of places as he does his lap. A couple of times since we've been here, something has interrupted him, and Dave just walked out and came back in again. I asked Rob about it during the first week and he said it was best to just ignore him until he says something first. I keep my head down and keep working.

The weird thing is that today, Dave never says anything to anyone. He just goes over to his station and starts organizing all his shit. There are a couple of minutes of silence where we're not sure what to say. Blaine walks in and looks around.

"Whoa, keep it down in here party animals. You'll disturb the guests."

"What's up man?" Greg says with some relief that the awkward moment is over.

"What's on the menu tonight boys?" Blaine asks, coming over to our stations to check out what we are doing.

"Steak, salmon, or risotto," I answer.

Blaine dips a spoon in the risotto that's warming on the stove.

"Fuckin' A boys. That's sweet," he compliments. "Dave, by the end of the summer, these wieners might actually be able to cook thanks to you."

Blaine walks over to where Dave has been silently working for a few minutes and puts his hand on his shoulder.

Dave looks up at Blaine, and all he says is, "Yeah," in a kind of far-off voice.

"You all right man?" Blaine asks.

"Yeah. Just in the zone," he responds, turning back to his chopping.

"Alright then," he says, turning and looking at both Greg and me. "You guys need some tunes or something in here. It's like a fucking library." He turns and walks back out to the dining room, grabbing a roll on the way out.

Greg looks over at me with a questioning look on his face. I shrug my shoulders.

"You OK if we put on some music, Dave?" Greg asks hesitantly, still looking at me.

"Sure. None of that pop shit though," he says, without looking up.

I pick a mellower playlist that seems to suit Dave's mood. One thing I can do well is pick a playlist to suit the occasion. I should really be a DJ.

I don't know what was in that bag, but it seems to have chilled Dave out majorly. We're half way through *Champagne Supernova*, when Courtney comes in, followed by Ariel and Christine. She stops just inside the kitchen and looks at the dishes we have stacked ready for them. Without saying anything, the three of them load up what they need and turn to leave.

Just as she's at the door, Courtney turns around. "This music sucks," she says, then walks out.

Dave doesn't even look up, but he says, in a calm voice, "You suck."

Greg and I look at each other for a second, then burst out laughing. This might be an interesting dinner.

Chapter Thirteen

CRAIG

"SOMETIMES I DO *not* understand my brother," I tell Terry as we get back to our cabin.

"In what way?" she asks.

"Him taking us all out today," I answer.

"Yeah, that was really nice."

"I know! That's what I mean."

"He's not pure evil, Craig. He has his moments."

"But even those moments tend to include something for him," I add.

"I think what's in it for him, is just being able to take everyone out and kind of be in charge of it all; probably makes him feel important. You know he likes that!"

"Yeah, I guess. He just usually has a girl to impress when he takes out dad's boat."

"What time are we having dinner?" Terry asks, changing the subject.

"We're meeting mom and Chantelle at 6:00," I answer. "I

bet it was also Daniel's way of 'putting in his time' during the day. I wouldn't be surprised if he doesn't show up at dinner."

"Let's not overthink it babe," Terry says, coming to wrap her arms around me. "I'm sure he'll be there. And if he's not; he's not."

"You're right."

"It was a nice first day. Just relax and enjoy the rest of it," she says looking me in the eyes and running her hand through the back of my hair. I lean down and kiss her. I've always had issues relaxing. Whenever Terry and I take a vacation, it takes a couple of days for me to be able to slow down and do nothing. Terry's hands gliding up my shirt are doing a great job now at helping me forget about my brother.

I unbutton her jean shorts and touch that fabulous ass. It sounds terrible and unromantic to say, but it's the truth; that ass was what first caught my attention with Terry. We met at a mutual friend's house one night. She was wearing these yoga pants that looked like they were custom made for her figure. She caught me staring as she leaned over to open a drawer. My mouth was probably hanging open like an idiot, but she just smiled and went on with what she was doing. It took me about half an hour to get the courage to introduce myself.

Undoing the tie at the front, Terry reaches her hand down my shorts as she gives a playful bite to my bottom lip. I'm as hard as a rock when someone knocks on the screen door.

After a second, Chris says, "Hello?" and peeks his head in.

Terry and I are standing there; me pitching a massive tent in my swim shorts, and her holding up her jeans with one hand. Chris gives an embarrassed chuckle.

"Sorry," he says, looking at the ground with a smile. "Terry; you just left your phone at our place. I'll set it down here." He places it on the little table by the door. "See you later," he adds, shutting the door behind him.

Terry looks up and laughs. She shuts the inside door, takes my hand and leads me to the bedroom.

For dinner, we all planned that Sarah and Chris would eat with dad; and Daniel, Terry, Chantelle and I would eat with mom. This will probably be the first time that mom and dad will be in the same space since last year. After being divorced for five years, you would think that most of the tension would be over, but mom hasn't really let go. In most messy divorces, the former couple would only see each other in the presence of lawyers. But in our case, once a year, mom and dad both come back to the Resort. Every year, they are thrown into this weird vacation setting where they have years of memories and relationships built. To mom, the week at the Resort is a reassurance that she still has connections to the people they used to hang out with. In their own ways, each does not want to give up to the other person, what the Resort represents for them.

Terry and I pop next door to see if Daniel is ready to walk to dinner with us. Annette is there, reading a magazine. She tells us dad is resting and that she hasn't seen Daniel. Hand in hand, we stroll over to mom's cabin. At a nice, slow pace, it takes about five minutes to get from our side of the Resort to the other side, where mom and Sarah have their cabins. A dirt path winds through the trees and down a little hill to the lake. We pass the boathouse and the beach. There are a couple of boys playing in the water as their parents sit and chat. The boys look like brothers; maybe one or two years apart. The younger one is trying to copy the older one as he balances on a flutter board.

"Is that you and Daniel about twenty years ago?" Terry asks.

"Pretty much," I admit. Growing up here, it was always kind of like an extended family vacation. Kids played together and adults looked out for all the kids. I guess that's why so many people come back every year. That sense of community is getting harder and harder to find. Unless they live in a cul-de-sac, not many parents let their kids outside just to play anymore. The Resort is a bit like a time warp to the days when kids ran around and played outside, skinned their knees and got stung by bees; and where you could walk up and talk to any adult without fear of it being a weirdo.

Without really planning it, I say, "Maybe that'll be our kids in a few years."

"If you're lucky," Terry responds without missing a beat.

We've talked about maybe getting married sometime, but we haven't really discussed any serious plan to start a family. But I'm pretty sure it's what we both want soon.

We reach Sarah's cabin first. She and Chris are chatting on the porch with a couple I recognize from last year, but whose names I can't remember. Not entirely ready to see them, we give a little wave and keep going to see mom and Chantelle. Chris raises his beer and gives me a little wink.

*

The four of us walk over to dinner and find our seats. The dining room is about half full. Some tables have already eaten; most likely the couples with young kids. Others haven't arrived yet. It's like this most evenings. The final night of the week is the only night where everyone eats at the same time; it's a bit of a celebration of the week. People who've been here before know to dress it up for that one.

"Hi guys, is it just the four of you today?" greets Michelle, our waitress when we eat at mom's table. She's efficient, reliable, and cordial. Across the other side of the dining room, at dad's table, Courtney's our waitress. She's pretty reliable too, but totally different in tableside manner.

"I think Daniel is coming too, Michelle. So we should be five eventually," mom answers.

We order drinks and chat while looking over the menu. Nobody really presses Chantelle too much to find out why she decided to come, and she's certainly not about to just tell us. While we're only six and a half years apart, I know very little about her life. We chat and text every now and then, but it's usually chitchat; never the details of what's going on in her life.

From the other side of the dining room, Sarah, Chris, and dad walk in. Annette is just behind. In a matter of seconds, there's a shift in energy at our table. I'm not a terribly spiritual person, but moments like that can make anyone believe that there's something around us, other than just us. As my mom looks across the room and sees my dad and Annette come in, it's almost like she actually changes the air around us; it's heavier, denser, and more electric. The air changes colour from seafoam to lipstick red. The temperature rises two degrees in an instant. Everything goes from standard definition to HD as I blink. Someone else is controlling the speed of everything around me, and it all goes in slow motion.

My dad looks across the room at us and waves. He turns and says something to the rest of the group. Chris and Annette turn to walk towards their table and my dad and Sarah start walking towards us. It seems like an eternity for them to cross the dining room. When I glance at mom, she's looking down at her menu. To break the interminable silence that has become the soundtrack to them making their way across the seemingly endless space, I feel like I need to start some conversation.

"I think instead of having the risotto this year, I might try the salmon."

Nobody says anything. Terry gives me a look that tells me it's probably best to just shut up.

"Hi Chantelle, how are you sweetie?" my dad asks as he nears the table.

Chantelle gets up to give him a hug. "Hi Dad. I'm good," she responds.

"Son," he says as he hugs me, then moves on to Terry. "How are you Terry? It's so nice to see you."

"Hi Stephane. You're looking well," she responds as she sits back down.

"Hello Marion, how are you?" he says to mom.

I glance over at a table next to us. A family of five has sat there for the past three years. We've talked to the couple several times. Their names are Randy and Reilly Holden; both are principals. Their three kids, Robby, Reese, and Ricky; probably eight, ten, and eleven, are all little shits. They run around the Resort and dominate every space they're in. The whole table is looking over at us. It's at that moment that I realize that half the dining room is watching.

At moments like this, I'm sometimes struck with something completely absurd. I think it's a defense mechanism. I imagine that we are all gathered around a little jack in the box and the lever has been turned. You're pretty sure that something's going to blow, but not sure when or how big it will be. Maybe there isn't even a scary, little clown inside; maybe it's a harmless, little, stuffed rabbit that just slowly peeks out. Or maybe the box will never even open.

Mom slowly looks up from the menu and says, "fine."

"Good. I hope you are enjoying your week," he adds.

"I see that *she* is too ashamed to come over to say hello to Chantelle," mom adds.

"Marion, you know that had she come over, you would have told her she wasn't welcome," my dad rightly points out, giving the lever another little turn.

"Don't you tell me what I would or wouldn't do," mom spits.

"Not here," Sarah says, stepping closer to the table and giving both our parents a glare.

This is normally where dad gracefully backs down. I think we're all expecting him to say a calm goodbye to us all, turn, and walk confidently back to his table. We're all taken aback when he speaks.

"Since I'm paying for you being here, I think I should have the right to speak my mind."

"HOW DARE YOU COME OVER HERE AND SPEAK TO ME LIKE THAT. Isn't it enough that you come here and parade around with that tramp?"

From a few tables over, there's a huge crash. Everyone, including my dad, looks over to see that one of the waitresses, who has apparently been watching the whole scene, has dropped a tray full of salads, crab cakes, and drinks. He turns back, but not quite in time to dodge the glass of white wine mom has thrown at him. She then storms out of the dining room, leaving the entire room speechless, with their collective mouths open.

Chapter Fourteen

MICHELLE

THE CRASH OF the tray echoes through the whole dining room. Every head turns to look at Ariel, who is totally frozen. She looks like a nervous kid who has to make a presentation to the class and has completely forgotten everything. I've dropped things before while waiting on tables, but never a whole tray. A couple of guests near her get up to help.

"Thanks so much, but don't worry; we'll get it," I say, hustling over to the crash site. "Ariel, let's get this cleaned up quickly," I add, giving her just a little squeeze on the arm. She snaps out of her daze and starts to pick up dishes. Pascal comes out of the kitchen with a broom and dustpan to help. After cleaning up all the big stuff, I take the tray and lead Ariel back to the kitchen.

"What the fuck happened?" I ask, shutting the kitchen door.

"I just dropped it," she replies defensively.

"When shit like that happens and guests are arguing, you can't stand and gawk at them!" I tell her, placing the tray on a counter. "And when you drop something, don't just stand there like a fucking statue. Clean it up!"

"She didn't mean to do it, Michelle. You don't need to be such a bitch about it," adds Christine, coming in from the dining room.

"Stay the fuck out of this," I snap. "It's not that she dropped something, it's *why* she dropped it; and the fact that she couldn't even figure out what to do *when* she dropped it."

"Sorry we can't all be perfect waitresses like you," Ariel says as tears well up in her eyes.

"Don't be such a fucking drama queen. You've been here less than three weeks and you still have no clue how to wait on tables. You screw up orders, stand around when you should be working, and you just broke, like 10 dishes."

"Plus those glasses last week," Greg adds.

"STAY OUT OF THIS ASSHOLE," Ariel yells.

"Holy shit. Keep it down. The whole dining room will hear you," Pascal says, peeking out the kitchen door.

Ariel is in full on break down mode now. She moves closer to Christine, gaining strength from some support. "You're right. I'm not as good at this as you are Michelle," she says with a sneer. "I also have a life and I'm not going to get old and bitchy being *just* a waitress like you."

There's silence as we stand and glare at each other. I'm ready to lunge at her and rip her eyes out, and it doesn't take long for her to see it in my face. She scans the room and inches closer to Christine.

"Whoa," Pascal says.

"Yeah," Greg adds.

"I've been helping you, you little bitch. Your tables complain to me about you, and I say that you're just new and you'll come around. Everyone here knows you're a useless, little twat." I slowly take a step towards her. "You are on your own now. If you ever speak that way to me again, I'll break your fucking nose."

"Whoa," Pascal repeats.

"Yeah," says Greg.

"You can't threaten her!" Christine adds from behind Ariel.

"I'll tell Stanley. Everyone here heard you," Ariel says, pointing around the room. Pascal and Greg look at each other.

"I am *not* getting involved," Pascal says, shaking his head.

"Don't look at me," Greg adds.

From the other side of the kitchen, there's another loud crash. I turn around to see Dave standing over a pot of risotto on the floor. I hadn't even noticed that he was standing at his work station the whole time. In his hands, he's holding a tray of salmon. Without any expression on his face, he flips the tray over and dumps it right next to the risotto.

"You all need to figure out your shit. I'm done with it all," he says turning to leave. "Good luck with dinner."

With that, he walks out. Pascal looks at me with complete shock on his face.

"What the hell are we going to do now? We have half the Resort to feed and that was two thirds of our food," Pascal shrieks, in a very high pitch.

The back door to the kitchen opens and Stanley walks in, followed by Courtney. He looks at the food on the floor and the tray of broken dishes on the counter. He scans the room and stops at me.

"What the heck happened?"

"There was some trouble in the dining room, Ariel dropped a tray, we had an argument in here, then Dave dumped the food and left."

Stanley walks over to the door and looks into the dining room.

"We still have a room full of guests out there. Whatever the problem in here is, it can wait. Boys, clean this up and get started on more food. Ladies, get out there and reassure everyone. Stall with drinks. We have to get this poop parade back on the tracks."

"Does that even make sense?" Pascal asks softly.

"You know what he means," I whisper.

"That was the end of the fish though," Greg tells Stanley.

"I have no clue how to make the risotto," Pascal says.

"I think Rob can make it," Greg suggests.

"Good," Stanley says, trying to get everyone on the same page. "I'll help him. Michelle, get Rob in here. Tell Blaine to take over his tables for him. Let the guests know that we're out of fish and that the risotto will take a bit longer."

I leave the kitchen and step out into the dining room, not looking at Ariel or Christine. As I walk out, still feeling the blood burning in my face, some guests pretend like nothing's going on; but there's clearly a tension in the air.

Chapter Fifteen

BLAINE

"SERIOUSLY DUDE, YOU missed a full-on disaster today at dinner," I tell Zack.

It's about 9:30 and some guests are starting to show up to trivia night. Zack's the social director at the Resort during the week. Stanley likes to let the guests settle in for a couple of days before any organized shit happens, so Zack gets the weekends off. He usually comes back by Sunday night to introduce himself to the guests and run the trivia night.

"No shit. Did she really throw a glass of wine at him?" he asks.

"Hit him right in the chest."

"What happened after Ariel dropped the tray?"

"She stands there like she's just puked all over herself in a school play or something. Then Michelle comes over and drags her to the kitchen," I tell him.

"No shit," Zack responds.

"Then we hear yelling from in the kitchen. I basically had to settle down the whole dining room."

"Where does Dave come into it?" Zack asks.

"I guess he just got fed up, dumped all the food on the floor and took off," I reply.

After the blow-ups with the guests, and in the kitchen, everyone was on edge. I kind of felt like it was my job to settle everyone down a bit. Usually, there's no music in the dining room; Stanley always says that the acoustics in the room suck and it gets noisy enough with everyone talking. Tonight, I put on some chill Spanish guitar music. Stanley never said anything; I think he realized we needed something.

I have no idea how tonight is going to go. Personally, I think the best way to get through all the tense shit is for everyone to come out for a few drinks; loosen up a little and talk it out.

By 10:00, staff and guests are starting to arrive and the bar is filling up. People are getting their teams ready. Emma Watson, the younger daughter of the Watson family, sits at the bar and orders a gin and tonic. Apparently, their family has been coming since before she was born. Emma is super-hot. Both the Watson sisters are tall and fit. They're swimmers so they have a strong look about them, but not a butchy, field-hockey kind of look; they still look feminine. Their mom is from some tropical island, so they have this dark, creamy looking skin tone that's kind of exotic. It's the type of skin colour that makes you think how great it would look after shooting your load right up their backs.

"How's everyone doing?" she asks.

"Not too sure. I haven't really asked anyone. And nobody is talking too much."

"That was quite a scene," she adds. "I hope Sarah and Craig are alright. I would be horrified if my parents fought like that in a public place."

"Everyone knows there's nothing *they* can do," I assure her.

"Yeah, but it would still suck."

Just then, Daniel LaPointe comes in and heads over to us.

"Emma, how are you? You are looking more and more fabulous each year," Daniel says as he greets her with a hug. "What's up Blaino?" he asks, shaking my hand. Daniel and I have had more than one conversation about Emma Watson and how much we each want to fuck her. I think neither of us has a particularly good chance, but if one of us ever did, it would be a conquest for the other to be majorly jealous of.

"How are you doing, Daniel? You alright? How are your parents?" she asks.

"Haven't seen my mom, but my dad was a bit upset. I guess there was a bit of a scene earlier," he responds.

I hadn't really clued in, but now that I think about it, he wasn't there earlier.

"Yeah, you missed a good one," I tell him.

"Have you talked to Sarah? She must be upset," Emma asks.

"No. I was out meeting a client for golf and dinner this evening. Just got back and spoke to my dad before coming here. Way too much drama if you ask me."

He leans against the back of Emma's chair and changes the subject. "How was your year?" he asks.

"Great. Montreal is such a cool city," she says.

The three of us chat while more guests arrive. She tells us about living in an apartment in Montreal, how wonderful the university is, and how her sister's wedding was. Zack waits until about 10:30 before he starts the competition.

When guests come to the Resort for the first time, they look at the schedule of events and arrive where they're supposed to be at the time that's listed. The reality is that Resort time is a bit like Jamaica time. Trivia is scheduled for a 9:30 start; but in the four years that I've been here, it has never started before 10:00. The guests who are type-A's have trouble with that at first; it's kind of funny. Some people just can't handle the lack of structure, and others are totally fine with it. There's probably some deep psychological shit to explain it. Maybe I'll ask Emma about it later; she's been studying psychology for a couple of years. Chicks love to talk about themselves, and bartenders are classic listeners. Might be my way in.

As is usually the case, the day's tensions are basically forgotten after a few drinks. Ariel is sitting with Courtney and Christine. With all the drama and commotion of the day, there's little hope of getting Christine alone later. Pascal and Greg are on a team with Rob and a couple of guests. Neither Dave nor Michelle ever comes to these things, so there's really no chance of confrontation. I'm chatting with Zack about possibly going out on the boat later when Chantelle LaPointe comes in. She waves at her brother, who's sitting with Emma and the rest of the Watson family, and comes straight to the bar.

"Aren't you the friendly bartender? Billy is it?" she asks, clearly messing with me.

"You got it. And you're Shannon right?" I respond with my best smile.

As I had seen earlier in the parking lot, a hint of a smile comes across her lips. It's clear that she works hard to put up a tough front; but I can tell that when she does let that drop, she has a great smile.

"Can I get a drink?" she asks.

"I'll do my best," I say. "What would you like?"

"How about a shot of tequila and a 50?" she orders.

I can't hide the surprise on my face. "That's pretty hard ass!" I say. I regret it as soon as I say it; it sounds a bit too critical.

"No. Two shots and a double whiskey would be hard ass," she responds without any sign of being offended.

"A shot and a beer it is," I say, turning to grab her drinks.

"You're going to have something too right? I would hate to

drink alone," she says as I pour her a shot of Cuervo. I look over, trying to judge her face. I have to admit that she has thrown me for a loop. The expression on her face is hard to read. That was clearly a proposition, but she's still giving off a frostiness. I also get a mental flash of hanging out with Daniel. We aren't exactly close, but we hang out and party the week he comes here. I don't really know how he'd feel about me hooking up with his little sister. Based on his behaviour, I doubt he'd care; but you never know if there's a protective brother thing in there somewhere. I know her sister, Sarah, would be pissed; but that's not really a major concern.

"I would love to; but drinking on the job is the number one no-no for bartenders," I reply.

"Shame," she shrugs.

It's not like I've never had a drink before while working, but I try to avoid it until the last hour of my shift. It's still early, but I don't see much harm in one little shot.

"Maybe just one would work," I say, pouring a small shot for myself.

Like a pro, Chantelle licks her wrist, pours the salt, licks her wrist again, downs the shot, then grabs a lemon wedge; not a flinch.

I love to have a few beers. I sometimes even go crazy and drink some vodka. But I've never really been a fan of tequila. I try my best not to scrunch my face up like a pug while I take my shot. I mostly succeed.

"How long does this trivia shit last?" she asks.

"Should be done by midnight," I answer. "You got big plans after?"

"Avoiding going back to my mom's mostly," she responds.

"Is she alright?" I ask, trying to seem as interested and sincere as possible. I guess I try a bit too hard.

"Is this sensitive bartender thing an act or do you really talk like that?" she asks flatly.

"Total act. I'm really an insensitive dick," I say jokingly.

"Thought so."

"Seriously though, how's your family doing?" I ask.

"My mom's mostly calmed down. She's surprisingly not very concerned about putting on a big scene in the dining room. My sister's probably the most stressed."

"Everyone will forget it by tomorrow," I assure her.

"Yeah, right," she responds sarcastically.

"Well, Zack and I were planning on taking a nighttime boat ride later if you're interested," I offer.

"Maybe."

*

The rest of the night is pretty normal. The trivia is won by Emma's family. The wait staff starts dancing after midnight. Pascal and Greg pull out their 'N Sync moves. Stanley pops in to talk to several regular guests to make sure they're alright. From what I can see, nobody really gives a shit about it by the end of the night. I think what Stanley really wanted to do was talk to Michelle or Dave, but since they weren't around, he comforted himself with talking to everyone else.

By about 12:45, the guests are clearing out. Courtney, Ariel, and Christine head off together. The other staff hangs around for a while before turning in; breakfast prep comes pretty early. Pascal is chatting up one of the chamber maids, and looking like he sucks at it. Zack and Chantelle are sitting at the bar as I clean up a bit. She's had a few beers throughout the night, along with that early shot of tequila; but she's still as alert as she was when she walked in. At nineteen, you can tell that she's not a rookie when it comes to having a few drinks.

"Is this boat thing happening?" she asks.

"For sure," I respond.

Zack looks a bit hesitant. He never likes to take the boat out at night; it usually takes a couple of minutes of convincing, but he eventually caves. I finish up in the bar and we take a walk down to the boat house. The moon is pretty full tonight. I remember there's some fancy word for it, like a waning gibbon or something. It's perfect for boating at night; not too bright so you can see everything, but bright enough you can tell where you're going. After working here a few years, I know the lake well; I could probably get around it blindfolded if I had to.

We throw some life jackets and flashlights into the boat and coast out a ways from the dock before I pick up speed. Chantelle cracks open a beer and hands it to Zack. Again, he looks a bit nervous, but takes it anyway.

Sometimes when I take girls out on the boat, they get all scared if I really open up and let it fly; but Chantelle doesn't seem bothered at all. It looks like she's out for a Sunday drive with her grandma. Her tough girl, hard-to-get attitude is really working. All I can think about is getting rid of Zack and fucking her right here on the boat. Somehow, the concern over Daniel's feelings has faded.

"Someone's flashing a light from the shore there," Zack says, scanning the side of the lake.

"Just someone out partying on their cottage dock," I reply.

"Maybe we should slow down a bit. If people see the Resort boat flying around the lake in the middle of the night, they might get pissed," Zack worries.

"No way they can tell it's us dude," I say. "Plus, there's no law against boating at night."

"No, but you could get in shit for operating a vessel in a

dangerous manner, and operating a vessel while impaired," says Chantelle matter-of-factly.

Zack looks at her, even more worried, and then looks at me.

"Thanks," I say to Chantelle.

"Lawyer family," she says, and shrugs.

I go just a little farther before turning around and heading back to the Resort. I take it a bit slower on the way back. It's a clear sky, so we tie up the boat outside the boat house and I sit up on the bow.

Zack has hopped out to tether the boat. "I'm going to turn in. I gotta be up at breakfast to go around and introduce myself to all the guests," he says.

"Later," I respond. Chantelle nods.

There's a moment of silence after Zack leaves. I'm deciding how exactly to handle this girl. On one hand, she insisted I have a drink, sat and chatted most of the night, then came out on the boat. At the same time, she's not showing any of the signs that a typical nineteen-year-old would show when I put on the charm; no giggling or hair flipping. As if reading my mind, she says:

"Don't even think of getting all macho and treating me like some bimbo waitress or something," she says.

"Oh, I know you're no bimbo. I just can't figure what you *are*."

"Good. Don't try," she states.

"So why *are* you here?" I ask.

"Didn't you hear what I just said?" she asks.

"Yeah, but I'm curious. It doesn't seem like you are super close with anyone in your family. You haven't been here in years. Yet you decide to come up by yourself. Something must have happened."

"Fucking Nancy Drew again," she jokes.

I'm glad she's not getting angry. I feel a bit like I'm teetering on the edge of either breaking through or pissing her off.

"I prefer a Hardy Boy," I say, running my fingers through my hair dramatically. "Something did happen though, didn't it?" I ask again.

She looks me in the eyes. Even in the moonlight, I can see that there's emotion there. She's holding something in; and I realize that there's no way she's ever going to tell me. She doesn't want to. All I am to her is a distraction.

That's completely fine with me; it might be what I'm best at.

"Alright. How about a beer?" I ask reaching into the cooler we brought.

"Thanks," she says, touching my hand as she slowly takes the can. In that touch, I know she's not just thanking me for the beer. We sit back and look up at the moon.

"You ever wonder how the hell anyone ever imagined a cow jumping over the moon?" I ask.

"Not really," she answers with a slight laugh. "But I did use to worry about the moon drowning in the lake and not being able to get out."

"That's a bit dark," I say without thinking.

"Interesting childhood," she responds.

Not sure how to continue, I sit in silence for a while, drinking my beer.

"My turn to play Nancy Drew," she says suddenly.

"You think you can match my detective talents? I doubt it."

"This is usually the point where you would be making your move, but I'm different from the bimbos you're used to and you're not totally sure what move to use."

"That's actually pretty good," I admit.

"If I were someone different, what would you be doing right now?" she asks.

"Probably asking you if you were cold? I might throw you a couple of compliments, or try and impress you somehow."

"And you don't think any of that would work?" she asks.

"I'm pretty sure it wouldn't," I respond.

"How about just saying, 'I think you are really hot and I'd like to fuck you'?" she suggests.

"Direct. I like it. But it seems a bit crass."

"What are you hoping we do? Make sweet love in a fresh meadow? Isn't most of the shit you've been thinking about all night pretty crass?" she asks.

I look over at her. "I think you're really hot and I'd love to fuck you."

She slowly sets her beer down, gets up from her seat and stands over me. I make a move to stand up, but she leans over and pushes me back down. Looking me right in the eyes, she reaches down and undoes my belt. She makes no move to kiss me as she unbuttons my jeans and slides her hand down my pants, grabbing my cock. After three firm strokes, I realize something.

"I *don't* have a condom," I say, disappointed in myself.

Still stroking my dick, she reaches into the front of her jeans, pulls one out and hands it to me. I look her in the eyes and realize that she came to the bar tonight expecting full well to be here right now. She knew exactly what she wanted and made sure she got it. I find that very hot!

I undo her jeans and she slips them off. She steps over and straddles me, lowering herself down. She's warm and wet against my cock. I lean up to kiss her, but she pulls her head back, looking at my eyes the whole time. Taking the condom out of my hand, she opens it and slips it on me. There's no subtlety in her intentions, and it turns me on more than I think it would. Before I have a chance to think, she's riding me hard, grinding back and forth with an aggression and anger that takes me by surprise. Going with the mood, I give her ass a good, hard slap and thrust deep inside her. She lets out a little squeal and grinds even faster. There's no stopping myself from exploding.

As I'm recovering my breath, she leans back and looks me in the eyes. She tilts her head forward and kisses me for the first time; not lovingly or tenderly, but firmly and with some heat.

"Any chance of getting a bite to eat before round two?" she asks.

Chapter Sixteen

SARAH

UNSURE OF WHERE I am, I blink a few times to try to clear my eyes. The room is familiar, but it's not our cabin. It takes a minute to remember I slept at Maman's. It must be the stress of the last few days, but I feel like I've been hit by a truck as I drag myself out of the little, twin bed. It's hit and miss with the quality of the mattresses here. Stanley and Melissa have been replacing them gradually over the past few years; but this one is clearly not one of the new ones.

After Maman stormed out of dinner last night, I followed her back to the cabin. When dad and Annette are involved, she just loses it. There's no reasoning with her once she gets a head of steam. What surprises me most is dad's behaviour. He usually tries to keep the peace and stay away. Maybe he thought mom wouldn't make a big scene in the middle of the dining room. Or maybe he figured by now she should be over it all. Whatever he thought, he was wrong.

After getting back to the cabin, we sat and had a glass of

wine as I listened to her rant. Stanley stopped by to check in later in the evening. He asked how Maman was doing and listened to her without ever trying to put blame on her. He's always been so good at ensuring everyone feels at ease.

Maman's not up yet, so I quietly head back to our cabin. There's no response from Telle on my phone from the texts I sent last night. There's not much danger at the Resort, so I know she's safe, but I'm still worried. I hope she hasn't done something stupid. Chris is still sleeping when I get back. Right now, the thought of coffee doesn't really appeal to me, so I grab a glass of orange juice and sit on the deck. Texting Craig and Daniel gets no response. There's a restlessness that I just can't shake. I don't want to read; so I grab my earbuds, pick a playlist, and sit and look out at the lake.

It's nice to have a moment to relax; but I just can't stop my brain from thinking. I've always been a worrier. I have no idea where it comes from; my dad has always been an easy going man who takes life as it comes. Sure he made some mistakes, but he owned up to them and moved on. Daniel is clearly the apple that fell directly under the tree. Craig is a bit more like me, but much more reasonable. And I have no idea what's up with Telle; she doesn't seem to worry about anything. I guess, apart from me, Maman is the biggest worrier in the family; although I don't think it's worrying as much as it is having intense freak-outs. When Craig was in public school, he was getting bullied by an older kid. Maman found out and stormed right to school to confront the boy. She saw him get off the bus, approached him and said something in his ear that scared the shit out of him. I don't know what she said, but the message got through; Craig wasn't bullied any more that year.

Now that I think about it, I guess what happens is that everyone in my family worries about their own problems, in their own way; but I'm the one who worries about the problems of everyone else as well as my own. Issues with mom and dad are alright to deal with over the phone when we're each at our own houses; but here at the Resort, they're right in my face. I can't ignore them.

The more I think about it, the more sense it makes for Chris and me to skip the trip next year. I'm not going to fool myself into thinking I'd be able to detach completely during our week if the rest of the family came, and we didn't; but I know it would be better than feeling exhausted and sick to my stomach the whole week.

Chris opens the screen door and comes out in his pajama bottoms and no shirt.

"Hey babe," he says, giving me a kiss on the cheek. He clearly hasn't brushed his teeth yet. "Did you sleep Ok?"

"Not really. That bed is a piece of shit."

"Sorry. Why don't you go in and snooze for a bit before breakfast?"

"Nah. I've been up for a while. I'd never be able to get to sleep," I say.

"Maybe a nap later then. Might rain anyway," Chris suggests, looking at the sky. He puts his arms across his chest and shivers. "Chilly this morning. I'm going to get a shirt. Do you want a coffee?" he asks.

"No thanks. My stomach's a bit off."

"Want me to go for a walk so you can have some privacy to take a poop?" he asks with a smile.

"No thanks."

I'm just putting my music back on again when I see Chantelle walking around the side of the main lodge, shoes in hand and wearing the clothes from last night.

"Hey sis," she says cheerily, coming over to our deck.

"Where were you?" I ask, feeling irritation.

"Had a sleepover," she answers with a cheeky smile.

"Why didn't you text someone to let them know where you were?" As I say it, I realize I sound exactly like an overprotective parent. I know that's the dynamic of our relationship that she hates, but I just can't help it.

"Didn't realize I was supposed to check in."

"Didn't you think we might worry?" I ask.

She stands for a minute and looks at me. I'm sensing an argument coming on and regret being the one to start it, but I know if she starts yelling at me, I'm going to be yelling back. When she speaks, she's very calm.

"I don't check in with you, or anyone else, on any other day of the year. So I don't see why it should be any different just because I chose to come up here."

I take a breath. I don't actually want a fight, so I try my best to stay calm. "I know you're right, but I just want some help from the rest of this family. It would have been nice to have you here so I didn't have to be the only one to stay with Maman."

"You didn't *have* to do that. She's a big girl, Sarah. She didn't have to make the choice to have a public freak-out."

"Come on. Someone *had* to be here. You must see that," I say. "It's really hard for her to come here and see dad and Annette together at the Resort that our family has been coming to for, like twenty years."

"It's been five years since they split, Sarah! She *has* to get over it."

"But she's not."

"Maybe she should stop coming here then," Chantelle suggests.

Chris comes out in his robe, with two mugs of coffee.

"Chantelle. I saw you and brought you out a coffee." He gives her a hug and hands her the mug.

"Thanks Chris. You're awesome."

Chris looks at me, then at Chantelle, then back at me. His arrival kind of broke the flow of our conversation. Picking up on the vibe, and wanting very much to be away from it, Chris says, "I think I'll have a shower before breakfast."

He turns to me, mouths the words, 'Are you ok?' and kisses my cheek.

"Yeah, good idea," I nod.

"Can I sit?" Chantelle asks, pointing to the two deck chairs on our deck.

"Yeah," I answer. I wait for her to sit and have a sip of her coffee before asking her; "Where were you anyway?"

"I told you – sleepover." She looks over and smiles guiltily. I'm pretty sure I can push for more info without her getting angry.

"Where exactly?" I ask.

"Would you believe Hugo and Beryl Weber?" she jokes.

"No. They're a hundred years old and were probably in bed by 8:30." I reply. We both have a laugh. "I'm not going to let it go," I add.

"I was out pretty late and ended up sleeping in the staff cabin."

"Really? The wait girls don't seem like your types," I say, surprised. It takes a second for the meaning of her guilty smile to sink in.

"You're right, they're not my type; too skinny. I prefer mine a bit more studly," she jokes.

"Please tell me you did not spend the night with Blaine," I beg.

"Ok. I can *tell* you that." She pauses. "But I might be lying."

I am genuinely disgusted. Blaine is a smooth-talking playboy who sleeps with as many staff and guests as he can. He and Daniel are like two rutting pigs when they're here together.

"Telle! He is the biggest player here!"

"I know. And it works because he's hot!" she laughs.

I give a sigh and sit back in my chair, crossing my arms.

"Sarah, it's not like I'm marrying him. Sometimes it's just nice to fuck some hot stud who knows how to use his shit."

"Do you have to talk like that?"

"Sarah, relax. At some point, you have to stop treating me like a little kid."

Once again, I know she's right. Chantelle has been living on her own for almost four years; but I can't help thinking of her as my kid sister. What the hell am I going to be like when I have my own kids?

"I know. You're right. It's just hard. Just no details please. I don't think I'm quite there yet; that I can sit and chat with you about your sex with Blaine."

"So you *don't* want to hear how amazing he is with his tongue?"

"OH MY GOD! STOP!" I yell, putting my hands over my ears.

"Shouldn't sisters be able to talk about sex?" she asks, laughing.

"Maybe one day we will. I just haven't seen you much over the past four years, so it's kind of like you're still fifteen to me."

"Well then you definitely wouldn't want to hear about Dimitri," Chantelle says.

"No? Why?"

"Nothing," she says quietly. I think she regrets mentioning it at all. To be honest, I don't think I can sit and listen to Telle talk about her sex life with that weirdo. "Like you said; 'maybe one day'."

"Telle, you can talk to me. Are you alright?" I ask.

"I'm fine. Now's not the time anyway. Let's just say, he got really weird after a while."

"Are you scared? Do you think he might hurt you?" I ask, feeling seriously anxious myself now.

"No. I'm pretty sure he doesn't give a shit I'm gone. He's not the crazy-possessive type. Just weird."

Once again, Chris comes out, looking tentative.

"How are we ladies? Ready for some breakfast?" he asks.

"I'm not sure," I say. I still haven't seen Maman yet today, and I never talked to dad after last night. I don't know what to expect at breakfast.

"It'll be fine," Chris reassures me.

"Let's go party!" adds Chantelle sarcastically.

Chris, Chantelle and I pop over to Maman's cabin next door. She is just back from taking Bijou out for a little walk when we arrive. I guess 'walk' is a bit of a stretch; Bijou trots about ten steps, does her business, then expects to be carried around.

Last night, we had discussed the breakfast plans. We had no idea where Chantelle was, so Maman and I planned for the two of us to eat with Chris. We thought it would be good to get to breakfast fairly early, but not be the first ones there. As planned, it's 8:40 when we pick up Maman; she's happy to see that Chantelle is coming with us. Maman acts as though everything is normal as we stroll over to the dining room, talking about the sombre clouds sitting off to the west. Looks like a storm is brewing.

Chapter Seventeen

DAVE

THE TOTAL NUMBER of texts I got from Stanley last night was fourteen. After I walked out of the kitchen, I left the Resort because I had to get away. At the time, I had no idea how to really explain what had happened. Hell, I *still* can't really explain what happened, so I never got back to him until this morning. Thinking about the dinner last night is just a fog in my head. I'd done a line of coke and taken some of the Benzos I had gotten just before dinner. My guy told me that the mix would help avoid being unable to sleep after doing coke. He was right; I got to sleep just fine. It's the time before sleep that concerns me.

Next time, just turn on the gas and light the whole fucking place.

When I had gotten to the kitchen, I was feeling fucking amazing. I had no clue of anyone else being there with me; I was in the zone and everything felt right. When those bitches started yapping, I felt like they'd cheated me out of a good high. Normally, I'm super OCD about order in my kitchen. Everyone knows it. Dumping all the food on the floor and walking out was completely out of my normal.

I've always considered my drug use as manageable; it's never been a problem. As long as I'm able to do my job, I know I'm good. Smoking a joint, or doing a line has always let me stay focussed on what I'm doing; it helps to prevent me getting too crazy with thoughts in my head. Whatever chemical mix I had going last night was different.

As I got into my late teens, our family doctor suggested some anti-depressant meds for me; but my parents fought against his suggestions. Again, after my trip to see the shrink, she suggested some type of pills and my parents said no. They didn't want me to become someone else because of some pharmaceutical shit a head doctor prescribed. I guess that attitude stuck with me because despite taking a variety of drugs over the years, I always steered away from the prescription shit.

What harm could it do? I'm so fucked up already.

After last night, that attitude is justified. I do remember feeling absolutely fucking amazing about myself for a while there, but ultimately I was not myself. I know there's no way I'm not taking those pills again, but I gotta be smarter about mixing. For right now I'm staying sober to go to Stanley's office to speak to him. He's always been cool with me, so I need to reassure him that I'm good. He's standing at the door to his office when I come in.

"Dave, how are you? Are you alright?" Stanley asks with concern.

"Yeah, Stanley. I'm good. I'm really sorry about yesterday. I never should have walked out like that."

"Don't worry about that; water over the bridge. I just want to make sure you're alright," he says, leading me into his office. "Is there anything I can do?"

It's amazing to me that Stanley has been able to keep the Resort running all these years. He's one of the kindest people I think I've ever met. Over the years, I've seen lots of people take advantage of that kindness. If he didn't have Melissa to be the strong, sensible one, Stanley would have either gone bankrupt or been fleeced for everything he owned, years ago.

"If you need to take a little time off or anything, you know you'd be missed and everything, but we'd find a way to make it work," Stanley adds.

"I appreciate that Stanley. I'll think about it. Maybe a couple of days might be good. For now, I'm going to have a chat with the boys in the kitchen; apologize for leaving them like that, then get back to work."

"Yeah, those boys stepped up nicely yesterday. They did a great job."

"They are pretty good guys," I add.

"Ok, well don't hesitate to come and talk to me at any time. My door is always unlocked," he says.

"It's 'open' Stanley," I correct him.

"What's that?"

"You door is always *open*."

"Right. You can come and talk any time, I mean."

"Like before I feel like dumping a bunch of food on the floor?" I ask.

For a second, Stanley looks a bit unsure of whether I'm joking. I give him a slap on the arm and a smile. He relaxes.

"If possible, yeah, that would be good."

"Don't worry, we'll make a great breakfast and everyone will forget yesterday completely," I assure him.

"Alright then," he says, putting his arm around my shoulder. "You haven't seen Michelle have you?" he adds.

"No. She OK?" I ask.

"Not sure," he responds. "She didn't say much during the rest of dinner, and then left pretty quickly after her shift."

"I'll give her a call."

"Ok, I'll see you a bit later. I need to have a quick word with Ariel."

"I don't think she's going to last, Stanley."

"It seems like she's struggling. But it's still early; she could turn it around."

"Always the optimist, Stanley! We'll see." I give him a little wink and head to the kitchen.

*

Despite getting a decent sleep, I'm dragging my feet this morning. The temptation to zip back to my room and do a line is strong. But after yesterday, I know it's best to take a little break; at least a few hours. Maybe I can catch a nap later and recharge before dinner. I've always been pretty lucky that I *do* have some common sense and willpower. I've known some people who just couldn't resist whatever their substance of pleasure was. It's pretty easy to recognize the type. I've not studied at any fancy University; but having toured around for a few years, I've had the chance to see lots of people. Plus, I spend most of my free time reading, usually either some philosophy or psychology; it keeps the mind occupied.

The potential for addiction is often visible early. You know that kid from elementary school who just can't say no to anything? Give him a plate of cookies and he'll eat the whole fucking thing. Later, he could never get enough of those video games; sneaking down in the middle of the night to the PlayStation to play when his parents went to bed. In high school, he's the guy who takes to drinking a little too hard, too early, then moves on to whatever he can get his hands on.

I'm kidding myself if I think I'm any different.

I've worked with lots of guys like that, and a few girls too. It's sadder in self-destructive girls. They inevitably get involved with the type of guy who is more than happy to take advantage. I was working in a piece of shit kitchen, in a little, piece of shit diner, in a little, piece of shit town years ago. One of the waitresses had just left home and ended up there. She was rebellious and looking for an adventure. She hooked up with the town dealer; a greasy little biker wanna-be with a death wish. In four months, she went from a misguided teen to a drug addicted, cheap-porn making disaster. She ended up asphyxiating during some sex scene they were filming. Then, as if in some twisted, modern-day Romeo and Juliet play, he shot himself. It was a few months later that another guy in the kitchen showed me a video of the two of them on some Internet porn site. Their situation was sad as hell, but the fact that a video of him fucking her, while smacking her around, had gotten a hundred thousand views is even sadder.

I'm too much of a pussy to get myself a little slut like that.

I don't know why I've been able to keep it together; mostly anyway. I guess it's because, in a way, I enjoy the anticipation. Waiting for a high makes it more rewarding. I don't think I could stay high all the time; there wouldn't be anything to look forward to. I've seen a few different people lose themselves to addictions; each with his or her own reasons.

Some people have a waking life that's just *so* bad that it's necessary to be constantly living in another reality. These people don't usually *want* to die; they just don't give enough of a shit about staying alive to ensure they don't overdo it. That's the saddest one to watch, but I often think that if I were in those situations, I'd probably do the same.

Then there are those who just need to reach even higher levels of intoxication. For me, I'm happy getting high, but I always keep at least some wits about me; I don't often lose control. When some people get high, they need to get as high as absolutely possible. Lots of people have a buddy that will say 'sure' to anything offered to him. Most of those people *don't* die because they have a group of friends that actually cares enough to not let them get too fucked up. Those who don't have that support are the ones who choke in their own vomit, or overdose on a combination of six different drugs.

The greasy little biker wanna-be was a third type of addict. He was the modern version of Billy the kid; I just knew by looking at him that he wanted to die in some dramatic way. After meeting him one time, I would have bet my meager life savings that he wouldn't make it to twenty-five years old. He was angry at everything around him, including himself. His whole existence was basically a big 'Fuck You' to life in general.

I'm so lost in my thoughts that I don't even notice that I've arrived in the kitchen; and I'm standing at my station. I look around and Pascal and Greg are both working away. Did I walk straight here, or did I do my lap first?

"Boys, how are we doing this morning," I say, sounding as 'normal' as possible.

"Pretty good Dave. You?" Greg asks, looking up to see how I'm doing.

"Alright. Listen, I'm sorry I left you guys in a shitty situation like that yesterday," I say, walking over to their counter.

"No worries," assures Greg. "It was actually kind of fun with the pressure."

"Yeah, but don't do it again, please," adds Pascal timidly.

"It's all good," I reassure them. "Let's just make a great breakfast so the whiney wait staff can't have anything to bitch about, and the guests forget all about yesterday."

"I think I'll need a cup of coffee first," Pascal says.

"Late night last night?" I ask him.

"Oh yeah. Loverboy here was out with Maria until late,"

Greg jokes, giving Pascal a nudge. This clearly embarrasses him because his face goes a bright red.

"Hardly," he responds. "I suck with chicks."

"Well you sure came back late," says Greg.

"Yeah. We sat around a talked all night. I have literally no moves. *She* actually gave *me* a kiss on the cheek to say goodnight when we walked back to the cabins."

Greg can't help but laugh. I feel kind of sorry for the kid. He clearly comes from a solid family that's raised him right. He's sensitive, quiet, and shy; and he's probably been called 'gay' more than once in his life. Kids like him get bullied and picked on by obnoxious, loud assholes in schools all over the country. The fact is, the world would be a better place with more people like him; but in our society, extroverts rule. It doesn't even matter if they're right, as long as a few people are loud, they'll dominate.

"Don't worry, skinny. There's nothing wrong with taking it slow. The fact that she kissed you shows she's interested," I try to reassure him. We all get back to doing some prep for breakfast. Pascal puts on a pot of strong coffee.

"I guess you're right. I just don't see how any other night is going to be different from last night," he says.

"Maybe you should ask Blaine for some tips," Greg suggests.

"Ugh, don't do that," I grunt. "He's a decent guy, but you're not like him. Probably shouldn't aspire to be."

"He sure gets lots of action though," says Pascal. "I saw him walking with a girl last night. They were heading from the kitchen to the boathouse… Late."

"Then he brought her back to the cabin at about three AM. I'm pretty sure I heard them going at it in the showers."

"Hmm. Sounds like it might be fun to be him for just *one* night," I say.

Chapter Eighteen

CHRIS

A BIG BREAKFAST COUPLED with a dark, cool day only means one thing for me at the Resort; nap time. We take our time eating breakfast this morning. Before we came, Craig had texted Sarah to say that their dad wouldn't be at breakfast, so there's really no rush. By the time we come out of the dining room, it's mid-morning and the clouds that were lingering over the lake earlier have slowly rolled in, leaving the grounds dark and cool. Leaves are turning over, ready to soak in the oncoming rain, as a breeze picks up. Sarah and I walk Chantelle and Marion back to their cabin and go back to ours. We shut the blinds and are both in a deep sleep within minutes.

*

I'm coming home from work on a Friday, except our home isn't our actual home. Sarah's there, completely naked, standing at a desk in an office that looks like something out of a Sherlock Holmes movie. Fancy books are on shelves; there's a dark, oak desk and a window overlooking a beautiful green yard. Like a stud in a romance novel, I stride over to her without saying a word, pick her up and place her on the desk. I'm kissing her neck as she undresses me. When I pull my head back and look her in the face, it's not Sarah, but Terry. I take a step back and look around. Sarah is sitting in a chair in the corner, playing with herself and watching us as Terry strokes my dick. Just as Sarah gets up and takes a slow, sexy walk over to the desk to join us, a cell phone rings.

*

I've had sex dreams about Sarah before, but this is the first time Terry has made an appearance. I guess you don't have to be Freud to explain the dream. I couldn't help but notice her body in that bikini, when we were on the boat yesterday. That, combined with me catching her and Craig red handed, was enough to get my imagination going, I guess. I'm just hoping my subconscious decides to do a rerun at some point down the line; this time without the show being interrupted.

My dick is absolutely throbbing as I sit up. From the sound of irritation in Sarah's voice at the conversation she's having with a client, there's not much hope of persuading her to come back to bed to help me release some built up tension. I get up and stand over the toilet for a few seconds while my erection goes down. Pissing with a hard-on is never easy; you have to lean over and aim differently. Sometimes the piss comes out in two streams. I usually end up pissing all over the seat.

It's 2:30 in the afternoon and the day hasn't cleared at all. It must have started raining while I was asleep, and it doesn't look like it will be stopping soon. I grab a couple of glasses of juice and sit down at the little table while Sarah finishes up her conversation. For a couple of years, she's been working as a legal consultant. After she finished her degree, she decided not to take a job at her dad's firm. Along with not wanting to work with her dad and Daniel, she doesn't really want the strict schedule. We both want a family at some point, and she thinks that once she commits to a 'real job', she won't be able to stop to have kids.

"Everything alright?" I ask as she hangs up and joins me at the table.

"Yeah, just work stuff. You have a nice nap?" she asks.

Sarah's not really the jealous type, but it's probably not the best idea to let her know about my little dream involving a threesome with her and her brother's girlfriend. "Yeah. How 'bout you?"

"Alright. Uneasy though. I just can't seem to relax. And I've been having weird dreams."

I guess I'm not the only one. But from her tone, I don't think Sarah's dreams are as fun as mine. "It's probably just stress," I assure her. "You *do* take on most of the stress of your family."

"Yeah, I guess," she admits. "I think I'm going to head into town today. You OK if I go by myself?"

"For sure. Get away for a bit and have some time to yourself. I'm sure I'll be able to find something to do."

*

Sarah walks up to the car and drives off to town. It takes about half an hour to drive there, so she'll be gone for a couple of hours. I can't really blame her for wanting to get away; she always stresses so much about her parents. Throwing Chantelle into the mix this year just adds another thing for her to worry about.

It's still raining out. The small deck is only partly covered by a little overhang; but the rain's been coming down pretty consistently for a few hours, so everything is wet. I don't really feel like sitting inside our cabin, so I grab an umbrella and walk over to the main lodge. I like most of Sarah's family, but I don't really feel like spending time with any of them right now. There's no activity as I walk by Marion's cabin. I'm guessing Chantelle is probably asleep. Apparently she was out late with Blaine. Seems like a weird mix to me, but I'm not going to judge.

Sarah and I have been married for three years, and we dated for another three before that. In that time, I've never really had a meaningful conversation with Chantelle. I'm not exactly a talker, and she's pretty secretive; so if you put us in a room together, we'd probably sit there in silence and both be OK with it.

The lodge is pretty packed when I arrive. Some people are sitting in loungers and couches, chatting. A couple of people have laptops out, either doing some work or just surfing the Internet. The lodge is the only place with reliable Wi-Fi. For adults, it's not hard to find something to do on a rainy day. The people I feel sorry for are the ones with young kids. One day isn't bad; usually parents can throw a movie on a laptop, play a game, or go for a drive somewhere. It's those weeks when it rains for three or four days straight where you see parents start to lose it. In the basement of the main lodge, there's a room that could be best described as a giant rec-room. There are old board games, none of which probably have all the original pieces for the game. There are some crappy old toys for toddlers to play with. It's the type of room that kids love to just screw around in; while parents dread the thought of having to spend any time there. There are always those parents that don't really give a shit about it, so they send their kids on their own to go and entertain themselves. I'm not sure I'd be able to do that. I'd be that poor sod who ends up sitting in there and watching everyone else's neglected demon children.

Usually, Monday afternoon at the Resort involves some kind of beach activity. I think the officially listed event is beach volleyball. Zack, the social director for a few years now, does a great job of judging the mood and going with whatever the guests are feeling. Sometimes it's volleyball; other times it's diving off the dock. Whatever it ends up being, Zack talks to everyone and tries to get people pumped up and involved. Sometimes on rainy days, he'll throw together a card tournament or something. Today, it looks like most people are content to just chill out. Zack is sitting at his little desk area talking to a couple of teens about having a game of 'capture the flag' later if the rain lets up.

I grab today's paper and find a seat near the fire. Halfway through an article about the financial crisis in Greece, I hear a woman's voice just outside the lodge, repeatedly calling a name. She walks into the lodge, looking concerned.

"DYLAN?" she calls, looking around. Zack gets up and goes over to speak with her.

"Are you alright?" he asks.

"I can't find our son. He was at our cabin, then I looked around and he just wasn't there," she says, getting more frazzled as she speaks. All eyes are on her. Several people get up and go over to her.

"It's alright. He's here somewhere. We'll find him," assures Carl Harris.

"How old is he?" asks Zack.

"He's four. He was watching a movie in our cabin and I was sending a couple of e-mails on my phone in the other room. I just looked up and he was gone."

"We'll all split up and look. What does he look like?" asks Maxine Bennett, a kind, older lady who has been coming here forever. I feel a little badly for joking with Sarah about poisoning her earlier.

"He has glasses and short, brown hair," she responds, starting to tear up.

"Don't worry love, he's fine. What was he wearing?" Maxine asks.

"SpongeBob pajamas. He just got up from his nap."

"And what's your name, dear?" Maxine sounds so calm and reassuring that I'm sure she's settling everyone down, not just this woman.

"Serena," she responds.

"And where's your cabin, Serena? Is there anyone else there?"

"White Dove; just up the hill to the left. My husband went out fishing. He says it's good to fish in the rain."

"Ok, dear. You and I will go back up to the cabin now to see whether Dylan has wandered back yet. Gene here will get everyone organized to have a look about," Maxine says.

"Absolutely, dear," Gene replies. "We'll have him back in a jiffy."

I have no idea whether Gene and Maxine actually feel that confident about it, but their calm demeanor is perfect for the situation. Maxine leads Serena out of the lodge and back to Serena's cabin. Gene doesn't really ask who would like to help look; he just assumes everyone present will participate. Nobody makes any objection. There really is a sense of community here that you don't often get in other places.

"There's about twelve of us. Zack and I will stay here and look around the lodge. In pairs, if you could all either go down to the beach, down the road in one direction or the other, over to the tennis courts, or down the back alleys, we should have most of the Resort covered. Anyone you find along the way, have them join in." Without questions, we all pair off and head out.

I grab my umbrella and head out side with Tariq. He and his wife have been coming for a few years. They have four kids, all close in age, who run around together the whole week with minimal supervision. His kids are probably all down in the rec room right now. I'm actually kind of surprised one of *them* hasn't gone missing. We volunteer to walk down one of the back alleys.

The lodge is big enough that there are three little dirt roads leading to some of the more remote cabins. From all over the Resort, sounds of guests calling Dylan's name can be heard. I'm sure Gene and Maxine are right, and that the kid will be fine; but I can't help imagining him walking down to the beach. On a cold, wet day like this, there would be nobody there, and it would be easy for the little guy to just fall in. Or maybe he wandered out to the road and got hit by some guy in a speeding pickup truck who just kept on driving. Or maybe some pervert happened to drive by.

"I'm sure the kid's fine," says Tariq. I realize that I've been walking along chewing on my nails. Maybe some of Sarah's worrying has started to rub off on me.

"Yeah, I'm sure you're right. Just amazed the kid could just disappear like that."

"You don't have kids do you?" he asks.

"No. Not yet at least."

"You really can't keep your eye on them at all times. Eventually, they have to figure things out on their own."

"I guess. But, at four?" I ask.

"My two boys were two and four when they got out of the house while my mother was supposed to be watching them. They made it a block and a half to the corner store and were trying to buy an ice cream with some pennies they had taken."

"Sounds scary. I don't know how you parents do it."

"You learn. When you have your first kid, you'll want to bubble-wrap it and keep it safe from everything."

"And by the fourth?" I ask.

"You try your best and leave the rest to God."

"Not sure that fills me with much confidence," I admit.

"If you try too hard to protect them, then they'll never be able to make decisions on their own. Plus, they'll never experience anything. Think about it; what were you doing as a kid? I'm sure you have some crazy stories about times you were doing something, and things could have gone wrong."

I think back to my own childhood. My sister is five years older, so we never really got into any trouble together; she was too busy being a second mother. But my cousins and I were known to cause some shit.

"I guess you're right, but times are different. It seems like there's just so much that can harm a kid these days."

"And you know that every generation says the exact same thing. Accidents happen! You have to try to make things safe for them, but kids also have to be challenged. If they never get hurt, they'll never learn how to deal with hurt! Everyone's all worried about law suits now, so the safest thing to do is just not allow kids to do anything even half dangerous. That's why so many kids have emotional issues these days; they're scared of everything and they don't get a chance to try to deal with anything themselves. No matter how safe you are, there's always something that can harm them. There always has been and there always will be. May as well let them be adventurous and learn how to deal with life. It's for the best."

"You are a very wise man, Tariq," I say sincerely.

We walk around a corner, sheltered by some trees and see Daniel walking down the path with a little boy on his shoulders. The boy is wearing glasses and a SpongeBob shirt.

"Dylan?" I ask as we approach.

Daniel picks him off his shoulders and places him on the ground. Dylan shyly hides behind Daniel's leg.

"Yeah, this is my new buddy; Dylan," Daniel says, patting

him on the head. "I guess he wandered up the hill to follow a bunny. He wasn't too sure where his cabin was, so we were headed to the main lodge to see if we could find his mom."

"She will be very happy to see you," says Tariq.

"He's in White Dove. Your mom is there now, Dylan," I add.

"Hey, I know where that is Dylan. Let's go buddy." Daniel takes him by the hand and walks up a little path leading to the cabin. I join them, and Tariq heads back to the main lodge to let everyone know Dylan has been found.

The three of us come around the cabin and find Serena and Maxine sitting on the front step. Serena leaps up and runs to us. Dylan lets go of Daniel's hand and runs to hug his mom.

"Thank-you, gentlemen. Very good work," says Maxine, approaching and giving us a motherly pat on the back.

"Yes, thank-you both so much," Serena adds, still holding her son.

"I actually did nothing," I say. "Tariq and I were walking along and Daniel had found Dylan."

"I guess he had seen a little bunny and decided to follow it. I heard him crying. Just lucky to be passing by I guess."

Serena takes Dylan inside, reminding him to always tell her before leaving the cabin. Maxine returns down towards the main lodge.

"I think I'll go back and get ready for dinner," Daniel says, turning to walk back to his cabin. I follow.

"So you just happened to be out walking in the woods and found him?" I ask, a bit suspiciously. I've known Daniel for a few years now and still can't quite figure him out. He has never seemed like the type to enjoy peaceful walks in the woods on a rainy day. Nor has he ever really shown interest in kids; yet he interacted with Dylan like he had been doing it his whole life. I guess he is an older brother to two siblings; but from everything

Sarah has said, Daniel was never really the caring, older brother type. And lastly, it's a bit unlike him not to take a bit more credit for something like that.

"Kind of," he replies. "I was taking a short cut through the woods, coming back from a cottage just up the way. If you take the road, it's like an extra ten minutes. Poor little guy was just sitting there crying."

"How did you get him to sit on your shoulders? He seemed pretty shy."

"Told him I needed his help being a lookout."

"Nice job," I say.

"Thanks buddy. Anything crazy happen around here today?" Daniel asks.

"Nope. Pretty boring, rainy day. Unless you count the lost child."

"Well, hopefully that's the end of the rain. This place gets pretty dull when the weather's shit."

We say our goodbyes and I walk back across the Resort towards the cabin. It's only after a minute or so that I wonder why Daniel hadn't just taken his car to the cottage up the way. Hard to see why he'd walk through a damp forest when he could just hop in his car and drive.

Chapter Nineteen

MICHELLE

"I REALLY APPRECIATE YOU coming back this morning, Michelle."

After breakfast, Stanley asked me to speak with him in his office. I told him that I needed to leave quickly, but that I would be back in time to see him before dinner. When I left here yesterday, I was furious. Coming back this morning, I wanted to see what the mood was like, and how I was going to feel about being here. I'm also a bit pissed at Stanley; he's hired these kids to be waitresses and they have no training, or even common sense in some cases. It seems every year, I have to train a group of even stupider, self-absorbed girls.

"I'm not going to just not show up. You know I take my job more seriously than that."

"I know. And I'm sorry there aren't more workers like you here."

"So why do you keep hiring people who can't do their jobs, Stanley?"

"You know it's tough Michelle. The people who want to

work at a place like this are usually kids looking for a summer job. They come here to make some money and have fun."

"Fine, but there still has to be a way to up the standards a bit. If you hire people who are shit at their job, then that becomes what's expected. Every spoiled little shit who wants to screw around and make some easy cash will end up applying. If you expect more, then people will begin to expect higher standards. Don't hire anyone without work experience and solid references. Slowly, the culture will change and you'll have more hard workers."

"You sound like Melissa," Stanley says.

"Have I ever told you how much I like Melissa?" I ask. We look at each other for a moment and both chuckle.

"I know you're right Michelle. I will talk to the other ladies. They crossed a line and should be showing you more respect. I think Ariel was mostly embarrassed. You know these kids have been babied growing up, and they don't know how to handle the real world; this might be the place that helps them learn some maturity."

"I hope this isn't the part where you say; 'you were like them once, Michelle'."

Stanley gives a laugh. "No, I wouldn't go that far. You've always been a hard worker Michelle. I hope you know how much I appreciate you around here."

"Thank you Stanley. But I'm done with being any kind of help to any of them. I'll show up, take care of my tables and that's it."

"I understand. I wouldn't expect anything else. And if you're interested, maybe you could have a part in hiring next year's staff. Maybe you could be dining room manager or something like that."

"That sounds like a promotion. Do I get a raise?" I push.

"We could negotiate," Stanley responds.

We sit for a few seconds as I consider it. Stanley leans back in his chair. My first impulse is to say no. I don't want to have a say in hiring people. That makes it sound like I'm making more of a commitment to the place. I've been here for seven years, but I don't really want to lock in to working here forever. Although being able to pick the wait staff could mean never having another Courtney or Ariel to work with.

"How about we see how things go for the rest of the summer?"

"Sounds fair," Stanley replies. "For now, we'll let the sleeping dogs lie."

"Sure," I say.

*

After our conversation, I walk out to the dining room to start the preparations for dinner. None of the other wait staff is there, but Blaine is stocking the bar. Despite being an irritating, horny, arrogant, frat boy, Blaine is actually not that bad. He lightens the mood and keeps the peace. There's no way that I'll ever tell him though.

"Mich, what's shakin'?" Blaine greets as I pass by.

"How am I supposed to even answer that?" I ask.

"Oh, there's lots of good ways. You could say to me; 'your fat ass' if you wanted to be a bit mean. You could say, 'Nepal'; but that's kind of mean too cuz a lot of people died in those earthquakes. Or you could just go with the standard, 'not much'."

"Not much."

I grab some linens and start setting up my tables.

"Wonder what's going to happen at dinner today," Blaine says.

"Hopefully nothing much. I wouldn't mind a nice, boring dinner."

"I don't know. It's been kind of a fun week so far."

I give him a glare and get back to work.

Chapter Twenty

STANLEY

AFTER MY CHAT with Michelle, I had to get out and have some peace. I find I think best when I'm puttering around the grounds and getting stuff done. The rain seems to have let up for a while. I start by putting the hanging baskets back up. All around the main lodge, Melissa and I have hung up baskets of geraniums, begonias and lantana. They're a big part of the look of the Resort; all summer, guests comment on how lovely they are. It works out perfectly for us, Melissa and I each do what we're good at; she picks them out and I take care of them. When I know we're getting a rainy day like this one, because they're partially sheltered by the eaves on the main lodge, I take them all down so that they can get a good soaking. The time it takes to take them all down and then put them all back up again seems crazy, but it's actually shorter than what it takes for me to water them all.

I know Melissa wants me to talk to her about selling the place, but I don't know what I'd do if we sold. I can spend entire days doing odd jobs around the place; it's what I am. How does someone just stop doing what he's been doing for most of his life? Even when dad owned the place, I would be the one to do all the little, odd jobs.

I'm wiping down the chairs out front when Walter Watson comes out the front doors. Walter and his family have been coming for well over twenty years. He's probably the wealthiest man I've ever met. He made a fortune in investments and in a variety of other business ventures. Every time I talk to him, he's got his hands in something new. Over the years, he's brought associates, clients, and extended family to the Resort with his wife and two daughters. Whoever he brings, he always pays. About fifteen or twenty years ago, the Resort was struggling to pay the bills. We had sunk a bunch of money into fixing things up, only to find two new problems with each one we fixed. Just when I was starting to lose hope, we got an anonymous donation of $25,000. It really did save the Resort. Walter has never even hinted at it being him, but I know it was. I could just never bring myself to flat out ask him; and then the years went by and it seemed I'd missed my chance.

"Stanley, old friend, how are you doing? We haven't had the chance to catch up much yet."

"Hi Walter," I say, shaking his hand. He has the strong, confident handshake of a man who has shaken hands with important people his whole life. "It certainly has been an eventful week."

"How are you holding up?" he asks. "I haven't seen you out and about as much as usual the first few days.

"I know. It seems like I've spent the past two days being a councillor or something."

"Well, the place looks great, as always," he says, gesturing towards the flowers.

"Yeah, it's been pretty smooth so far. Last year, it seems like whatever could break, broke. We had a burst water line, a septic leak, and about six water heaters died."

"Let me guess, you fixed most of it yourself."

"I certainly tried. You know I love that kind of stuff."

"You are a better man than me, Stanley. I can barely fix a loose doorknob. You have a gift."

"Thank you, Walter. I can fix a water heater, but I could never do what you do either. Without Melissa's business sense, I'd probably be living in a little hut in the forest," I joke.

"How long do you plan on running the place, Stanley?" he asks. The directness of his question throws me for a bit of a whirl. I don't know whether he's just making conversation, or he's noticed that I'm thinking about the whole situation. I'm not completely sure how to answer, so I let out a sigh and shrug my shoulders to stall for a second. I know Walter is asking out of kindness. I might as well be honest with him about it.

"Not too sure about that, Walter. The thought of not running this place is a bit scary to be honest."

"No doubt. Is there anyone in your family interested in taking over? Wasn't your nephew interested? He spent a couple of years here, right?"

"He was useless and hated every minute of being here," I say with a laugh, remembering how Spencer would complain about having a grain of sand on him, or shriek when a bug came near him.

"Didn't get much of the old Henderson blood then did he?"

"I'd say no," I answer. Spencer is the son of my eldest sister, Linda. He goes to some preppy, private school and dyes the tips of his hair blond. There was no way he was ever going to take over the Resort. Linda thought he was getting too spoiled, so she sent him one summer so he could experience something different. He complained the entire time.

"If it were up to me Stanley, I'd never see you pass this place on to someone else. But that's only if you're happy; you deserve whatever you want in life. You've created a special place here my friend; and everyone who passes through, whether it's just once, or they come back every year, is better off for having done so."

These are probably the nicest words that someone has ever said to me; and it almost brings me to tears.

"Thank you Walter. It's my pleasure."

"I know, Stanley. That's what makes it so special," he says, reaching out to squeeze my shoulder. "If you ever need anything; if you ever *do* consider selling the place, let me know. I could get you in touch with some good people, I'm sure. This place is special to my family too."

"I'll keep that in mind," I respond.

Walter lets me get back to my work. We make a tentative plan for Melissa and me to go over to visit one evening before the end of the week.

Walter's last words certainly give me something to think about. The main excuse I've been giving to Melissa for not looking into selling this place is that smarmy, rich kid who made the offer. I trust Walter. He understands this place and what it really means. Anybody he recommends would hopefully be able to understand it too.

I cross the street to the maintenance barn. The Resort is mostly on the west side of the little county road that circles the lake. On the east side, there's an old barn that's used for all the maintenance supplies. We fixed it up a few years back; replaced broken boards and painted it a deep, forest green. It looks pretty nice, but there's still lots of crap sitting around outside. It's best that it's on the other side of the road, and tucked behind some trees. Just up the road a few hundred yards are the staff cabins; nothing glamorous there. In fact, with the kids we usually get working here in the summer, it's often a complete dump. I know it makes me sound like an old man yelling for kids to get off my lawn, but kids these days don't know the meaning of the words 'work ethic'. I can only imagine the look I'd get from most of them if I tried to convince them of how great it feels to come home after a day of good, hard work; with sore muscles, sun in your skin, sweat on your brow, and that satisfaction of knowing you got something accomplished.

I pull the tractor out of the barn and head towards the road. After a day of rain like this, I usually like to go down to the beach area and give it a rake with the tractor. As I'm waiting to cross, a car pulls into the parking lot. Marion LaPointe and her son, Craig, get out, along with his girlfriend. Her name escapes me. I spoke to Marion after her little incident in the dining room, but haven't seen her since, so I pull up to them and cut the engine. I notice they are each carrying a box.

"Hi folks! Found something to do on this rainy day?" I ask.

"Oh yes, we visited that lovely antique place up the highway," Marion tells me. "I know Craig had a marvelous time," she says jokingly.

"Actually was pretty fun. Saw a record player I might pick up on the way home," adds Craig.

"Can I offer you a lift? We could put the boxes in the bucket."

"Thanks, but I think we'll walk. It's nice to be outside after all that rain. And besides, I'm not putting my new, antique clock in that filthy thing," Marion says with a laugh, and pointing at the front of the tractor.

"Understandable. We'll see you later."

As they walk away, I remember that Craig's girlfriend's name is Terry. I really should have known that sooner. Maybe I am getting too old for this. I've always been a master with names.

On my way to the beach, I pass cabins where people are on the decks, shaking off towels and wiping off chairs. A bunch of kids clothing was left out on the railing of Partridge and is now completely soaked. A few guests are taking a walk around the grounds. A group of kids are splashing around in the lake. The water is probably freezing right now. We've had some nice days, but the sun hasn't been out for long enough to really heat up the lake yet. It's funny how some kids just don't give a hoot about it though. It's kids like that, who'll splash around in freezing cold water on a cloudy, rainy day, that are the ones that make it all worthwhile.

*

On my way back up from the beach, I see Stéphane LaPointe with Annette, walking back from their car. It seems lots of people decided to take a day trip today to avoid the weather. Stéphane is another guest that's been coming here forever. I've watched his family, and Walter Watson's family, grow up here every summer. The three of us are fairly close in age, so we hit it off in those early years. We'd fish, golf, or just sit and drink beer on the patio. Over the years, families grew and we stopped spending as much time together. At least once in the week, the three of us will usually still sneak away for a beer, or a boat ride.

"How's it going kids?" I ask, approaching.

Annette looks up and smiles. "Hello Stanley. How is everything?"

"Can't complain really. It looks like it's clearing up, and the rest of the week promises to be great weather."

Stéphane gives my hand a shake. "We need to find some time to catch up; if you can pull yourself away from all your work."

"Absolutely. I actually just chatted with Walter. Maybe we can make it out fishing this year."

"That would be nice," Stéphane says.

As I look at him, he seems tired. I'm sure the little incident in the dining room yesterday affected him. He's always prided himself on being able to get along with everyone.

"What did you get up to today?" I ask.

"We actually took a drive to look at some properties on the lake," Stéphane says.

There's no real sense to it, but I can't help feel a bit saddened. If Stéphane buys a cottage somewhere, then it won't be long before his whole family stops coming here. They've been a part of the Resort for pretty much the whole time I've been in charge. There certainly seems to be a wind of change blowing around me, and fighting it is becoming tiring. Melissa sometimes talks about signs. There've been a couple of things happening around lately that could be seen as signs. Could be time for a new rent on life.

Stéphane can clearly tell I'm affected by what he said. "I think it's getting a bit hard on everyone to have both Marion and myself coming here the same week."

"For the last couple of years, we've talked about staying away," Annette adds.

"I know. It just sucks," I say, sounding like a little kid reacting to some crappy news that he doesn't want to accept. "Have you talked about it with the kids?"

Annette looks up at Stéphane, then answers, "Not yet."

"I imagine Daniel and Craig will understand. I don't think Sarah will like the idea though," Stéphane adds.

"At least we'd be close," Annette reassures.

"The value of properties around here certainly has gone up recently," Stéphane says.

"I know. They've gone up dramatically in the last five or ten years," I add. "That little, white cottage across the lake sold for about three hundred grand last year."

"People are realizing it's a beautiful place to be," Stéphane says.

"Well, keep me informed," I tell them. "And I won't mention anything to anyone else."

"I know you wouldn't Stanley," Stéphane tells me, touching my shoulder. "I think I'm going to have a little nap before dinner," he adds.

With that, he and Annette walk off towards his cabin. I pull the tractor into the barn and cross over to the kitchen to see how things are going. Some weeks, I can get tons accomplished in a day. This week, however, things take me twice as long because I'm constantly stopping and talking to guests. It slows me down; but it's also what makes this more than a job. I'm not sure I could fill that hole.

Chapter Twenty One

PASCAL

I'M KIND OF bummed out that Maria didn't come out tonight. After an uneventful dinner, I went back to the cabins to shower and get ready for the evening. The Resort is pretty much exactly what my mom feared it was. When I told her I wanted to come and work here, she didn't really know too much about it. She wanted to do some research and ended up speaking with Stanley's wife, Melissa; which was probably the best person for her to talk to. Melissa is straightforward, kind, and doesn't take any crap. She told my mom how the staff here was responsible and it would be a great experience for me. That's mostly true, but there's no way mom would approve if she knew about some of the stuff that happens at night.

I don't usually drink too much when I have to get up the next day, but it's only Monday night now, and my day off isn't until Thursday. My plan is to have a few drinks tonight, recover with a nice, long nap tomorrow, take it easy tomorrow night, then party harder on Wednesday. Tonight is talent night. There's no way I'm going to get up and perform a talent in front of the whole

Resort, but it's fun to sit and watch others. Tuesday night is disco night, and I'm not really into that; so I'll gladly avoid it. Maybe I'll actually crack open the book that I brought. Wednesday is a classic at the Resort; this band from the area comes and performs. The past two Wednesdays have been a blast, so I'm happy that I'm able to have Thursday off to recover.

I grab a second beer from Blaine at the bar and head back to the table in the back where Rob, Greg and I are sitting. The bar is starting to fill up with people greeting each other and chatting; but I haven't really gotten to know any of the guests. Since this is only the third week of my first year here, I'm meeting people for the first time. Some of the other staff have hung out with these people in previous years. I've always kind of sucked at meeting people. I never really know what to ask, and I get all nervous talking about myself. I'm glad Greg and the rest of the guys are pretty good at talking to people. I just sit back and nod, sometimes throwing in a comment.

We're having a deep conversation about whether Crosby is ever going to win another Stanley cup when Courtney, Ariel and Christine walk in. They're dressed like they're planning on performing some song or dance tonight. They have a look around the room, then cross the bar over to our table.

"Ladies," Rob greets them. "You look like you're ready to put on a show. What do we have to look forward to?"

"You'll have to wait and see," Courtney answers, sitting down.

I'm a bit surprised they're joining us; although they do get along with Rob pretty well. Since the little blow-up in the kitchen, things have been a bit icy with all the wait and kitchen staff. Courtney, Ariel and Christine have never really spoken to Dave much, but now they completely avoid him. Michelle doesn't even make any kind of acknowledgment that the three other girls exist. Greg and I have been stepping up our game, getting salads and stuff ready so that they don't really have anything to complain about with us. And since she dropped the tray, Ariel has been laying pretty low. I have a feeling Courtney took her aside and told her she needs to cool it for a while.

"How about you boys? Any big talent to show off?" Courtney asks.

"None we'd like to reveal to all the guests," Greg answers.

"Didn't I see you guys dancing the other night?" Christine asks me with a smile.

"Maybe; but not in front of *everyone*!" I answer.

I'm surprised that Christine gives a little laugh and a smile. Maybe the tensions between everyone are starting to ease. Maybe it's the couple of beers, but I'm feeling kind of good about talking to them. It's too bad Maria isn't here; I might actually be able to be somewhat charming.

At around 10:30, Zack sets up the microphone on the tiny, little stage area in the corner of the bar. Even as I sip my third beer, the thought of getting up there and performing *anything* in front of this crowd scares the crap out of me. I don't know how some people do it. The first person to get up is a guy named Marc. He and his wife Carrie are pretty outgoing. They have two little kids that they take care of during the day, and at night, they get someone to babysit. I think they've been out every night until pretty late. He takes the microphone and tells a few jokes; some are pretty bad, but a couple are actually pretty funny. He ends with a really dirty joke about four nuns crashing their car and then trying to get into Heaven. A few people look seriously offended, but most of the crowd either laughs or groans.

Next up is the old couple; the Webers. Hugo plays the ukulele and Beryl sings in this really high pitched voice. I think they've been coming here for like fifty years or something. I wonder how many times they've performed that song.

A couple of younger teens do some average break dancing; then another guest does some pretty crazy yoga-type poses before the talent show takes a little break. A couple of guests, like the Webers, call it a night. Other people grab some more drinks and walk around to socialize. I've always liked sitting and watching how all the people behave in a bar. Being kind of shy myself, I'm amazed at how some people can just walk up to a group and jump right into a conversation. As I'm watching, I hear a little cheer from a few people sitting near us. I look at the doors and see Daniel LaPointe coming in. I guess he found the little, lost kid earlier today.

He shakes some hands and has a laugh with a few people before heading over to the bar. The whole time, I notice Courtney watching him too. Without taking her eyes off him, or saying anything to us, she gets up and walks over to the bar. Approaching from behind him, she places her hand on his shoulders as she passes, and greets him with a big smile. He leans over, gives her a one-armed hug and says something in her ear. Daniel's got that 'muscular, cool, rich, handsome, classy, mature, older guy, stud' vibe going on; whereas I'm rockin' the 'skinny, nerdy, shy, geeky' thing. It doesn't seem fair. It sounds stupid, but I'm jealous of him, and I don't even like Courtney. But her going up, putting her hand on his shoulder and smiling at him makes me depressingly think to myself that I will probably never be greeted like that.

"You alright buddy?" Greg asks me.

I snap out of my little pity party and smile. "Yeah, great."

"You want another beer?" he asks.

"Why not?" I answer.

"Cool, will you grab me one too?" Greg says, turning to the others and laughing.

I could complain, but I think having a little walk is probably a good idea.

"I gotta piss anyway," I say, getting up and walking towards the bathroom.

*

When I come out, I go over to the bar where Blaine is chatting with Daniel, Courtney, and Zack. I ask for a couple of bottles of beer.

"You up for a boat ride later, bud?" Blaine asks as he grabs them.

"In the dark?" I ask.

"Best time for it," Blaine responds. "Daniel here thinks he can beat me once around the lake, and I beg to differ."

I've never really been much of a boat person. I can swim pretty well, but I'm no superstar. I don't really want to go, but with all of them looking at me, I don't want to say 'no' either.

"Sure," I hear myself saying.

"Sweet. We'll head out after the show." Blaine seems to be talking to everyone. Zack looks about as excited as I feel.

I walk back to the table to join Greg, Rob, Ariel, and Christine. Zack steps up to the mic again and introduces the next 'act'. Michelle and Emma Watson do this patty cake thing, but it's a million times more complicated than that. There's some song that goes along with it and I'm surprised at how impressed I am.

Next up is someone who does this double jointed routine, ending with her using her own arms to skip. It's actually kind of gross, but I can't look away. I think the talent is starting to run out.

The last ones to perform are Courtney, Ariel, and Christine. The three of them stand up on stage with Courtney in the front and the other two behind. The music kicks in and they start dancing to Taylor Swift's *Shake it off.* You can tell that they love the attention of having everyone watch them. Courtney looks over at Daniel several times with a sexy look.

After the show, people finish off drinks, say goodbye and trickle out. At the end of the night, I'm left with Courtney, Daniel, Blaine, Zack, and Ariel. Christine didn't want to go out on the boat. I kind of wish I had the balls to just say no myself.

We have another drink as Blaine cleans up a bit. Daniel tells a story from a trip to Belize he took last year. I'm pretty sure I couldn't find Belize on a map. The most exotic place I've ever been to is Halifax.

*

It's a calm, clear evening as we head down to the dock. The clouds from earlier have cleared and the moon is shining. Daniel states that he and Courtney will take his boat while Ariel, Zack, Blaine and I take out the Resort boat.

I take a seat at the back of the boat with Ariel. Blaine coasts out and takes us around the corner from the Resort. Daniel's flashy boat pulls up beside us.

"Once around the lake and back to this point," Blaine shouts over to Daniel.

"I'll try not to splash you too bad as I'm pulling away."

Ariel gets up and moves to the front of the boat. I think about following, but the back seems a safer option. I wonder for a moment why boats don't have seatbelts. Then I realize it's probably because of the danger of getting stuck in it and drowning if the boat flips. Now I feel worse.

Daniel's boat is newer and faster than the Resort boat. He

pulls away from us quite easily along a long stretch of water. When he has to slow down to make a turn, Blaine gains some ground. After a couple of turns, I settle down a bit; Blaine drives the boat aggressively, but he seems to be in control. It's a bit like being on one of those roller coasters that passes through a giant puddle. We hit a part of the lake that's quite narrow, with lots of turns. Daniel slows in front of us, allowing Blaine to catch up. He pulls us up close and tells Zack to take over.

"What? I really don't want to drive Blaine. I had a couple of beers."

"Just keep us close," Blaine says. He goes to the front of the boat, where Ariel has been sitting.

"Woo! We got you now," Blaine yells out to Daniel.

"No chance!" Courtney yells from their boat.

Up ahead, Daniel starts to veer to the left, preparing to take his boat between a small island and the shore. Zack sees them turn, but the excitement of the chase gets the better of him and he cranks the wheel to try to make the turn sharp enough to pass on the inside. Just as he does it, Ariel must have been adjusting her seating position because as the boat takes a sharp left, she flies across the bow and smacks her head on the corner of the little windshield. She bounces off and continues tumbling towards the edge of the boat. Blaine is just able to reach out and grab her by the belt before she flies over the edge. Zack releases the throttle and we come to a stop; a bit too quickly. I'm thrown forward into the back of Zack's seat and Blaine falls forward, still holding Ariel, who falls on top of him in the front seat.

As Daniel's boat zips away, I can hear Courtney cheering. Oblivious to what has happened, they disappear into the darkness. I pick myself up from the floor of the boat and give my head a shake.

Looking up, I see Zack standing at the wheel, looking at the front of the boat. "HOLY SHIT! She's dead!" he says.

"She is not. Settle the fuck down," Blaine says. He sits up and places Ariel next to him on the seat. She's out cold and her head is bleeding badly. Blaine grabs a towel and covers the top of her head.

"Get the first aid kit," Blaine directs Zack.

I'm not sure if it's the blood, the fear, the waves, or the four and a half beers; but I turn around, grab the side of the boat and vomit those four and a half beers, along with the Chicken Parmesan that I had worked so hard on earlier, over the side.

Chapter Twenty Two

BLAINE

"DUDE, I DON'T want to get sent home," Pascal whines.

"Relax. You won't get sent home. Ariel's fine. Remember, we were standing on the boat and Ariel slipped. She hit her head on a sharp corner. Simple as that."

After Ariel hit her head, I drove us back to the Resort. Luckily, we were pretty close. She came to as we were pulling into the dock. The blood down the front of her shirt freaked her out, but I was able to calm her pretty easily. The cut on her head is big, but nothing compared to what it could have been had she hit her eye or something. I've cracked my head open tons of times. If you hit it just right, it splits like a tomato and bleeds like fuck; but it shouldn't leave too bad of a scar. She had no memory of being out on the boat, which means she's probably got a pretty bad concussion; but it also means that she won't be able to say anything about what actually happened.

We walked her up to her parents' cabin and woke them up. Seeing the blood as they opened the door obviously freaked them out, but her dad's a doctor so he was pretty calm about it. He wrapped a blanket around her shoulders, gave her an ice pack to put on her head, and drove her to the little hospital in town. Her mom on the other hand, looked suspicious the whole conversation. She will definitely be talking to Stanley in the morning.

When we got back to the staff cabins, I lit a fire in the pit outside and sat Zack and Pascal down for a talk. The two of them are like scared, little girls. I have to get them to relax.

"I don't know man, someone *must* have seen us out in the water," Zack responds, looking nervous as hell.

"I really don't want to be sent home," Pascal repeats.

"Listen. Both of you. I talked to Daniel. He and Courtney are cool with saying they went out on his boat by themselves. If someone says they saw a boat going out, it was just them. Ariel is not going to remember anything. The three of us need to stick together." I lean forward and look them each in the eye for a good couple of seconds, trying to put them at ease. In a calm, slow voice, I go over our story. "We were sitting on the boat having a beer. Ariel stood up and slipped on a wet spot on the floor. She tried to stop herself, but her hand missed the windshield. She whacked her head and split it open. End of story."

The two of them look at each other. I lean back and cross my arms.

"The other option is to tell Stanley that Zack was driving the boat, racing Daniel, and caused Ariel to split her head open; probably needing several stiches and leaving a big, ugly scar." I know it's dirty, but if they want to tell the truth, that *is* the truth.

"Ok. I get it," Zack says, looking more scared than ever.

"Skinny?" I ask Pascal, using the nickname that Dave sometimes uses in the kitchen.

"Yeah, Ok. I *really* don't want to be sent home."

"I know buddy. You'll be fine. Go get some sleep. I'll talk to Stanley in the morning first thing. He'll come and check things out with you then. Just relax and keep it simple."

"Yeah. Ok. I do need to sleep. I'm bagged," Pascal says, looking exhausted. He gets up and heads inside. I might set my alarm super early tomorrow just so that I can check in with him before Stanley does. I can see him cracking under the first sign of pressure.

"She'll be alright, right?" Zack asks, almost looking like he's about to cry.

"She'll be fine. It seems bad now, but it's just a cut. She'll get a couple of stiches and have a story to tell for years," I assure him. As long as nobody gets scared and rats us out, we should be fine.

Chapter Twenty Three

CRAIG

JUDGING BY THE sun blazing into the room, it must be late. It's taken a couple of days, but I've started to relax more. Yesterday was a pretty nice day considering it rained for most of it. Terry and I took Marion to this little antique place up the highway. Having a chance to spend some relaxing time with Terry is nice. We've been super busy over the last couple of years. My garage is starting to get a reputation for good service, so I often find myself working six days a week. Terry is taking courses to help her get ready for teachers' college in September.

The three of us were in no rush, and ended up having a great time eating lunch and looking at antiques. After we got back, the weather was clearing up a bit, but it was still cloudy and cool. Everyone else in the family seemed occupied, so we went back to our cabin, shut the door, went to bed, and for an hour or so, made full use of our time alone.

Some of the girls I was with before Terry were kind of shy and reserved. Sex was good, but never like what it is now. Terry is confident and free; it's not uncommon for her to walk around our apartment in nothing but her panties in the middle of the day. Plus, she genuinely enjoys sex. It never feels like a chore for her, or that she's just doing it for me. There are lots of other ways that our relationship is great, but the sex is right up there.

After dinner, neither of us felt like going to the talent night, so we put on some pajamas, curled up by a fire in the little fireplace in our cabin, and did a crossword together before turning in early.

I must be relaxed because it's 8:45 and I don't think I woke at any point in the night. Terry is up already, walking around, tidying the little cabin in a tank top and her little, retro, pink shorts.

"About time," Terry says. "I was wondering how loud I was going to have to be banging around in here, before you finally got up."

"Aren't you the one always telling me to relax?" I ask.

"I guess you deserve it."

"You been up long?" I ask.

"About half an hour."

"Let me have a quick shower and we'll head up for breakfast."

"Good luck with your water pressure!"

Terry's right. The water coming out of the shower can only be described as a dribble. There are a couple of times throughout the day where if you don't have a shower early enough, you get no water pressure. Mid-morning is one of them. I try my best to actually rinse the soap off my body under the pathetic drip, before giving up. It would have been better to have taken a quick dip in the lake.

When I come out, Terry has changed and is sitting on the front deck, drinking a cup of tea. I go back in and use the leftover hot water in the kettle to make an instant coffee, then I join Terry on the deck. It's a beautiful morning; the sun is up high enough to warm the air, but still low enough that it's peeking behind the tree tops. People are mulling about, drying towels and clothes on balconies, wiping the moisture off deck chairs, and getting ready to start the day.

"It's Tuesday, right?" I ask Terry.

"Yup! Wonder what today is going to bring."

"Yeah. It's been interesting so far. My family's fucked up!"

"Not really, babe. Everyone's family has its own shit going on. You just don't see it all."

"Do they really though?" I ask skeptically. It certainly feels like we have more issues than most.

"Totally. People just put on a show that everything is normal and perfect. You know how everyone always says that stuff is '*so great*'. And then you experience it yourself and it turns out to be a pain in the ass?"

"Like what?" I ask.

"Like Disneyland."

"You don't like Disney? I never knew that."

"It's crowded, smelly, expensive, and you have to wait in line forever."

"Ok. And?"

"Well people's families are the same. Everyone has a drunk uncle, or a cousin on Ritalin, or a grandad that shouts at birds."

"Your grandad shouts at birds?" I ask.

"Maybe. Who are you to judge?" Terry jokes.

"What does he yell?"

"Not important. My point is, at a place like this, I bet half the people here have some kind of family drama they're working through under the surface; you just don't see it."

"I guess. But I swear Sarah and I are the only normal ones in our family. Mom is either fully menopausal or bipolar, Daniel is an egomaniac, Chantelle is a mystery, and dad has been acting pretty strange. And this week, even Sarah's been acting weird; more high strung and edgy than normal."

"She could just be stressed by your parents," Terry suggests. "Or maybe she and Chris are working through something."

"Hope nothing too serious. I really like him. He adds a bit of normal to the family mix."

My dad's cabin is just behind ours, so as we sit on the little deck, we can't see it. As we're looking out through the trees at the water below us, Annette and Daniel come around the corner along the little path that leads to the main lodge and dining room.

"Heading for breakfast?" I ask.

"I am," Daniel responds. "Annette is going to grab some for dad and bring it up."

"Is he alright?" I ask. "He hasn't been out and about too much."

"He's fine, just a bit tired," Annette says. "He's been really busy recently. Even when we've been here, he's had to go to some meetings and talk to clients."

"Maybe we can all head out on the boat later," I suggest.

"That sounds good. He actually wanted me to tell you both that he'd like to talk to you and the girls later today. Will you pass on the message to Sarah and Chantelle?"

"I will. I'm on my way to meet Sarah and mom right now. She's sent me a hundred fucking texts already," Daniel says. "Our sister has seriously got to chill out, bro."

I ignore Daniel's comment and ask, "You sure he's alright, Annette?"

"Oh yes. Just wants to share some news. We'll see you later." With that, she and Daniel walk down the path to the dining room.

"Can you and I just sit by ourselves at dad's table and eat this morning?" I ask Terry.

"Sounds great to me."

*

Terry and I stroll down to the dining room. The rest of the family is sitting across the room at mom's table. We give a wave to Sarah, who looks over as we come in, and then we sit at dad's table. I just can't bring myself to sit there and listen to the same shit from everyone.

"Sarah looks a bit pissed that we're not going over there," Terry mentions.

"Yeah, I noticed. I'm going to choose to ignore it."

Terry gives my hand a squeeze. "What do you think about Daniel finding that lost kid yesterday?" she asks, changing the subject.

"I think if anyone was going to find him, it would have to be my brother."

"I don't fully understand what he was doing wandering around in the woods though."

"Wasn't he looking for the kid?" I ask.

"Apparently not. I guess he was just walking through the woods and found him."

"Daniel? Just walking through the woods by himself? That's weird."

"Yeah. I guess Chris was out looking with another guest and they saw Daniel just walking out of the woods with the little guy."

"How do you even know this?"

"I spoke to Chris at dinner yesterday. I think you'd gotten up to go chat with someone."

"Daniel has never been one to take a leisurely stroll through the woods. Wonder what he was doing."

"I guess he told Chris he was coming back from someone's cottage?" Terry says.

"That makes no sense. Even if he did know someone close by, he'd drive there."

"Maybe he's changing," Terry says naively.

I give her a look of disbelief. "Unless there's some purpose to going that way, there's no way Daniel just decides to walk to and from a neighbouring cottage."

"Maybe he was going to have a few drinks, so he didn't want to drive," Terry suggests.

"Are you kidding? If it's only a few miles up a country road like that, Daniel drives his car; even if he's completely smashed." I've seen Daniel get behind the wheel after having a few too many more times than I can count.

"Hey guys. How's it going?" Courtney, the waitress at my dad's table, arrives looking a bit frazzled. "Sorry about the wait. We're short this morning."

"No problem. We're not in any rush really," Terry answers.

"Can I grab you a coffee?" Courtney asks while absent mindedly looking around at a couple of her other tables.

"I'll have one. Tea for you?" I ask Terry.

"Think I'll just have an orange juice."

"No worries. I'll be right back."

Once she leaves the table, Terry turns to me. "*She's* looking a bit rough this morning."

Terry's right. Courtney is someone who usually puts a great deal of care into her appearance. She's one of those people who totally suits her name. I don't know why, but every 'Courtney' I've ever met has had a blond ponytail and a similar face. Today, it looks like she rolled out of bed, put her hair in a bun and crawled into work. It's a look I've seen before with waiters and waitresses at the Resort. When we were younger, Daniel and I used to party with the staff. Many nights were spent drinking around the staff cabin fire pit. Now, most of the staff seem like kids to me; although that doesn't seem to stop Daniel from hanging with them!

"Have you had a chance to find out what's going on with Chantelle?" Terry asks.

"Not really. I haven't seen her much since dinner the other night."

"Maybe she's just matured a bit and wants to spend some time with her family," Terry suggests.

"Could be. It sure does throw in a new wrinkle this year."

Courtney comes back with our drinks. We hand her the page where we've circled our order for breakfast and she hurries off to another table. Terry gives me a dirty look as I dump the sugar into my coffee. I've reached the point where a double-double isn't sweet enough anymore. Terry's trying to get me to cut back on sugar; she says it's highly processed and it'll make me fat and diabetic one day.

"You gonna be my partner today?" I ask her, trying to take attention away from my coffee.

"Is it that stupid corn bag game today?" she asks.

"How dare you?" I say, acting offended. "Cornhole is a sacred game here."

Apparently Stanley's dad spent some time living in Ohio. When he came back, he got his dad to build some boards and cornhole became a tradition at the Resort. Over the years, boards got old and new ones were made. Stanley has three or four sets now; one he made himself years ago, and a couple that some guests have donated. There's a whole vocabulary that goes along with the game. Last year, Terry sucked at it. She threw a couple of Sallys, where the bag doesn't even make it to the boards; along with lots of Screaming Eagles, which means launching it clear over everything. She's normally pretty athletic so it really pissed her off being so bad at it.

"Maybe you can find another partner this year," Terry says.

I'm instantly torn between not wanting to offend her, and being happy that I might find a partner that could help me win.

"You know I'd prefer to play with you," I decide to say; hopefully sincerely enough.

"I'll pass. My plan is to sit in the sun."

"Ok. Only if you're sure." I immediately think about who would be a good partner. Maybe Chantelle might give it a go. It's been a few years, but I think I remember her being pretty good at it.

*

Breakfast is good, but not spectacular. The bacon's a bit soggy and the hash browns are overcooked. If the kitchen staff got up to whatever Courtney was doing last night, then maybe they're all pretty burned out today.

On our way out of the dining room, we see a fairly large boat heading towards the dock. I hold my hand up to block the sun while my eyes adjust to the brightness.

"Is that a police boat?" Terry asks.

Chapter Twenty Four

DAVE

MY HEAD IS fucking pounding as I make my way to the kitchen. I managed to get about two hours of sleep last night. I spent most of the night at Shawna's place. She's a messed up druggy who lives in a piece of shit, little cottage about five miles away from the Resort. She's not particularly attractive, nor is she very nice. But she lives close, likes to get high, and fucks like someone who's just gotten out of jail.

I hadn't planned on ending up with her, but a night of shooting pool at the bar in town took a turn that way after a few lines in the bathroom. Now I'm dragging my ass into work to cook breakfast for a room full of rich snots, and work with a bunch of useless college twats.

Pathetically dragging myself home after a pathetic night. Again.

When I got back to the Resort at about three in the morning, I made my way to the little room in the main lodge where Stanley has let me stay for years now. On the upper floor of the big, main building, there are a few rooms where people can stay if they don't want their own cabin. They're nothing fancy. There's a little balcony that either overlooks the lake, or the forest. Few people book those rooms for a whole week; most of the time, it's people visiting others here that end up staying in one. At one point, I used to stay in the staff cabin with the waiters, bartenders, and some maintenance guys. That didn't last too long. Having a room of my own lets me do what I want without having to always deal with other people. When I made the change, it kind of alienated me from the rest of the staff, but it's worth it for some privacy.

I'm the first one in the kitchen. I always try to make it that way. There's something about unlocking the door, turning on the lights, and walking in first that makes it feel like it's *my* kitchen. I walk around the perimeter once, touching each part of the room. The deep fryer is first, close to the door to help vent the greasy air quickly. Sink and counter are next; for prep work. The stove is in the corner; a sturdy gas stove that's been at the Resort for decades.

Once I'm done my lap, I grab my apron and head to the walk-in. It's only a couple of minutes before Pascal comes in with Blaine. It's completely strange to see Blaine here this early.

"I'll go talk to Stanley now and explain what happened," Blaine is saying to Pascal. "I'm sure he'll pop by and check in on you in a bit. Just relax."

"What happened?" I ask as they head towards me.

"Nothing," Pascal says quickly.

"No. Not nothing," Blaine says with a shrug of his arms. "Tell him what happened."

Pascal just looks at me for a second then back at Blaine. Something is definitely up with him.

"We were sitting on the boat last night and Ariel slipped, fell, and cracked her head open on the windshield in the boat.

She had to go get some stiches. No big deal. She'll be fine, right Pascal?"

"Yeah," is all he says.

"At the moment, I don't really give a shit about Ariel hitting her head. I have a head ache myself, so none of that music shit today. Get to work," I tell Pascal.

"Somebody's on the rag today," Blaine jokes. I'm not in the mood.

"Unless you're going to be cooking, get the fuck out of here," I tell him. "And you get to work," I add to Pascal.

The door opens and Stanley walks in. He looks like he got up, threw on some work boots and came immediately here. His white hair is a mess, and he's wearing some pajama pants that must be fifteen years old.

"Blaine. I'm glad you're here. Perhaps you could tell me what exactly happened last night with Ariel," he says to Blaine, concern evident in his voice. "I got a call from Celeste."

"Not in here!" I say loudly.

"Alright, sorry Dave," Stanley says. "Blaine, let's sit down in my office."

Pascal looks like he's about to shit himself, or perhaps he already has. Blaine follows Stanley out the door. I don't really want to get involved, but I'm curious about what's going on. It's at least taking my mind off the fact that I feel like crap and that I really want to zip upstairs to my room to grab a couple of pills.

"You alright there, skinny?"

"What?" Pascal jumps. "Oh, yeah. Good."

"What really happened?"

"What do you mean?" he asks in a pathetic attempt to sound casual.

"I mean there's more to the story than what our buddy Blaine just said right?"

Pascal looks at me in silence for a few seconds before glancing at the door where Blaine and Stanley just left. Unable to find the support from the closed door; his strength sucked out of the room, he turns back to me and blabs the entire story.

I guess they were speeding around the lake, racing Courtney and Daniel LaPointe, when they took a corner way too fast and smashed Ariel's head open. I can't say I feel too badly about Ariel. Hopefully it knocks some sense into her. I'm sure Blaine will schmooze his way out of it. Pascal will probably worry himself sick and then blab everything to Stanley. It's all pretty funny. I'm actually kind of looking forward to springing it on Courtney one day that I know all about her being involved.

We start getting breakfast ready. Pascal gets called out by Stanley a while later. I guess he manages to stick to the story, but he still doesn't look too good when he comes back.

Everything around me pisses me off this morning. I'm irritated by Greg chopping potatoes at the next table. Pascal keeps talking about how he's scared about this or that, and I'm ready to pick up a saucepan and crack them both on the back of the head. The wait staff is snippy and irritable because they're shorthanded. All of this shit together makes me feel even worse. The feeling hits me suddenly. I barely have the time to make it out the kitchen door before I'm spewing my guts out into a bucket. Thankfully nobody is walking by; a chef puking just outside the kitchen door is not a good look.

Why not just get in the car and drive?

I go back inside and go straight to the washroom. I rinse the bits of puke out of my teeth, and the taste out of my mouth. Splashing water on my face, I look in the mirror. I look tired and old. The darkness around my eyes has a depth to it that

I haven't seen before; my eyes are sunken and dull. I give my head a shake and make my way back out to the kitchen. I'll get through this meal, then re-evaluate.

We manage to get through breakfast. It won't go down as one of our best. The clean-up is quick and shoddy. After working in a kitchen for so long, I know how important it is to clean up well so that the next meal has a good start. Today, I just can't bring myself to do it. I'm just about to leave when Stanley comes in.

"I hate to do this right now folks, but we need to have a staff meeting in the dining room in ten minutes," he says, very seriously. Without waiting for an answer, he crosses the kitchen to go out to the dining room.

Once again, Pascal looks like he's about to pass out. Since I'm forced to wait around for a few minutes, I do some more clean-up.

When Pascal, Greg and I walk out into the dining room ten minutes later, two provincial police officers are talking to Stanley. My heart instantly doubles in speed. I have to grab a chair and take a few breaths to stop myself from falling over. I fucking hate cops. There's a part of my brain trying to tell me that their being here has nothing to do with me, but it's a tiny, little mouse squeaking against a choir of voices screaming in panic. One cop looks right at me as if he's reading my thoughts.

Fucker can see right through me; hates every molecule in my body.

Blaine sees us come in and saunters over to Pascal, taking him by the arm and sitting with him at a table off to the side. Feeling like there's a spotlight on me, I put my head down and sit at a table with Michelle.

"Sorry to keep you all, but these officers have something to tell us," Stanley starts.

"We wanted to talk to you all at once," begins one officer. He looks to be in his forties, but could be a shitty-looking thirty-something. He's a typical cop; even has the fucking mustache. If you've ever seen a video of a stocky cop with his knee in the back of some scrawny teenager, smiling like he's just caught America's most wanted criminal as he slaps the handcuffs on, then this is that guy. "We've had some complaints about boats racing around the lake at night. Some of the cottage owners are worried there'll be an accident. Last night, a boat matching the description of this resort's boat was seen, and heard, possibly racing another boat around the north branch of the lake."

I glance around the room. Stanley is looking at the cops as they talk. Blaine is sitting with his feet up on a chair, looking as calm as can be. Pascal has turned as white as a ghost. Courtney is biting on her nails. Hearing the cop talk calms me a bit, but I still can't relax in their presence.

"That's terrible," Blaine says, leaning forward and putting his elbows on his knees. "Are you certain it was *our* boat?"

"We can't be certain at this point," the officer replies. "However, we are still investigating."

"Do you know who was driving the boat?" Blaine continues, seeming very concerned about finding the bastard who would do such a thing. He definitely is a cool customer.

"Once again, we are still in the process of investigating."

"Well I certainly hope you find out who it is. We would hate to have anything bad happen on our little lake here," Blaine says, looking around at the rest of the staff. Stanley gives him a long look.

"We wanted to make everyone aware that we will be stepping up our monitoring of the lake at nights. If this does happen again, we will prosecute the individuals involved to the full extent possible," adds the other officer, who is somewhat younger.

"In addition, if it is the boat from this resort," the other cop starts.

"Or any *other* resort," Blaine interrupts.

"Or *any* resort," continues the cop, "then we will also press charges against the facility."

There's a moment of silence as people either glance around the room, or look at their shoes. I shift in my seat and put my arm around the empty chair next to me. I notice that, for no real reason, my hand is shaking. Certain that someone will notice it and assume it's because I'm guilty, I quickly cross my arms. As I look up, my eyes meet the eyes of the older cop. The urge to puke rises again into my throat as I hold his gaze for a second. I swallow hard and look away. I fucking hate cops.

The cops leave with Stanley, in the direction of his office. Without speaking, I get up and calmly head for my room. When I get to the stairs, I take them two-by-two. Once my fumbling hands are able to get the key in the lock, I open the door and then lock it behind me. In the bathroom, just behind the toilet, I pop open the loose board and find the bag. Dropping at least one pill on the floor, I'm able to toss a couple in my mouth. I know that dose dumping is stupid, but I'm so desperate to have them ease my anxiety attack that I chew them and swallow the bitter powder. Sitting on the bathroom floor, with my eyes shut, my back against the wall, and my head next to the toilet seat, I'm slowly able to control my breathing. I think I have a problem.

Chapter Twenty Five

CHRIS

"THESE THINGS ARE heavier than they look," I say, holding one of the boards that are going to be used for the cornhole tournament. This has become one of my favourite events of the week. Over the past couple of years, I've actually gotten competitive. The first year I came with Sarah and her family, I was her partner for the tournament and I was dog shit. She didn't hesitate to let me know I had let her down.

"You got one of the old, hardwood ones too," Craig says.

"Had those ones probably fifteen years," Stanley adds, as he pulls a couple more boards out of the storage shed. "Those are heavy like a dead donkey."

We carry the boards to the back lawn. There's a bit of a slope to it, but it's a nice, big, open, grassy area that's perfect for games. We set the boards up sideways on the slope. Stanley has custom built a little ledge to place under one side of the boards to counteract the lean.

It's about two fifteen and some guests have sidled over with beers in hand. Some people like to sit and watch the event; so they set up chairs around the outside. Zack takes names of those who want to sign up. It's the usual people, plus some new guests.

Sarah and I throw a few bags to warm up. Craig is partnering with Chantelle this year instead of Terry. She was a rookie last year and stunk it up pretty badly. After my pathetic first year, I was determined to improve for Sarah's sake. I guess Terry decided she's not willing to put in the effort to redeem herself.

For the last two years, Daniel and Blaine have been unbeatable as partners; but it looks like Daniel is going to partner with Courtney this year. They seem pretty flirty. We'll have to see how she throws; but not having Blaine with Daniel should give Sarah and me a better chance.

"Is your mom going to come?" I ask Sarah as we take some practice tosses.

"I doubt it. Even when we were younger, she never came out to this."

"How about your dad? Didn't he play last year?"

"I think that was the year before. Annette would never play this, so I doubt he'll come. He used to always play with Walter Watson, but they kind of drifted apart after the divorce."

"As long as we get a nice, tomato-can opponent for the first round," I say.

"Zack knows better than to set us up against anyone he knows is good," Sarah says confidently. "I'm sure we'll be able to take them."

Sure enough, our first round opponents are a nerdy looking couple that I've noticed walking around almost completely covered all week. They look skinny, pale and weak; perfect for a first round. They end up being surprisingly decent. Sarah is a bit off her game, but in the last inning, I score three points in a row, also known as a slippery granny, to secure the win.

Sarah and I have a seat with Daniel, Courtney, and another

waitress named Christine. Craig and Chantelle play against Carl Harris and his two granddaughters, who take turns throwing from their side. This game is perfect for the Resort because of the social aspect. For each game, opponents who position themselves at the same end get a chance to chat for however long the game takes. Some people end up chatting away so much while their partners are throwing that the game ends up taking forever. When you're not playing, you sit and chat with spectators and other players; probably having a drink or two. In the early rounds, most teams are just out to have some fun. By the semi-finals, the social chatter dies down and the matches become more competitive.

"How has the summer been so far, ladies?" Sarah asks Courtney and Christine. They look at each other for a moment and smile.

"Interesting," Courtney says, turning to glance at Daniel.

"Pretty crazy actually for only being the first couple of weeks," Christine adds.

"Seemed like you guys were a bit short handed this morning," I say, not sure what they're talking about, but assuming it has something to do with work. "Did you lose a waitress or something?"

"Yeah, Ariel fell and hit her head," Christine answers. "She has a pretty bad concussion and won't be coming back."

"Stanley will find someone soon," Daniel says. "There are always tons of people wanting to work here."

"I notice you're not with Blaine this year," I say.

"He couldn't make it," Daniel answers. He turns to Courtney and puts his arm around her shoulders. "I definitely upgraded this year though."

"You got *that* right," Courtney says, giving her hair a flip.

Craig is absolutely on fire during his game. The girls, Eclipse and Nova, barely hit the board, but have a blast playing; as does their grandad, Carl. Some other teams play and the afternoon rolls along. The sun beats down and most people set up their chairs under the two huge Oak trees.

"I'm going to zip back to the cabin for a piss. Should I bring a couple of beers in the little cooler?" I ask Sarah.

"Not for me," she responds. "I want to stay sharp."

*

It's about 4:00 before we're down to the semi-finals. Craig and Chantelle have destroyed everyone they've played so far. They'll play Daniel and Courtney, who sucks miserably, but is being carried by Daniel. Sarah and I have played a couple of good games and a couple of lucky ones. In the semis, we'll be facing two guys who have been pounding back beers since they arrived. They've played four matches and have gotten louder each round. In their last game, they played the Watson sisters, and just barely squeaked through; spending more energy hitting on Emma and Michelle than playing the game. Both of their wives are looking after their young kids on the beach.

The drunk guys are pretty good. I spend the match on one side with Darryl, who owns a roofing business. Sarah looks a bit uncomfortably with Charlie, a loud investor from Toronto, who's the drunker of the two. Our match is entertaining simply because of their drunkenness, but the other match is way more intense. Watching the interaction between Daniel and Craig, I can imagine them when they were younger. I doubt Daniel ever took any pity on Craig or let him win anything. They are at opposite ends of the court, Daniel standing with Chantelle, while Craig is with Courtney.

"Nice shot little bro," Daniel taunts after Craig's throw slides up the board and over the edge. "You actually hit the board on that one."

Craig shows no sign of responding, but I can see the determination on his face.

Possibly because I'm distracted by the other game, I'm not very good and we lose to Darryl and Charlie, who knocks one of his own bags into the hole with his last throw to seal the game. This results in several high-fives and some loud "BRO's". We shake hands and have a seat.

"I can't believe we lost to *those* guys," Sarah grumbles as we take a seat.

"Sorry, probably my fault," I respond. "I was distracted by your brothers."

"That's nothing. My whole childhood was spent listening to that, and far worse!"

After Chantelle lands one just in front of the hole on her toss, Daniel says, "I guess we know who the star on your team is!"

"Just shut up and throw," Chantelle responds. There's still no answer from Craig. He's not even making conversation with Courtney at his end.

It's tied at seventeen going into what looks like the final inning. The teams change sides.

"Hey Smudge," Daniel says as he passes Craig, using a nickname that I've only heard once or twice, and one which I know drives Craig insane. "How about a little side wager? Hundred bucks maybe?"

Sarah leans in and speaks softly to me. "This is where Daniel cranks up the mind games."

"How about five hundred?" Craig answers immediately, his face completely expressionless. Daniel is clearly thrown. He covers it really quickly, but for a split second, the smile drops from his cheeks.

"Big spender! Let's go then bitch." Daniel replies.

Craig gives a confident nod and a smirk. Chantelle whispers

something in his ear before they walk to opposite ends. I really wish I knew what she said. I'll have to remember to ask later. It could have been anything from, 'Are you insane?' to 'Let's kick their asses'. Craig's reaction reveals nothing.

Courtney and Chantelle do the classic best-two-out-of-three rock-paper-scissor to decide who starts. Out of the four of them, it's actually Courtney who looks the most worried. I'm not sure she planned to get involved in a high-stakes game of cornhole when she got up today. Chantelle wins the rock-paper-scissors and the game begins.

Chapter Twenty Six

STANLEY

SITTING AT MY desk, going over the last couple of days, I'm starting to feel old. It used to be that I was like a cool uncle to the staff here. Then I became more of a father figure, which took a while to adjust to, but ended up being pretty nice. Now I'm starting to shift into grandad phase; I just can't relate to them. Building this place up from the little fifteen-shack place it used to be has taken years of blood, sweat, and tears. Now my bartender is taking too many liberties, possibly putting guests at risk; the waitresses are spoiled, and my chef is just plain losing it. I've always loved working, but some parts of the job are just not as fun anymore.

Blaine walks up to the open door of my office and knocks on the frame. "You wanted to see me boss?" he says in an accent like he's in a seventies mob movie.

"Not the time to joke Blaine," I say. I've never been very good at talking to people like this; confrontation makes me uncomfortable. Having Melissa here helps with my confidence.

"What's up Stanley?" Blaine asks, as though he really has no clue something is wrong. He walks in and sits across from my desk.

"Listen, Blaine. This is serious business. Ariel gets injured on our boat, late at night. Cops show up saying that there were reports of boats racing around the lake at all hours of the night. We're lucky Max and Celeste don't sue us."

"Stanley, I don't know what you want from me. I am as concerned as you are."

"Were you speeding around the lake when Ariel fell and hit her head?" Melissa asks, getting straight to it.

"Absolutely not," Blaine replies confidently. I know Blaine is very smooth, and he very likely could be lying, but Melissa and I decided we'd give him a chance to say more about the incident; and if he chose not to, we'd let it drop. I look at Melissa.

"Alright. We do need to let you know that if something comes up to suggest that you are not being honest with us, we'll have to let you go," Melissa says calmly.

"I would expect nothing less," Blaine replies.

"Well, for now we are going to lock away the boat after dark. I've put two new padlocks on the doors, and Melissa and I have the only keys," I tell him.

"Very smart, Stanley," Blaine says. "But we can't lock up *all* the boats, can we? The cops said there were most likely two boats blazing around."

"No, but we've posted a sign saying that all boats must remain in the docks after sunset."

"Sounds good," Blaine says. "Now, what are we going to do with Ariel's tables? I like helping out and all, but you *are* looking for someone to replace her, right?"

This morning at breakfast, Blaine took charge of some of Ariel's tables. He's a competent waiter, but clearly not a permanent solution.

"Yes, we have several people we're talking to," Melissa says.

"Good stuff," Blaine adds, standing up. "If that's all you need, I think I'll catch a little nap before dinner."

"Thank you Blaine. We'll see you later," Melissa says, pretty formally.

*

"He's lying isn't he?" I ask Melissa after Blaine leaves.

"Most likely yes," she answers calmly.

"You want me to call Courtney or Pascal in again to talk to them?" I ask.

"Do you?"

"Not really. Ariel has a concussion, but she'll be fine. Max and Celeste are not pushing it. If we keep digging, we'll just be sticking our noses in a wasp's nest."

"I think you mean poking the hornet's nest dear. And I think letting it drop is probably best," Melissa says.

I'm a bit shocked. "Really?" I ask.

"Yes. However, maybe we reconsider whether Blaine is hired back next year."

"Fair enough," I admit.

"I think you should take the rest of the day to just putter around. Cut some grass. Fix that screen at Partridge. Don't worry about dinner. I'll make sure everything is alright."

"Yeah, sure," I answer. "Some time outside will be nice. You sure you'll be alright?" I ask, knowing full well she can handle things better than me.

"We'll be fine, dear. I'll let you know if we need anything."

I know she's just saying that to make me feel needed. There's very little that Melissa could need from me over dinner, unless the stove won't work or something.

"I love you," I say, giving her a hug before heading outside.

*

It's hot and sunny on the back lawn. The cornhole tournament is still on; it must be almost done by now though. Those two guys from Toronto who drink all day are being very loud, playing against Craig and Chantelle. I won't be able to cut the back lawn for a while, so I decide to take the golf cart to the barn, grab some supplies and do a couple of odd jobs that have been waiting. The last few days have taken up too much of my time with talking to people.

The first job I tackle is fixing a roof on one of the cabins on the outskirts of the Resort. I noticed that the family staying there is down at the beach at the moment, so I know I can get something done without disturbing them.

Up on the roof of the little cabin, nailing in some underlay is really where I'm supposed to be, not holding staff meetings and calling people into my office. I hate that darn office. I hated it when I was a kid, and I hate it now. Melissa always reminds me that I could easily have it re-done to change the atmosphere in there, but I leave it the same on purpose. It's a reminder of what the Resort was; old, mildewy, and uncomfortable. If I keep it like that, then I'll spend more time doing the stuff that really matters – making the place better. I guess it's kind of like the ex-smoker who holds on to one last cigarette, almost as a test. Plus, I can't justify spending money on my office when there's so much other stuff that could be done first.

If we do ever decide to sell the place, I know I could get some work as a handyman. I've made so many connections with people who either live around the lake, or have cottages there, that I could keep myself busy all summer. In the winter, I could start up a snow removal business and plow some driveways. But then, how would that really be different from doing what I'm doing now?

As much as I love getting my hands dirty and putting in a solid day's work, I've noticed that the work is starting to be a bit more challenging on the old body. Being on the roof, on my hands and knees, makes my hip tighten up like a rusty pipe. I still love to get stuff done, but I can't help wonder how much longer I got in me.

After nailing the last tile on the roof, I turn over and have a seat. Cabins like this one are raised quite a few feet above the lake. The trees here are pretty thick, so the lake is just a glimmer through the trunks. I can't explain where the thought comes from, but I briefly imagine myself falling off the roof on my way down. I'd break an arm or a leg, maybe some ribs too. I doubt I'd break my neck, but you never know. I take extra care as I grab my tools and climb down to the golf cart.

Falling off the roof and breaking my leg would certainly suck, but I'd still be able to get around and do some stuff. Falling off a roof and breaking my *neck* would be about the worst thing in the world to me. If I ever had to sit in a chair and have Melissa take care of me, I'd be steering that chair into the lake the first chance I got. That's kind of why the thought of dropping dead of a heart attack while working here doesn't sound like the worst way to go. When dad died, he didn't even make it to the hospital. With the time it took to call an ambulance, and for them to arrive, there was never any chance for him. If I'm going to go, I want to go quickly.

When Melissa's dad died a couple of years ago, it was long and drawn out. Peter Olmstead was 83 when they found out he had cancer; not bad really for a guy who smoked a pack a day for 50 years. Peter and the rest of the family decided to go through with the chemo and the radiation. Over the course of the year, Peter deteriorated before everyone's eyes. The stubborn old bat held on and fought it for a year and a half before dying in hospital. The toll it took on the whole family was heavy. Even though I have no family other than Melissa, I don't want that to be me.

I remember watching that old Billy the Kid movie and hearing that Bon Jovi song about being gunned down in a glorious blaze. I'm not much of a fan of Bon Jovi-type music, but I have to admit I like that song. The thought of being struck down on the spot like that has its appeal. Of course I wouldn't do any stealing or anything that would get me in trouble. Maybe I could get shot down saving some women, while fighting all the bad guys in black.

Maybe that's what's going on with all those shootings happening in the States recently; just some cowboys with some messed up ideas about how to get to a quick death. They're like modern-day Billy the kids, only with a twisted mind that makes them think it's OK to take a few dozen people with them. I guess the glory part depends on your interpretation.

It's kind of weird how little people actually talk about death even though we've all experienced it along the way. Everyone loses a grandparent when they're growing up; if not a grandparent, then maybe a great-grandparent. Some kids have to work through a mom or dad dying; that must suck. Usually kids are sheltered from the actual death. They might pop in and visit grandpa in the hospital for half an hour when the family knows the end is coming; but ultimately we don't really *see* it. Death happens in rooms way up high on the eleventh floor of the hospital.

In other countries, that's not the case. People live with death all the time. I wonder if they appreciate their lives a bit more. And in the old days, before fancy scans and regular doctor visits where they put on a glove and stick a finger up your behind; did people have a better understanding of what death was all about?

I've never really tried talking to Melissa about all this. I think I know what she'd say – that I'm being morbid, and selfish with my attitude to die a quick death. But I don't see it as that. I think putting her through a long, drawn-out sickness or something like that would be more selfish. Asking someone to take a year out of their life to take care of you while you die seems selfish to me. Besides, my last checkup said my cholesterol was pretty good and that I'm in good health. If I want to be clutching at my heart and saying, 'Elizabeth, this is the big one", then I'm going to have to eat a bunch more fried food.

While doing all this thinking, I've managed to fix a roof, replace three ripped screens, oil some hinges, and unclog a storm drain; all in all a pretty productive afternoon. That's part of the reason I love getting out and doing some odd jobs. Not only do I get stuff done, while making the place look nice; but I like to let the mind wander and see where it goes. If I had the time, I might even write some of it down. That would require sitting down at a computer though - not my favourite activity.

It's dinner time before I pack it in and drive back to the barn.

Chapter Twenty Seven

SARAH

I KNOW IT'S TIME to just come out and say it. Chris and I have been back at the cabin now for at least half an hour. There's not really much excuse; I'm pretty sure I know what his reaction is going to be. It's just that saying the words feels like it'll be so final. Once it's out there, I can't take it back. I open the bathroom door and step out.

"Almost ready?" Chris asks.

"Almost. Can I talk to you first?" I ask, timidly.

"For sure," he says, putting down his magazine. "What's up? You alright?"

"Yeah." I take a deep breath. How is it possible to practice something in your head dozens of times, be certain that it sounds perfect, then second guess how it's going to sound at the last minute?

"I'm pregnant."

I can almost see the words leaving my mouth and floating across the room.

"Are you sure?" Chris asks.

"As sure as I can be. I took a test and I looked at it, like ninety-five times."

A big smile comes across Chris' face. He gets up, takes a couple of steps and engulfs me in a huge hug. "You're excited right?" he asks, pulling away and taking hold of both my hands.

"Of course! Maybe a little scared, but really excited. How about you?"

"You know I want this," Chris says. "I can't wait to be a dad."

"I know. It's just a big change."

"But I think it's a change we *need*."

He sits on the little, wooden chair and guides me down to sit on his lap. I look into his eyes. He's always had such a confident gaze; brown eyes with flecks of green shooting out from the middle. I know we're as ready as we can be. But it doesn't change the fact that it's scary. Now that the concern of telling Chris is over, I feel a bit overwhelmed by thoughts of whether the baby will be alright, whether I'll be able to breastfeed properly, or whether I'll become majorly depressed and want to kill my husband.

"Yeah. No telling anyone though, right?" I say.

"No, yeah. When are you supposed to wait until?"

"Three months."

"What? That's a really long time away. No way you'll be able to keep quiet that long!" Chris says jokingly.

"Whatever! You'd be the one to blab."

"Wanna bet?" Chris challenges.

"Sure. First two weeks of diaper changes you tell someone first."

Chris laughs and makes a face of disgust. "That seems extreme. How about a blow job?"

"If it's a blowjob for you, then a month of diapers!"

"OK, maybe not as part of the bet then. Just a celebratory blowjob?" he jokes.

I smack him on the arm and laugh.

"First two weeks of diapers for whoever blabs first. Unless we get to three months, then we tell people together," I clarify.

"Fine," Chris agrees, holding out his hand for me to shake. "Wonder how fat you're going to get?" he adds, touching my stomach. Once again, I smack him on the arm; harder than the first time.

"I am going to eat right, exercise constantly, and do yoga throughout the whole pregnancy. I am not getting *fat*."

Chris puts one hand gently on my leg and pushes my hair behind my ear with the other. He kisses me softly on the neck.

"I know. You are going to look fabulous the whole time," he whispers in my ear. "And I hear that sex is really good for the baby."

"I've actually heard that too," I admit. I put one arm around his neck. He pulls his head back and looks me in the eyes again. I hope our baby has his eyes.

"You know you're going to be a MILF right?"

"That's depressing," I say, letting my arms drop to my sides.

"No way! That's hot!" he insists.

Just then, my phones buzzes on the table next to us.

"It's my mom," I say, kissing him on the lips, then getting up and grabbing my phone.

"Hi Maman," I answer.

"Sarah, dear. Are you coming soon? I did tell Craig we'd meet him at 6:00."

"On our way mom," I assure her before hanging up. I turn to Chris, who still looks like he's wanting sex.

"We gotta go," I say, sounding apologetic.

"I know," he sulks. "We're putting a pin in *that* though," he adds, raising an eyebrow and tapping his lap.

"Oh, yeah," I agree.

*

When we arrive at Maman's, she's waiting at the door with Chantelle.

"Took you long enough," Chantelle complains. "What were you doing, arguing or having sex?"

Maman turns sharply and looks at Telle. "Darling, that's not very appropriate."

"We're all adults here, mom," Telle says. "Right Sarah?"

"I guess. But still not really before-dinner conversation."

"I think some people need to loosen up a bit in this family. You're both a little prudish," Chantelle says. She's not really saying it confrontationally, just like she's stating fact. "Don't you think, Chris?"

My husband looks like he was just asked a question in class, when he has no idea what language the question was even asked in, and his entire life is based on his answer. Thankfully for him, Maman steps in quickly.

"Chantelle, please," she says in a parental kind of way. "Let's not start dinner by picking fights and making people feel uncomfortable."

She takes Telle by the arm and walks off towards the dining room.

*

When we take our seats, the dining room is pretty full. Daniel is sitting with dad, Annette, and another couple who regularly come to visit dad during our week here. Craig and Terry arrive after a couple of minutes.

"Sorry we're late," Craig apologizes as he pulls Terry's chair.

"Sex or fighting?" Chantelle asks.

"What?" Craig says, confused.

"Chantelle, dear, please stop," Maman says with clear

irritation in her voice. I think the last two days of having Chantelle around is beginning to get to her.

"Craig, don't you think that this family is a bit tight assed? I mean, wouldn't it be nice to be a bit more honest and up front?"

Craig stays calm and just looks around at us. "Is there something going on that we need to talk about?" he asks Chantelle.

"Nope. I just think that everything is always so superficial with us all being together. Nobody really talks about anything. I make a couple of simple jokes that family should be able to make, and people get all jittery." Telle then turns to Terry. "You know what I'm talking about right?"

"Sure," Terry responds without flinching. "For the record, we weren't having sex. We had a nap after all the corn bag drama. Congratulations by the way," she says to Chantelle, touching her on the arm.

"It's cornhole, babe," Craig corrects.

"That *was* pretty impressive," I add.

For now, the tension has eased. Craig relives the glory of beating Daniel on the final throw of the semi-final game; but there's clearly something coming with Maman and Telle.

"Folks, how are we doing?" Blaine asks, approaching our table to take drink orders. I can't even look at him since Chantelle came back the other morning. She can obviously tell that I'm uncomfortable because she gets up and taps him on the ass as she passes by on her way to the bathroom. She also throws in a, "howdy," as she taps him. As disturbing as that is to me, it's also pretty funny to see him blush and squirm as the silence lingers over our table.

"Well Blaine, I'd like to order us a couple of bottles of the St Henri Shiraz," Craig says, breaking the silence.

"Wow!" Blaine sounds shocked by the order, and glad that the attention is off him. "Special occasion?"

For a moment, I think that somehow, someone has found out that I'm pregnant. I glance over at Chris, who winks and blows me a kiss.

"Just celebrating a victory," Craig answers with a smile. "And can you send over a bottle of the Pino Grigio to my brother?"

"Sounds good," Blaine says before leaving.

"Is that smart?" I ask him. He knows full well how much that will piss Daniel right off.

"It's fine!" Craig answers.

"I agree," says Terry. "I think Daniel could use being knocked down a peg. Today was exciting."

"I suppose," I add. "We were definitely cheering for you two."

"Oh totally," Chris pipes in. "That was exciting shit today. Sorry Meme."

"Understandable dear. I heard it was quite thrilling."

*

Dinner is nice. The food is good and the wine does a nice job of loosening everyone up. I have to make an excuse for not having any, and I think Terry picks up on something, judging by the look she gives me. Maman fills us in on some gossip about a family that hasn't made it back this year. Apparently the teenaged son got arrested for dealing drugs and the dad was caught having sex with his assistant.

Craig is clearly elated at having won the cornhole tournament; he's laughing, joking and having several glasses of wine. After coming back to the table, Chantelle is quiet, but not argumentative either. I'm not sure if it's the calm before the storm, or she's actually settled a bit.

After dinner, Craig and Terry go over to join Daniel and dad for a coffee. Maman takes Bijou for a little walk. It's disco night tonight, so Chris and I leave dinner to go and get ready.

We aren't really dancers, but this night is always fun; Chris gets right into it. Telle leaves with us.

"Are you planning on going to the disco night tonight?" I ask her when we get to her door.

"I think that might be entertaining."

There's a silence that hangs for a few seconds. I look at Chris, then back at Telle.

"Why don't you come over, have a drink and get ready?" I ask, unsure of what her reaction will be. I think that's the hardest thing about my relationship with Telle. I never really know how she's going to react. Every time I make an effort to reach out to her, I'm uncertain of whether she'll accept, act indifferent, or lash out in some way.

"Thanks. As long as I won't be cramping your style." She looks directly at Chris when she says it.

He shrugs it off. "Not at all."

I know that he's a bit irritated. He got his engine all revved up earlier and was probably hoping to squeeze in a quickie before we went out. He can wait.

Chris goes inside to get ready, so Telle and I sit on the deck.

"Beer?" she offers.

"No thanks," I answer.

"Why? You pregnant?"

Once again, her bluntness surprises me. It wouldn't really matter if she found out, but I would really prefer to wait a while.

"Can't I just decide *not* to drink for a day, and not be pregnant?"

"Not on vacation, no."

"Fine," I say and take a beer. I take a few small sips, then place it on the railing. I'll just nurse it a while and maybe dump some out when I go inside in a bit. I'm not really sure when it's bad to drink during a pregnancy, or how much is acceptable. I just always assumed that all drinking is bad during the whole thing. I should look into that later.

"Listen, if you're so interested in everyone in this family being more real and honest, then why don't you start by telling me what exactly happened with you and Dimitri."

Hopefully I can make her feel uncomfortable for a minute. At least I can distract her.

It works; she looks over, then stares off at the lake.

"I don't think you would like to hear it all."

"Try me," I say, not entirely sure myself.

"Alright! He started to get kinky, then violent, then weird. He knocked me up, then insisted I get an abortion; said he'd do it himself if I didn't. I did. Then a week later, I found him fucking our neighbour in our apartment."

"Oh, Telle. That's awful. I had no idea."

"That's not the best part," she says with a little chuckle, sipping her beer.

"How could that get worse?"

"Our neighbour's a guy."

I literally have no idea what to say. Chantelle takes a long swig of her beer. Without thinking, I do the same. "What did you do?" I ask, after discreetly spitting some beer back into the can.

"Well, I left. I thought about going back while he was sleeping and slitting his throat, but I figured that probably wasn't smart."

I actually don't know how serious she is. "I'm glad you didn't."

"I went back when I knew he was out, grabbed all my stuff, took a shit on his pillow, and came here."

"Oh, Telle," I say, "that's disgusting!" It's all I can think of saying.

"I think he deserved it."

"Why didn't you say anything sooner?"

"Because I knew you'd get like you are now!"

"What do you mean? I'm just concerned."

"I know, Sarah. I'm surprised you don't have an ulcer already because of everyone else's problems."

"It's not wrong for me to care about my family."

"True, but you can't control everything either," she says, looking at me. "I'll be fine."

My phone rings. I pick it up and see that it's Craig.

"Hey, Craig. What's up?"

"If you girls are free, dad would like to speak to us all. Can you and Telly meet us at the boat?"

"Alright. Chris too right?"

"Nope. Dad just wants the four of us. Terry's going to head over to your place to hang out with Chris while we're gone."

"Alright. See you soon."

"What's up?" Telle asks once I've hung up.

"Dad wants to talk to the four of us. We're supposed to meet the boys at the boat."

"That should be a blast!" she says sarcastically.

Chantelle finishes her drink. I take mine inside and dump most of it down the sink while she's not looking. Chris has had a shower and is wearing his silver disco outfit. When he was in university, I guess he bought this god-awful silver jumpsuit for a Halloween party. He had an afro wig and platform shoes too. He called himself Dr. Disco. After he found out there was a disco night at the Resort, he was so happy he hadn't ever thrown it away. He's since ditched the wig, but he still rocks the shoes and the jump suit on Disco night.

"Looking sharp there Chris!" Chantelle jokes.

"Oh yeah! Can you dig it cat?" Chris answers.

"We are going down to the boat to see my dad. Apparently he wants to talk to the family."

"Alright. I'm going to sit, have a drink and enjoy some peace and quiet before I get my boogie on."

"Hope you don't mind Terry coming over for your peace and quiet," I tell him. "Craig just said she's on her way."

"That's fine."

*

Telle and I walk down to the boathouse. It's about an hour before dusk; the lake is calm and peaceful. Dad, Daniel and Craig are getting ready to take the boat out. Annette is not there. After some chit-chat, dad pulls the boat slowly out of the dock. I can't remember the last time the five of us were together on dad's boat. When we were younger, we would spend most of the week out fishing, waterskiing, and sometimes just touring around the lake.

"So is there a specific destination in mind here, or are we just going for a spin?" I ask.

"Or are you taking us all out to the middle of the lake to finally get rid of us all?" Chantelle adds.

"No Chantelle," my dad answers calmly from the driver's seat. "I've invested way too much money in all of you." He turns and winks.

"Then where *are* we going?"

"Just a few more minutes sweetie. There's something I would like to show you all."

We take a few more turns, and then dad cuts the engine. He turns to face us.

"I wanted to show you this," he says, pointing to the shore.

"You mean that tree that looks exactly like every other tree on the way here?" Chantelle asks.

"Not exactly," Daniel says. "Just up the hill, behind the trees."

"I purchased some property on the lake here," dad says. "We are building a cabin there."

"That's great dad," I say.

"I just wanted to tell everyone at once that Annette and I won't be coming to the Resort anymore. We've been talking about it for a few years now. It's obvious to everyone that when your mother and I are both here, it's not really enjoyable for anyone."

"I'm surprised you've all lasted this long, to be honest," Chantelle adds.

"What's *that* supposed to mean?" I ask.

"It means that I stopped coming here four years ago. It was awkward as shit right after the divorce, and it hasn't gotten much smoother since."

"That's not dad's fault though!" I protest.

"I never said it was. It just is what it is."

"I think it's for the best," Craig says. "Will you be around here all summer then, dad?"

"Off and on."

"How about for our week?" I ask.

"I don't know, sweetie. We'll have to see."

I know it's unreasonable, but I'm not happy. I know how difficult it is on everyone when we all come up. I've talked to Chris multiple times about not coming ourselves. But I still feel saddened at the thought of change. Chantelle hasn't really been here for years, except for these last few days, and if dad stops coming too, I know it won't be long before everyone just does their own thing.

"I think we should see it as a great opportunity," Daniel adds, sounding very much like he's making a presentation to a room full of people in suits. "We can start some new traditions. Dad has already said that we'll be able to make several trips up here throughout the summer. Right?"

"Absolutely. It will be big enough for everyone to come and stay together. There'll be some weeks where Annette and I spend some time alone here too. I've been starting to cut back my responsibilities at the firm over the last few years, so I plan on having lots of time off by next summer. We might also look into renting it out for some weeks."

"Will you two stay at the Resort next summer?" I ask Daniel and Craig.

"Haven't really thought about it," answers Craig. "I just kind of assume we're coming, so I'm sure we will."

"I'll need to avenge my cornhole loss, so I *have* to come back," Daniel says jokingly. He seems to have gotten over the loss.

I look at Chantelle.

"I have *no* clue," she says, shrugging her shoulders. "I'm not sure where I'll be next *week*." I think that's about the best I can hope for from her. At least she didn't completely shoot down the possibility.

"I'm happy for you dad," I say sincerely.

"I think it will be best for everyone," he says, turning back to the wheel.

We turn around and head back to the Resort in silence, enjoying the cool night and the stars that are just starting to peek out from the growing darkness.

Chapter Twenty Eight

PASCAL

I FEEL LIKE I'M going to die. Every time I get stressed, it always hits me in the stomach. During exam time, I spent days sitting on the toilet. This has been the longest day ever. I had a horrible sleep after the whole boat thing. I had to get up early for breakfast prep, feeling like crap. Stanley called me into his office and I had to lie to him. Then the cops came and I felt like I was going to barf the whole time. I managed to sleep this afternoon for like, an hour; but then dinner was really hard. Dave was super tense and snippy. Everyone was kind of on edge; the waitresses are all overworked because they have more tables. Even Blaine was not his normal, joking self. It felt like an eight hour shift just for dinner.

So here I am, sitting on the toilet again. I don't know how stress turns my shit into acid water, but it happens. Just the thought of having to wipe is painful.

Tonight is disco night, and I plan on crawling into bed and sleeping. The thought of having anything to drink right now just makes my guts do flips.

I finish up my business and drag my sore ass to my bunk. There's nobody else in the cabin, so instead of putting in my earbuds, I turn on my little Bluetooth speaker and play some Tragically Hip. Just as I'm starting to relax, my phone buzzes. I don't get too many texts up here, so I check it right away. It's Maria!

Will I C U out later?

For a second, I forget how crappy I feel. The fact that she's actually asking me if I'm going out has got to mean that she wants me to go, doesn't it? What should I say? How do I sound interested, but not too interested? Now I'm stressed again.

Hope so, I respond. What time R U going?

I think that sounds pretty good. Short and sweet; that's what Rob suggested. I trust his advice more than someone like Blaine.

Around 10 save a dance ☺

That means I have about half an hour; so much for relaxing. I grab my speaker, head to the shower, and crank up the volume.

I'm showered and ready in fifteen minutes. I take out a bottle of water from the mini fridge and go outside to join Greg and Rob sitting around the fire pit.

"Are you finally done on the shitter?" Greg asks.

"Yeah. Feeling better," I lie.

"Grab a beer," Rob says, opening the cooler next to him.

"No thanks," I say, feeling my stomach lurch at the sight. "Still not quite *that* good." I take a swig of water.

I have a seat in a canvas fold-up chair that has a built in foot rest. They continue their conversation about how weird it would be if Toy Story were true. It's perfect, mindless stuff to get my mind off everything.

"When Woody did that thing where he spun his head around, I was freaked out!" I admit at one point in the conversation. Greg then shares that he still thinks Jessie is hot.

Just after ten, we cross the road to the bar. I'm actually starting to feel better by the time we get there, so I get Blaine to grab me a beer. The dancing hasn't started yet, but quite a few people have already arrived. Not having actually come to disco night yet this year, I never realized that people get pretty into it. There are a few guests who are dressed up in fancy suits. I guess I've never really gotten the whole disco thing.

Some of the tables have been moved away to make a dance floor, so there's nowhere really to sit. I'm way more comfortable when I can sit down; standing in a bar is too much work.

Once Zack starts the music and dims the lights, people start dancing. I'm able to find a space against the wall where I can at least lean. Maria comes in with a couple of other girls. She sees me and waves. I can hear some other guy's voice in my head telling me to play it cool; maybe give a little nod, but don't act too interested. In that moment, I decide that I'm done with trying to seem cool. I'm just going to be myself and be honest. I smile and wave back. The decision is comforting. I'm not Blaine, or any other guy who's a 'player'. I just can't do that.

After getting a drink, Maria leaves her friends and crosses the bar in my direction. I don't really want to give up my leaning space against the wall, so I stay and wait for her to come over.

"Hey," she says sweetly.

"Hi Maria. You look really nice tonight." She's wearing a dark, pink dress that shows off lots of leg. She's wearing makeup, which I'm not used to seeing. It makes her look at least five years older. She's also got her hair down, which is really different than the bun she normally wears. I have a buddy who's always talking about how he loves blondes. Not sure why, but dark hair does it for me. There's something more exotic about it.

"Thanks, so do you," she replies. I know she's just saying it because I have no clean clothes, and I literally put no effort into dressing up.

"Thanks, but I feel a little underdressed. I didn't realize that people get so into dressing up," I say as I look out onto the dance floor.

"Or you would have worn *your* disco outfit?" she jokes.

"Absolutely!"

"Maybe next week then."

We spend a few minutes watching the people dancing. I start to realize that at least half the people on the floor are horrible dancers. It's more about putting together some really cheesy moves than actually looking good. After some small talk and a second beer, I'm feeling like I can do this.

"I'm not exactly a disco expert, but do you wanna dance?" I ask, not very smoothly.

"I'd love to. And I've seen you dance before. You're good."

She takes my hand, which I'm hoping is not too clammy, and we walk out onto the floor. I keep it fairly simple and reserved at first; minimal foot movement with some shoulder dips and a little bit of hip action. Maria moves really well; I can't keep my eyes off her and her moving body.

Over the course of the next two hours, Maria and I dance, have a couple of drinks, and talk. The night is perfect. I've completely forgotten about feeling crappy. At the end of the night, the final song is an Elton John slow song from the seventies. I've heard it before. It's the one with the line, '*How wonderful life is when you're in the world*'. I've always thought it sounded really cheesy when people talk about having a song with someone, but while dancing with Maria, to that song, I kind of understand it. I never want the song to end; and regardless of what more happens with Maria, I swear I will always think of this dance when I hear it.

I was pretty nerdy in high school, so I didn't get to experience it much, but slow dancing is the greatest thing ever; I get to hold Maria in my arms, my hand just inches away from her butt, and feel her moving her hips back and forth, every once in a while brushing up against me. Her hair smells like peaches when she puts her head on my shoulder.

The song ends and the lights come up. For a second, I feel anxious again. The dancing is over and now I have no clue what I should do.

"It's kind of hot in here," she says after a few seconds of silence. "Do you want to go sit outside?"

I snap out of my stupidness and nod. "Sounds good."

Once we get outside, I ask, "Are you getting picked up soon?" Maria doesn't usually stay at the Resort.

"No, I'm actually staying in the girl's cabin tonight."

"Cool. Maybe we could sit on the beach for a bit?"

"That sounds nice," she says.

People are starting to trickle out of the bar, wandering back to cabins. Feeling a burst of courage, or maybe it's the fresh air mixed with a few Budweisers, I take her hand as we stroll towards the beach.

There's a loud whistle that comes from behind us. We both turn around.

"Wooooo! Don't do anything I would, buddy!" Blaine calls from the bar door. Sometimes guys like him can be real assholes.

"Sorry," I say quietly.

"Why? You didn't do anything. You can't help him being a dick."

I look at her and smile. I know how guys are supposed to

care about getting in a girl's pants as quickly as possible; but I really don't want to screw anything up with Maria. This has been the best night so far, and I think she's really cool.

Once we reach the beach, we sit in a couple of deck chairs and look out at the lake. She tells me about her family, her home town, and what she hopes to do next year. I talk about my mom, lacrosse, and my school. The conversation flows so smoothly that an hour goes by before I know it. The Resort is quiet and lights are going out. Looking over, I see her yawn and give a little shiver. I realize how tired I am, and try my best to swallow my own yawn.

"It's getting pretty late," she says. "I should head back to the cabin. I have to help set up the dining room for breakfast."

"Yeah, I have to be in the kitchen super early," I add. "Can I walk you back?"

"Of course," she says. She gets up, takes both my hands and helps me stand. When I'm up, she doesn't move back at all. She's right in front of me, looking up into my eyes.

"I had a really nice time tonight," I say. Absurdly, I suddenly worry about my breath.

"Me too," she answers, still not moving.

I lean down and give her a kiss. She doesn't move away, but kisses me back, slowly raising her arms and putting them around my neck. I put my arms around her waist. She tastes of raspberry wine coolers and peppermint gum; and it's glorious. All the blood in my body rushes to two places, one of them being my head. I actually feel like I might pass out for a second, but it passes and I enjoy the moment. Feeling brave, I slide my hands down her back and slowly pull her body into mine. I have no idea how long we're like this. At the same time, it feels like it lasts an hour, and that it's over too fast. She slides her arms from my shoulders and takes a small step back, still holding onto both my hands.

We walk back towards the cabins, slowly; me floating more than walking. There's no conversation, but I don't care. I walk her to the door of the girls' cabin and give her one last kiss goodnight. After she goes inside, I turn and walk across the little field to the boys' cabin. Everything is dark inside. People are in the bunks. I pass them by and head to the bathroom. With all the sensations still fresh in my head, I masturbate for about thirty seconds before I'm shooting like a cannon into the toilet. A thought crosses my mind just as I'm doing up my pants; what are the chances that Maria is lying in her bed, doing the same thing right now, while thinking of me? Probably not very good.

Chapter Twenty Nine

MICHELLE

THE ROADS ARE always clear on the way to the Resort this early in the morning. Having the afternoon off yesterday, and a chance to spend it with Scarlett, was exactly what I needed. She's eight now and time is seriously flying by. During the school year, I work two jobs and she goes to school. We barely see each other during the week; then every other weekend is filled with playdates and gymnastics classes. The other weekends, she spends with her dickhead father. The money I can make at the Resort is too good to resist; but it means I only really get one day a week with her in the summer – usually Tuesdays. Stanley called me and asked if I could come in for breakfast yesterday, sounding completely desperate, so I did. I knew we were going to be short for dinner too, but I needed the rest of the day off. There was no way I was going to give it up.

After grabbing a coffee on my way, I get in at about 6:55. I have it timed perfectly now. As I walk into the dining room, I see Stanley there talking to a perky looking girl. Hoping to avoid an introduction to what I assume is a new waitress to replace Ariel,

I take out my phone and earbuds, and grab some stuff to start setting up.

"Michelle, I'm glad you're here," Stanley says, waving.

"Hi Stanley," I respond, still untangling the wire. Damn things always get all tied up in my pocket.

"Michelle, this is Stacey. She'll be starting this morning."

Stacey? Are you fucking kidding me? That's basically another Courtney.

"Hi Stacey," I say as coldly as possible.

"Hey! I'm super excited to be able to shadow you. Stanley has told me you're the best waitress he's ever had."

I turn and glare at Stanley, who looks very uncomfortable.

"I was thinking Stacey could start with two or three tables this morning, with your help. And she could also help you out with yours; you know, run some food and clear some dishes."

"Great," I say, and turn to go to the kitchen.

*

Dave is walking around the kitchen putting dishes away and getting set up for breakfast. He doesn't acknowledge me coming in.

"Mornin' Dave," I call out.

"Hey."

He looks like absolute shit. His face is pale and his eyes are dark. Despite it being nice and cool in the kitchen at this time, he looks like he's sweating.

"How are you doing today?" I ask, already knowing the answer.

"Shit. Just want to get my stuff done. Sorry."

We've never been super close, but Dave and I at least see things mostly the same way. Recently, he's been acting more jumpy than normal. Something's up with him, but it's not really my place to push it.

"Let me know if you need anything," I tell him as I grab

some dishes and head back out to the dining room. Stanley is just finishing up showing Stacey around, which is funny because Stanley doesn't really know shit about the dining room; that's more Melissa's domain.

"Stacey, why don't you grab some more side plates from the stack just inside the kitchen," I direct her. Stanley gives me a relieved looking smile.

"Alright, if things are good here, I've got some business I need to take care of," he says, bolting for the door. "No time to sit on the fence."

As Stacey walks towards the kitchen, I wonder if she's already been introduced to Dave. Assuming she probably hasn't, and knowing what kind of mood Dave is in, I decide to follow her. When I open the door, I see she's talking to Greg, who has just arrived.

"Well if there's anything I can do, just ask," Greg is saying.

"Thanks, that's super sweet."

"Are you staying on the Resort?" Greg asks, clearly smitten with her.

"No. My parents are picking me up. They might let me come and stay later in the summer though if things work out."

"Well, I hope things work out."

"Either take that shit outside, or get to work Greg," Dave calls from the other side of the kitchen, without even looking up. Stacey looks shocked, and a little hurt.

"Don't worry about him; not much of a morning person," Greg says in a quiet voice. "I'll talk to you later. Have a good shift."

"Thanks," Stacey replies, looking over at Dave a bit nervously.

I grab some more supplies and head out to the dining room. Stacey follows me out.

"Did I do something to piss him off?" she asks me.

"No. He's just very particular about his kitchen; best not to fuck with him."

"Uh, OK."

*

We finish setting up the dining room in good time. She's actually pretty fast and efficient, although she's a talker. I respond in minimal grunts, but she keeps chatting away. When Courtney and Christine arrive, they pull her aside and talk with her for a bit, giving my ears a break. It's hard to say what it is about Courtney that pisses me off the most. Stanley's right in saying that she's a decent waitress; but she's the kind of girl that if I met her under other circumstances, I'd be grabbing that blond ponytail and smashing her perfect teeth into the side of a table. Just as I'm getting ready to open the doors, I see Courtney look over in my direction and say something to the other two. Courtney and Christine give a little laugh and look away. To her credit, Stacey looks more uncomfortable than amused.

Breakfast is usually a pretty easy meal to serve at the Resort. Everyone has a couple of options for a starter, then three choices for their meal. We feed them pretty well in the morning. Lots of people only eat two meals each day, maybe snacking in the afternoon; guests are on their own for lunches. I make sure coffee stays hot and dishes are cleared. Usually that makes guests happy.

Stacey takes two tables to start. She's as bubbly and chatty at the tables as she's been all morning. I know that if she waited on my table, that would drive me crazy; but the guests at her tables respond well. I have to admit that she does a really good job. She checks in on all my tables and shows good initiative. It's one of the easiest breakfasts I've had all year. Maybe she's a keeper.

*

The last couple of guests are finishing up, and most tables are cleared and ready to set up for dinner.

"Michelle, can I ask you a question?" she asks.

"Sure."

"Is it always like this around here?"

"What do you mean?" I ask, not entirely sure what she's talking about.

"Everyone seems super edgy. The cook guy didn't even look at me once. Courtney seems a bit,…" She hesitates a moment.

"Bitchy?" I add.

"Well, kind of. You seem a bit irritated too. Did I do something? Or say something wrong?"

I actually feel kind of sorry for her, even if her asking seems more out of concern for herself than anyone else.

"It has nothing to do with you. It's been kind of a crazy week. Usually it's less tense."

"Ok. Good. Cuz it seems like it could be a super fun place to work."

I suddenly feel very old. Her perspective is so naïve and simple. I guess that's my biggest problem with a lot of the staff here. I've never seen this place as a 'fun place to work'. It's always been a necessity to work. A lot of these girls are here because their parents are rich and have been coming to the Resort on vacation for years.

"Yeah, just make sure you do your job before the fun," I say, a bit too harshly than I probably should.

She looks hurt. I try to feel sorry for her, but I can't.

"Thanks for your help today. I learned a lot," she says before turning to clear the last couple of tables.

The fact that I feel guilty pisses me off even more. I decide not to say anything more right now. I'll just say something nice before dinner.

Chapter Thirty

BLAINE

I'VE COMPLETELY MISSED breakfast, but that was a much needed sleep after the last thirty-six hours or so. It's hard to believe that's all it's been since the whole Ariel thing happened; it seems way longer. Today is the perfect day for a day off. After a couple of texts, Greg agrees to bring me back something from the kitchen so I don't have to go all the way over there. In the meantime, a quick trip into the woods behind the cabin to smoke a pinner helps to get the day started right.

While I wouldn't want anything serious to happen to Ariel, it's all kind of for the best that she's gone. She was a pretty shitty waitress, and she was always hanging around with Christine and Courtney. Maybe now I can get Christine by herself. Or better yet, maybe whoever they hire to replace Ariel will be hotter. Whatever happens, shit *has* to get back to normal around here. The first two weeks of the summer were pretty chill and uneventful; it was nice to see a couple of people again, and nice to meet some newbies. But the shine wore off pretty quickly. Now everyone has some beef with someone else, and people are all pissy. Not having me around at dinner tonight will totally just make things worse. Without me to bring a little humour to the place, it'll be like a fucking morgue in there.

Even though it's late morning, the temperature hasn't really gone up much. There are some grey clouds rolling over the lake and the few pitiful attempts the sun has made to break through have done nothing to warm things up. It doesn't look like it's going to be a day for hanging on the beach; I'll have to find something else to do. Maybe I can convince someone to drive to town and see a movie.

As I'm putting out my joint, I look up at the road and see Daniel walking out of the Resort driveway and heading up the road. He doesn't seem like the type to just go for a brisk walk.

"Sneaking away somewhere?" I call to him, stepping out of the woods.

"Blaine. What's up?" Daniel asks, crossing the road.

"Not much. Just starting my day off with a good perspective," I answer, making a toking motion and giving him a wink.

"Nice."

"So are you just out taking a stroll?" I ask again.

"Uh, yeah. Big breakfast," he says, patting his gut. "You got big plans for your day off?"

"Not really. Kind of hoping to get away and see a movie or something. How about you, me, Courtney and Christine go hang for the afternoon?"

He stands silently for a second, looking like he's thinking way too hard about a simple question. "I kind of have a plan already."

"No worries. Maybe I can persuade Rob to go."

Once again, he just stands there. He glances up the road in the direction he was heading. "Feel like joining me on my walk?" he asks.

"Why not," I say. I still haven't had breakfast yet, but since

I'm not starving, a little baked walk sounds like a good idea. "I have to admit that I never really pictured you as the 'going for a walk in the woods' type, buddy," I say as we start up the little hill leading away from the Resort. "But I guess it worked out pretty well the other day when you found that kid."

"Yeah. Want to hear a funny story about that?"

"Sure."

"There's a cottage a couple of miles up the road here. It's more like a big house than a cottage though."

"Yeah, I've seen that. Big double garage and shit?"

"That's the one. Well there's a couple who lives there. The guy's loaded. His name's Winston. He works in investments; probably scooped enough cash here and there from clients over the years to buy that house ten times over. He's a really nerdy guy; bald and skinny with glasses; drives a Porsche. But his wife, Gabriella, is a fucking knock out."

"I've seen the car drive by, but never the couple."

"Well Winston works a lot, and he golfs a lot. They come here in the summer and stay in that fancy house in the woods. I met Gabriella last year, right at the end of the season when my dad and I were looking at properties. She was out doing some shopping in town and I struck up a conversation in line. Turns out she's cooped up in that house most of the summer while Winston is out on the golf course with clients."

"Let me guess, you took her out and showed her a good time?"

"Not exactly. More like she brought me *home* and we showed each other a good time."

"While Winston was out? You dog," I say with admiration. "How old is she? Is she a cougar? She's not a snow leopard is she?"

"Fuck no! She's like forty and built like a twenty-five year old. They never had kids. I guess she married him for his money; he's in his fifties. He could never really 'satisfy' her, and it's starting to get a bit too boring for her to handle."

"So you thought you'd step in and fill a need?"

"It's the noble thing to do."

I give a chuckle. "How does this relate to finding the kid?"

"Well, I visited her a couple more times in the fall while my dad was sealing the purchase of some land on the lake. Then this week, she got in touch again. She texted me that Winston was out golfing and that she expected me there. I went over, like a good soldier, and got down to business. We're fucking on the kitchen counter when we hear the garage door open. It seems old Winston's golf game was rained out and he was back a couple of hours early."

"Shit!"

"I know. I grabbed my pants and shoes and bolted out the back door. I was cutting through the woods when I saw the kid crying. I'm just lucky I didn't end up driving over."

"You have some fucked up karma, dude. You found that kid because you almost got caught boning some rich guy's horny wife."

"Horny? You have no idea! This bitch is a freak!"

"Really?"

"Loves role play shit. One time, she told me to break into the house, find her in bed and fuck her good. She got pissed at me when I wasn't being rough enough with her. Told me not to stop, no matter how much she fought. By all the bruises I got, you'd have thought I'd been in an MMA fight."

"I guess Winston wouldn't be able to handle that kind of punishment."

"Nope. She says he's very 'traditional' in his sexual practices. She's told me a couple of times how much she would love to have Winston watch us, to learn how to give it to her right; maybe even join in if he were up for it."

"I assume you haven't seen her since the kitchen incident."

"Not yet," he says, turning and raising his eyebrows.

"Shit. You're going there now." I realize. He looks over and smiles. "Does she have a horny sister?" I ask.

"No, but I'd be willing to bet that she'd find the idea of *you* joining in a whole lot more exciting than Winston."

I stop walking. "You asking me to come with you to fuck some horny housewife?"

"Pretty much. She's talked about a threesome more than once. If you're up for an adventure, I guarantee you it'd be an epic story to tell."

I had two girls at the same time once before when I was really drunk, but I've never done anything with another dude involved. "I don't have to suck *your* dick or anything, do I?" I ask, mostly joking.

"Please don't! Trust me; she's got enough energy to take care of both of us."

"And we're sure the old man is really out this time?"

"Had to drive to Toronto for a meeting. He'll be gone all day."

"Lead the way!" I say, after thinking about it for about half a second. "Is there like a theme or something? Are we plumbers?" I joke.

"We'll see when we get there."

Chapter Thirty One

CRAIG

"I DON'T WANT TO jinx anything, but this week isn't turning out too badly."

Terry, who's lying with her head on my shoulder and her hand across my chest, looks up and kisses my chin. After breakfast, since it's a pretty cool and cloudy day, we snuck back to our cabin and had some late morning fun. We've managed to have sex three times already; plus I beat Daniel in the semi-finals of the cornhole tournament. Definitely a good week.

"I agree," Terry says, playing with the hairs on my chest. "Other than the one incident, your parents have not really interacted at all. That's made things a bit more relaxed."

"That's basically my dad's doing. I think he's tried pretty hard to keep his distance."

"Which makes it even stranger that he came over to your mom's table on Sunday."

"I guess he figured mom should have moved on more than she has. I think that little incident just finalised it in his head; it'll never be 'normal' here."

"He's got a point," she says matter-of-factly.

"It's pretty tough on my mom," I respond defensively. "Can't you imagine how she feels about Annette?"

"I know. I'm not saying it's not tough. But hasn't it been, like five years now?"

"Yeah, but at home, it's easier to stay busy and not think about it; but here, it's right in her face."

"I guess. Won't have any issues next year though, with your dad not coming."

"If *we* even come."

Terry rolls away just a bit and looks up at me. "You don't want to come back?"

"I have no idea. I'm sure we will; Sarah would never let that happen. But you never know. I just have a feeling this is the beginning of the end, you know?"

"Maybe you and I can go to Turks and Caicos instead?" she suggests excitedly.

"In the summer?"

"We can go in the winter; if we're not spending the money to come here in the summer."

"What would I do in Turks and Caicos?"

"Be with me?" she says, rolling on top of me.

"Well, that sounds nice. But we can't go on vacation and lie in bed *all* week. You know that sitting on a beach isn't exactly my thing."

"I'm sure they'd have some stupid bean bag game for you to play."

I give her a pretty hard slap on the ass. "You keep disrespecting cornhole!"

"Stupid, stupid game," she whispers again, leaning downing to kiss my bottom lip. I give her another slap, this time on the other cheek. She starts to move her hips, slowly grinding up against me. Four times in four days; this is shaping up to be the best week at the Resort in a long while.

*

Once we finally get up, it's early afternoon. We enjoy a leisurely coffee on our little deck, in a hoodie and pajama pants. Sarah texts over to ask if we'd like to play some Euchre in the main lodge.

"What do you say?" I ask Terry.

"Sure. I'll probably just end up having a nap if we don't do something."

We clean up a bit before walking over to meet Sarah and Chris. They're standing with mom between their two cabins while Bijou is flopped on the ground in front of them. It can't be more than thirty steps from where they are and mom's front door, and the dog looks like she's run a marathon.

"Hi guys," Terry calls over as we approach.

"How's your day going mom?" I ask.

"Fine dear. Although it is quite chilly today," she answers, pulling her cardigan together.

"Well, let's see if we can get a cup of tea and get inside then," Sarah suggests.

Mom tries to coax Bijou back to the cabin with a tug, but the dog doesn't budge, forcing mom to bend down and pick her up.

"That dog is the most spoiled animal I've ever seen," Terry whispers in my ear as my mom carries her to the cabin. When she's at the foot of the stairs, Chantelle comes out the door wearing black pants and a Red Hot Chili Peppers t-shirt.

"It's freezing outside dear; you'll need a jacket," mom says, passing her at the foot of the steps.

"I'm sure I'll be fine," Chantelle dismisses.

"I really think you should at least grab a sweater, Chantelle."

"Enough mom. Stop trying to fucking parent," she snaps.

"That language is really not necessary, dear."

"Yes it is! It helps to make my fucking point more emphatically! People swear mom. Get over it."

"Telle," Sarah says, giving her head a shake back and forth, signaling for her to stop.

"What Sarah?" Chantelle barks. "My fucking language too harsh for you too?"

"Let's just try to get along," Sarah says calmly.

"Fuck that! I'm so sick of 'trying to get along'." She spins towards mom. "Stop trying to parent me. I've been on my own for almost four years. I don't *need* your parenting, and I don't *want* it either." She turns to Sarah. "Stop trying to make everyone 'get along'. If I have something to say, I should fucking be able to say it! All this fake shit is so unhealthy." Then she turns towards Terry, Chris and me. "Sorry if I made anyone feel 'uncomfortable'." She spins and walks towards the parking lot.

"Telle!" Sarah calls.

"Let her go dear," Mom says. "There's no point in trying to talk to her when she gets like this. We learned that when she was thirteen."

After putting Bijou back inside the cabin to rest after all of her physical exertion, mom comes back out with a deck of cards. "Shall we?" she asks, gesturing towards the main lodge.

"Should we text Daniel to see if he wants to take Chantelle's place?" Terry asks.

"We already tried him a couple of times, but he's not answering his phone," Sarah answers. "Maybe you can try, Craig?"

"Sure, but I doubt he'll answer me if he's not answering you."

Our walk over to the lodge is a bit quicker than our normal pace walking around the Resort; the chill in the air gives us a push. There are a couple of circular tables that are perfect for cards in the main lodge. At one table, some guests are playing a board game; Settlers of Catan. They're regulars here, and they spend most days at one of those tables, or one of the ones on the large patio, playing some kind of board game that they ordered online. The other table is empty, so we claim it. There's still no response from Daniel.

"Shall we play something else since there are five of us?" Chris asks.

"I was hoping to get some practice in before tomorrow night's tournament," mom says.

"Why don't we take turns," I suggest. "I'll sit out first; maybe I can grab us a pot of tea."

"That would be great, dear," my mom says.

*

One of the best things about the Resort is that once you get to know Stanley and the rest of the staff, it's kind of like you're just part of one big family. I walk into the dining room to see if anyone is there. Zack, the social director is sitting with a waiter named Rob.

"Gentlemen!" I greet them.

"Hi Craig. What's up?" Rob asks.

"Just going to play some cards."

"Good day for it," Zack says.

"I was hoping to grab a pot of tea."

"For sure," Rob says, moving to get up.

"Don't get up. I know where everything is," I say, putting my hand on his shoulder.

"Cool," Rob says.

I head over to the corner of the dining room, right by the kitchen. As I'm filling the tea pot with water, I can't help but remember a resort I went to a few years ago. Before I met Terry, I was dating a girl I'd met in a college bar. She was a spoiled, rich girl who decided that dating a dirty mechanic guy would be fun. After a couple of months, she paid for us to go on a ski trip to a supposedly all-inclusive resort. Being so used to *this* Resort, I hated the stuffy, informal feel of the place. Everything cost money and took time. I wanted a bottle of water and had to wait at the front desk for a woman to finish a phone conversation, then had to pay $3 for it. Here, it feels like the whole place belongs to the guests. That trip was a sign that our relationship was not destined to last.

I thank Rob and Zack, for nothing really, then I bring the tray back to the family.

"That looks like a good idea," I hear from a couch as I walk by. Looking over, I see Hugo and Beryl Weber.

"It sure is a day for it," I say. "After I drop this off with my mom, I can go and grab you some if you like."

"Oh, don't put yourself out, son."

"No, I insist," I tell them, walking away before they can object. I drop off the tea with my mom. Their game is tied at one; looks like I'll have plenty of time to make another run. Nipping back into the kitchen, I let Zack and Rob know what I'm doing. I grab everything I need and bring the tray to Hugo and Beryl.

"Craig, you really shouldn't have," Beryl says, stopping her knitting.

I've had the chance to sit and talk to the Webers a couple of times over the last few years. For my whole life, they've been 'that old couple from the Resort'. I remember them always talking to us when we were kids; but I never really had an adult conversation with them until about three years ago. Now, I look forward to the chance to sit and listen to their stories.

"It's no bother, Beryl. It's my pleasure."

"You always were a sweet boy, you know," she says, pouring a cup for her and one for Hugo. "When you were a boy, you used to collect worms on rainy days so that they wouldn't drown. Do you remember Hugo?"

"Oh yes. You carried them around in a little, yellow bucket."

"I remember that," I say, sitting on the couch opposite them. "I don't know how many I actually saved though."

"Would you like a cup, my dear?" Beryl asks, offering me the cup that was meant for her.

I stand up again and look over at our table. "I actually have a mug over there. I'll just pop over and grab it, if you don't mind me coming back to join you."

"Of course not, son," Hugo says with genuine kindness.

Hugo and Beryl love to talk. A cool and cloudy day is right up their alley. They come from a generation of people who can tell stories, mainly because they have stories to tell. Who knows what today's twenty-year-olds will be talking about when we're in our mid-seventies. Somehow, I doubt we'll be able to talk like people born around the Second World War.

I pour myself a warm cup of tea with plenty of sugar, and sit back down on the couch.

"Did you both have a good year?" I ask. It's kind of a standard question at the Resort. Some people stay in contact now over social media, but it's still natural to ask about the calendar year that has passed since last summer.

"At my age, all the years I get through are good ones," Hugo jokes, with a wink. He's lived away from Germany for almost sixty years now, but there's still just a hint of an accent. "If we make it to next year,…"

"God willing," Beryl adds with a smile.

"… we'll be great-grandparents, you know."

"Wow! Congratulations."

"Can you believe it?" Beryl says.

"You certainly don't look it," I say. It's just one of those things that people say. They totally look like they could be great-grand parents.

"The grandkids sure do keep us young, you know."

Hugo starts in on a story about his grandson, Jack, now fourteen, who used to want to do nothing but throw a baseball with his grandad. 'My shoulder still hurts to this day', he insists. Beryl continues from there to talk about how their granddaughter is studying law.

"Can you believe it?" she asks. "From a couple of runaways like us, we have so many beautiful children and grandchildren doing all these great things."

Last year, on a cold, rainy day, I sat with Beryl and Hugo all afternoon and heard their life story; it rivals any Oscar winning movie I've ever seen. Hugo was born in Germany in 1941. His early story is one of hardship and struggle. In 1949, Hugo's family found themselves on the wrong side of a divided Germany. In 1957, his dad was accused and taken into custody for spreading propaganda. Hugo never saw him again. He decided to flee the country, so he stowed away on a train. As he tells it, he lay crunched up in a box for two days before he could get out, smelling like death itself.

After his escape, Hugo worked on boats moving goods around Europe. In 1958, Hugo Weber met Beryl White in France. Her family was on holiday and staying with some friends.

"I knew right there that I was destined to marry her," Hugo said.

But the White family did not like the idea of their daughter marrying some German sailor. They took Beryl back to England before she could even say goodbye. The young Hugo was heartbroken. Having no idea where she lived, Hugo believed he had lost the love of his life.

"But the fates had other plans," Hugo explained it.

One blustery night, after leaving Calais on a ship bound for Denmark, Hugo and his boat got caught in a massive storm. The boat was blown off course as the crew desperately tried to avoid being capsized by the brutal wind and waves.

"As that wind was pushing us, I had a moment when I felt that there was a reason for it. I yelled for the crew to stop fighting the storm; to let it carry us to safety. They thought I was crazy."

The storm ended up pushing them to the coast of England, near a town called Lowestoft. The crew managed to steer the boat to safety. After the storm, drawn by an inexplicable force, Hugo walked into town. He stopped in a pub for a drink and some food. When he walked out, he looked across the street.

"There she was, son. *My* Beryl was standing on the other side of the street looking at me, mouth hanging down to the floor in shock. I didn't take my eyes off her; I didn't even blink because I was afraid if I did, she'd disappear. I crossed that street, got to the other side, dropped down on my knee and asked her to marry me," Hugo told me.

"I thought he was absolutely mad," Beryl said. "I told him to get up off his knees and stop being foolish."

"But I wouldn't take no for an answer, you know."

Hugo never went back to his boat. He left everything behind, found work with a fisherman, and spent every free moment trying to convince Beryl to marry him. Her parents once again found out about the German sailor boy and threatened to have him arrested if he came near her again. But Hugo had done enough to convince her that he loved her. She hurriedly packed up some things and left her family behind. She was seventeen years old.

They moved around, found work where they could, and eventually ended up on a boat bound for America. They worked odd jobs and barely managed to afford a roof over their heads. After a couple of years, Hugo somehow managed to join the US army. In 1962, with Beryl pregnant with their first child, Hugo was sent to Vietnam. He survived nearly three years before getting shot in the leg. He got sent home.

"Nine months later, our second daughter was born," Hugo said, with his customary wink. At twenty-five, Hugo got a job with an older German man, making furniture. The following year, the Webers came to the Resort for the first time.

Hugo and Beryl Weber didn't accomplish great deeds in their lives. They didn't find a cure for some awful disease. They didn't publish great novels or write beautiful symphonies. They worked hard and raised good kids who went on to become good adults, who had good kids of their own. Beryl and Hugo Weber might have lived the fullest lives of anyone I've ever met.

Sarah calls over that their game is done. I tell them to play another. Hugo is halfway through a story about how they returned to Europe forty years after leaving. I can play euchre anytime.

Chapter Thirty Two

DAVE

ONCE AGAIN, MY sleep is choppy and unsatisfying. It's an hour before dinner and I feel like shit. The pills from yesterday mellowed me out, but by dinner I wasn't feeling great. This morning's breakfast was even harder. After yesterday's anxiety attack, I decided to do a self-imposed detox for a couple of days. It's not the first time. I've usually been pretty good about identifying when I need a break. Although, I have noticed that it's not getting any easier.

I hate everyone around me. I hate the room I'm in. I hate my dark, sunken eyes. I hate my receding hair.

Wednesday dinner is Beach Barbecue. Despite the sun starting to poke through the clouds, it's still cold out. Zack will probably light a couple of bonfires on the beach. We'll fire up the big barbecue that Stanley bought a few years ago. It'll be a grand old fucking time.

I'm kidding myself if I deny that the only question I have in my mind right now is what substance I'm going to take to make it through this. The self-imposed break will have to wait.

Smoking a joint will mellow me out, but I will *not* feel like working after a couple of hours. I'd have to step out and smoke another one at least once. An event like this needs something that lasts a little longer. Coke will get me pumped up and ready for the shift, but recently I've been having some trouble keeping my shit together with that. Mushrooms are definitely a 'no'. Xanax is what it has to be.

I get up. My back hurts. My head hurts. My gut hurts. My eyes hurt.

I grab a smoke, two pills and a bottle of water; and go out on the tiny balcony off my room. It's small and covered - perfect to sit and have a smoke. I smoke the cigarette in nine drags; the exact same as every other cigarette I've smoked in years. Add that to the list of my fucked up behaviour.

After a quick shower, I go downstairs to the kitchen. Of all the days, I have to be the first one there today. I know that the beach barbeque is a regular event at the Resort, but it really fucks with my head to have to cook in a tent down by the beach. After getting myself settled in the kitchen, I start to grab all the shit we'll need.

Have you ever thought about how much trust is involved in having someone else prepare a meal for you? Twice a day, a hundred people sit down here, to eat a meal prepared by me; and most of them haven't got a clue who I am. I wonder how much arsenic I'd have to add to the salad dressing to kill off the whole resort. Maybe cyanide would be better; within fifteen minutes of eating, everyone would be dead. Nah, I'd rather go classic and use Hemlock; an homage to Socrates. Everyone would be paralysed before they knew what the fuck was happening to them.

You never hear about any good poisonings anymore; not like in the old days of Cleopatra, or in a classic Agatha Christie book. I guess in a way, modern poisonings are just drug overdoses. If you want to off someone now, all you have to do is lace their pot with some Fentanyl.

"Dave?"

Someone is talking to me. I look up and Pascal is standing just inside the door.

"What's up skinny?"

"Not much man. Was there someone else here a second ago?"

"I don't think so," I say, looking around.

"Thought I heard you talking to someone."

I must have been standing here talking to myself. What the fuck was I even thinking about a minute ago? "I'm just getting everything ready to take down to the beach. Probably just thinkin' out loud."

"Yeah," Pascal says, looking doubtful.

"How about you grab the golf cart, load it up, and start making trips down to the beach. Start with the tent, fold-up tables, cloths, and all that shit first," I suggest. I know that Pascal doesn't usually get to drive the golf cart around. He's a bit like a puppy; give him a new ball and he'll be distracted and happy.

"Sure!"

Pascal makes a trip down to the beach while I get everything else ready. It's warmed up a bit as I load the second cart of shit to take down. The clouds have moved on and the wind has died down; might not be so bad to be outside for dinner. Being on display in the tent throughout dinner is not my favourite thing; but at the moment, I don't give too much of a shit about it. I pop a couple of beers into one of the coolers that's going down to the beach in the last load.

I would hardly even call this a dinner. I'll be stationed at the barbecue for about three hours grilling chicken breast and steaks. Pascal and Greg have made a few salads and prepared baked potatoes with my special oil and seasoning mix. This is really the only time I interact with the guests on any level. I'm way happier hiding behind the kitchen doors and not knowing who's eating my food.

Pascal and I load up the last shit and drive the cart down to the beach. Greg, Rob, Courtney, Michelle and that new girl are unloading and setting up.

"Well, hello gang!" I hear myself say. Where the fuck did that come from?

"Hi there," the new girl says. Everyone else looks a bit confused. "I'm Stacey. I didn't get a chance to introduce myself earlier."

"Welcome Stacey. I'm Dave."

"Are you?" I hear Greg say quietly.

Ignoring his comment, I add, "It'll be nice for us all to get out of the kitchen."

The looks on all of their faces are priceless. Nobody knows quite what to say, so Stacey pipes up.

"I agree; it'll be super fun." She looks around at everyone else, just kind of standing around. "Sorry," she adds, looking a bit embarrassed.

"Don't be sorry," Michelle says. "You're right. Let's not forget to have some fun."

Stacey gives a little smile. Courtney turns and walks away.

"Let's put on some tunes and get going then!" Greg exclaims.

"I'm on it," Pascal says, turning to get the speaker set up. "I put together a nice beach mix!"

I fire up the barbecue as that nineties song, *Steal my sunshine* plays. There are a few brave people hanging out by the water, making the most of a bit of sun on a cool day. The kids were probably nagging all day to go swimming and the parents eventually gave in once the sun poked through. Once the smell of steak hits their noses, they'll come over and place their orders with one of the servers. I try to avoid any of the guests actually coming over and talking with me; and most staff knows that.

In the past, beach dinners have driven me absolutely insane; people are all in my space. One week last year, I told Stanley I needed the day off just to avoid it. A couple of other people stepped up and cooked all the meat, and apparently it was a disaster. Another time a few years ago, I just refused to speak to anyone; I didn't say a word the whole time. But today, I'm feeling good. I crack a beer and keep it just to the side of the barbecue.

"One medium rare, one well done, and a couple of breasts, please Dave," Greg calls over from just outside the tent. "And did we bring any hot mustard down?"

"Check in the cooler here," I answer, brushing some barbecue sauce on a rack of chicken breasts. After everything is set up, the rule is usually that nobody is allowed in the tent. I set up tables and shit all around so that it's really hard to get in. There's only one opening and usually nobody dares to pass.

"Uh, alright," Greg says.

Seeing Greg in the tent, Stacey walks in also.

"Dave, could I get three steaks, please? All medium," she asks sweetly.

"Uh, usually, we give Dave our orders from over there," Greg says, pointing to the other side of the tables, with mustard in his hand.

"Oh, I'm sorry," she says to me before turning to leave.

"Don't worry about it, sunshine," I assure her. Out of the corner of my eye, I see Pascal mouthing, 'What the fuck?' to Greg. For some reason, I'm finding this all hilarious.

*

Another couple of pills and a beer help make the dinner more manageable and interesting. I don't talk much, but I listen to everyone else's idle chatter. Every once in a while, I throw in a comment just to see how people react.

Most guests have long finished and have moved on to roasting some marshmallows by the bonfire that Zack has got going, when a girl walks right up to the little entrance of my tented kitchen kingdom. She doesn't stop on the outside, but walks through the little opening so that she's just inside. The rest of the staff is off cleaning up, so nobody is there to stop her. She's dressed in jeans and a black shirt that just barely reveals a pierced belly button. She doesn't look like she belongs on a beach; she looks more like she's about to hop on a motorbike and speed away. Her jet-black hair is pulled back from a chiselled face.

"Am I too late to get a steak? I like it rare, so you wouldn't have to cook it long."

When she speaks, I recognize her as the younger sister of the LaPointe family. I haven't seen her for quite a few years, and man how she's grown up.

"I think I can manage that," I answer. She has to be about eighteen or ninetten; which is way too fucking young for me, but looking her up and down, there's something about her that makes me forget her age.

"Thanks," she says. "You probably hate this shit don't you?"

"Why do you say that?"

"Because you've built a nice little fort here to help keep everyone away from you."

"But you decided to just walk right in?"

"Maybe I like forts too," she answers, leaning against one of the tables.

"Can't say I'm a huge fan of all this. I do prefer my own kitchen."

"Well, you make some nice food in that kitchen of yours. Are you responsible for the poached eggs?"

"Oh yeah," I say proudly.

"You good there Dave?" Michelle calls over, having noticed my visitor.

"Yup," I answer.

"Body guard?" she asks quietly.

"You can't be too careful."

"How do you know *I'm* not here to kill you?"

"Just as long as you don't steal my recipes." I hand her a plate with her steak and a baked potato. "Enjoy."

"I bet a joint and a beer would be pretty good after this. Don't you?" she asks with a devilish smile. She turns and walks away.

"That *does* sound like a good idea," I say after her.

Chapter Thirty Three

CHRIS

"YOU GOING TO feel like going out tonight?" I ask Sarah as we get back to the cabin. We just dropped off Meme at her place; Chantelle did not come back with us. She was talking to some staff members for most of dinner. Despite it being a bit chilly, the beach barbecue was pretty good. Most places would just offer up burgers and hotdogs in a situation like that, but I had a nice steak with probably the best baked potato I've ever had. The salads were great too.

"Yeah, but I'm running out of reasons why I don't want to drink! I think Terry suspects something's up; and Telle flat out asked me if I was pregnant yesterday!"

"Does that mean you lose the bet?" I ask excitedly.

"No! I didn't tell her anything. I had to have a beer to cover."

"I guess it's harder to make excuses here than it would be at home."

"No kidding. Makes it apparent how much people drink on vacation."

"Maybe your family is just a bunch of lushes."

"No. I'm pretty sure it's everyone."

"Next year will definitely be different for us. We won't be drinking much with a baby here, that's for sure."

"Who knows what the heck will be happening with *anyone* next year!" Sarah says. She's always stressing about her family, and this trip has done nothing to help. Her dad has announced he's not coming anymore, Chantelle has added an interesting element to things this year, and Daniel is never really a big part of things. Sarah is left trying to have everyone get along.

"Well whatever happens, it will be kind of exciting to bring little Chris junior here for his first Resort vacation."

"Chris junior? There is no way," she laughs.

"Probably not, but we'll keep it on the table," I add.

"Not a chance," she says, knowing there's no way I'm serious. "But that's a lot of pressure coming up with a good name." She plops down on the couch.

"Babe, don't get stressed about that too. We have tons of time."

"Yeah, but think about it. We have the responsibility of naming a person. That name will follow them around forever; it *defines* them."

I love Sarah a lot, but her neuroses can be very tiring. "We will sit down, research it, and come up with something perfect," I try to soothe her. I sit behind her and rub her shoulders. I can feel the tension ease a bit.

"There is so much to think about! What if we're not ready?"

"We're as ready as we'll every be. We'll muddle through it, do our best and figure it out as we go; just like everyone else does with their first kid."

"But what if we do something wrong?"

"We totally *will*!" I exclaim; probably not the best way to calm her. "Everyone does. But we are intelligent, reasonable people. We'll figure it out without messing the kid up too badly."

"I hope you're right."

"All I know is that I plan on making the most of the rest of my time this year."

On Wednesday nights, a local band comes to play. They aren't really anything special, but the night is usually fun. They play pretty standard stuff, like *Sweet Home Alabama*, and *Brown Eyed Girl*; throwing in one or two new songs every year. Last year, between sets, I struck up a conversation with a couple of the guys. I've played the guitar since I was a kid. I'm no superstar, but I like to play; so they offered to let me join them for a song. I said no then, but told them I'd practice up a bit during the year so that I could play something this year. If I have enough to drink, I might even sing.

"Well, I don't know if I'll make it the whole night, but I'll come for a bit," Sarah says. "Maybe you can wait until later in the evening to get up on stage."

"That's harsh. You like when I play guitar."

"Yeah, but I don't know how I feel about you getting drunk, playing guitar, and singing in front of everyone."

"I doubt I'll even end up playing. They won't remember our conversation from a year ago."

Craig and Terry come by to have a drink before we all go over to the bar. Marion never comes out for this kind of thing; she'll probably sit and chat with one of her ladies. Daniel and Chantelle are nowhere to be found. We hear the music start just as I'm finishing up my drink, so we walk over in the clear, cool evening.

There are seats at a number of tables set up around the little stage in the corner, but when we arrive they're all full. The bar at the Resort is used for lots of different events, like euchre, dancing, and small performances; and it works pretty well with all of them. After grabbing a drink, the four of us find a stand-up table to the side of the room.

The three guys in the band are playing their version of a Coldplay song. It's too loud to talk, so we stand and listen to the music. The room is pretty full; most people come out on Wednesday nights, not because the music is spectacular, but because it's what people do. There's a certain comfort in the routine of something like this. I've only been coming here for five years and I already feel the connection to the place, the people, and the events. By Wednesday, guests have had the chance to settle in and relax. It's great to be able to spend time with family, sitting around relaxing; but there's only so much of that you can do. It seems only a couple of staff are here.

The Watson family is seated smack in the middle, and right up front. I think Mrs. Watson arrives right when Blaine opens the doors so that she can snag a prime spot for the whole family. I've had the chance to talk to Walter Watson a couple of times; he's a nice enough man, but he's so successful that it's hard for me to relate to him. His wife Selina has always seemed a bit cold, but their daughters, Emma and Michelle are nice enough. The Watsons always seem to have other people staying with them, whether it's extended family, friends, or business people. Right now, they're sitting with a young couple who look like they belong more in a five start resort on a pristine beach somewhere.

At the bar, Daniel is chatting with Blaine about something that looks intense. It doesn't look like Blaine is actually working though; Zack is making drinks behind the bar. When someone approaches to get a drink, they both stop talking, only to huddle up again when the person goes. The two of them are far more like brothers than Daniel and Craig are.

The two drunk guys from the cornhole tournament are here with their wives. They must have gotten a babysitter to look after their little ones. I wonder how long it will take me to get to the point where I feel like I can trust pretty much a stranger to take care of my kid while I go out and get drunk. I'm not sure if I ever will. The wives of Darryl and Charlie are basically the female versions of their husbands. They are loud and drinking heavily.

I'm always fascinated to meet spouses. When I met Darryl and Charlie yesterday, their wives were standing on the beach watching the kids. The men spent most of their time hitting on the Watson girls. For some reason, I assumed their wives would be timid women, doting over the children while their husbands were off chasing skirts. But it appears these two ladies have plenty of fire of their own. I imagine these couples as having the types of relationships that are either just crazy enough to work, or will end up exploding and ending with young parents who despise each other and won't talk.

The band finishes a pumped up version of *Losing my Religion* and takes a break. There's a flurry of activity as people get up to grab a new drink, go to the washroom, or just stretch their legs and chat with people. Markus, who plays the bass and sings a few songs, passes us on the way to the bar.

"Hi guys," he says, recognizing Sarah and Craig. "How is everyone?" He gives Sarah a hug and shakes Craig's hand. He looks in my direction and nods a hello. After turning away, he looks back at me and holds out his hand.

"Hi Chris, are you going to join us for that song this year?"

I'm shocked that he remembered our conversation from last year. I shake his hand, a bit thrown off. These guys play at the Resort on every Wednesday of the summer, along with any other gigs they have on the go. They have seen a different group of people each week, all summer, for probably ten years. I guess that's why they continue to draw a crowd, the feeling that we are part of the whole thing instead of just an audience.

"If you guys don't mind having me, I'll give it a go," I answer.

"Nice! Let me grab a few beers and we'll make a plan."

"Think I'll grab a drink too," I say, after Markus has left.

"Well I don't think I'm going to make it to your big moment, babe. I'm exhausted," Sarah says.

"That's OK, I'll record it," Terry says, holding out her phone with a smile.

"Oh great," I say.

After grabbing a glass of whiskey and a beer to help calm the nerves a little, I talk to the guys in the band. Markus suggests that I join them to play the first song of the next set, so I walk with Sarah back to the cabin and grab my guitar. It's probably good that I don't have too much time to think it over and get nervous; even though I have been practicing this song at home for a couple of months.

Before I know it, I'm sitting on a little stool, on the tiny stage with what feels like the whole Resort looking at me. I'm nervous, but not too bad; I have just enough of a buzz to calm myself. Vince, the lead singer and guitarist gives me a nice introduction. I take a deep breath and start to play.

Before you accuse me, take a look at yourself, …

Chapter Thirty Four

STANLEY

EVERYONE GIVES A big cheer when Chris finishes his song with the band. He looks so proud of his performance. Markus, Vince, and Trevor have always been so good at interacting with the guests on the nights they play; over the years, they've let countless aspiring musicians join them for a song or two. In thirteen years of playing here, they've never once asked for an increase in the small amount that we pay them, along with free drinks for the night.

A few years back, Trevor was diagnosed with lung cancer. The doctors caught it fairly early and he got through it; but he lost a ton of weight and most of his hair. For all three guys, it was a bit of a wakeup call. They were always a pretty fun-loving bunch; but now they really seem grateful for the days they have. All three guys have worked hard their whole lives; Markus farming, Vince as a brick layer, and Trevor in construction. They all have a passion for playing music, and genuinely love hanging out together. I bet they'd come and play for just the free drinks.

Chris takes his seat, high-fiving several people on the way.

The fellas start in on another tune. I've got one last thing to take care of before turning in.

"Blaine," I call, walking up to the bar. "How are things tonight?"

"Going well, Stanley. It's nice to sit on the other side of the bar for an evening and have Zack getting me my drinks," Blaine answers, looking to Zack behind the bar and raising his glass. "How about you?"

"Very nice. I was hoping you could do me a favour."

"Shoot."

"I'd like you to do the inventory and get the week's order ready tomorrow morning instead of Friday, if that's alright."

"OK, but is there a reason? You know I'm driving the boat tomorrow for skiing and tubing."

"I do, but that's not until early afternoon. I wanted to get our drink order in a day early just to make sure we are set for Friday's dinner. Last week, we ran out of a couple of things. And with the big 75th anniversary dinner, people have been tending to have an extra glass or two."

"Yeah, but last week, the entire Kowalewicz family was here with their friends. They drank more in the one week than most frat houses drink in a semester."

"I know, but I'd rather be over-stocked this week than be short."

"Sure," Blaine answers. He can be a cocky, pain in the behind sometimes; but he does step up and do a good job when he has to.

"Thanks, Blaine. I'd like to call in the order before noon. Then we can get a delivery on Friday morning."

"Stanley, you're killing me. That's going to cut into my beauty sleep."

"Well, you could always go to bed earlier," I answer, and turn away.

*

On the walk back to the house, I'm greeted by a deer standing just under a tree. Her eyes are glowing from the reflection of the little light on our porch. As I usually do when I cross paths with one of the many animals that live in and around the Resort, I take a moment to stop what I'm doing - to just stand still. Every deer, fox and eagle that visits is a reminder of the connection we have to the land where grandad built this Resort. I once had a guest ask me whether I'd ever shot a deer around here. I'm not one of those anti-hunting nuts, but I can honestly say that being around this place for as many years as I have, I've never once thought about getting a gun and killing anything I've seen here.

One year, I saw a moose just up the road. Melissa and I were going for a walk one morning and she spotted him on the edge of the forest - big antlers sticking up and steam rising from his shout. We froze and watched him for a few minutes before he turned and disappeared into the trees, both of us feeling more alive for having seen him. I would never want those antlers hanging above my mantle.

The deer and I stand and look at one another for a moment. Sensing I mean her no harm, she relaxes her posture, wiggles her ears, and walks off to find some food. With a deep breath of clean air, I go in the house and turn off the porch light.

Melissa has already turned in by the time I get in. When I grab a beer from the fridge, I see a note telling me to check e-mail; one of my least favourite things to do. Over the last ten years, ownership of the Resort has involved more and more computer things; and I'm lucky Melissa is good at it. I'm definitely the blind dog trying to learn new tricks.

Once I fumble my way to where I'm supposed to be, I see

a message from the real estate agent of the man who made the offer last year. She's contacted us a couple of times on his behalf.

> *Stanley,*
>
> *Omar asked me to get in touch with you again to see if you have had a chance to think over his last offer. He says he's willing to add on another hundred thousand, and that he's looking forward to hearing from you. Once you've had a chance to think it over, please get in touch.*
>
> *Eileen Vanderwick*

I close the email and walk out to the balcony. Sitting in my recliner, I shut my eyes and listen to the night; but all I hear is the music coming from the bar.

Omar is a man who is used to getting what he wants; I could tell that the minute I met him. For him, throwing another hundred thousand onto the price means nothing. What he doesn't understand is that the offer of another hundred thousand just makes me want to sell to him even less. But I can't deny that the kind of money he's offering would change our lives unbelievably. I've found myself thinking about what I would do with that much money.

Completely ignoring what my wife would want, I could see myself buying a place on a lake up near here; somewhere more quiet and secluded. I'd spend most of the year fixing it up, maybe do some fishing. I could find some work doing odd jobs to keep busy. Melissa would probably want to move somewhere closer to civilisation. In the winters, we could get a little place somewhere to the south, or maybe out west. I'm pretty sure she'd be alright with that part.

As nice as those thoughts are, I can't shake the feeling that it's just *wrong* for me to sell this place. I know life would go on if I did; Johnny Bigshot would come in and make the place all commercial, and people would continue to come. Maybe not the same people that come now, but people will come. They will have no knowledge of the history of the place, nor will they respect it. I just don't want *those* people to be the ones swimming in my lake, eating in my dining room, or walking on my lawn.

A particularly loud conversation from outside the bar area pulls me from my thoughts. The trees keep out most of the sound, but sometimes, when the partying at the bar gets loud, it makes its way to our balcony. Right now, it kind of makes me wonder whether I'm just kidding myself, and that the guests here now don't give a hoot about the place anyway. Maybe my mind just makes me believe that my owning this place actually matters to people. If I were to drop dead tomorrow, I'm sure they'd hold a nice ceremony; but next summer, they'd all be back.

All this thinking has made me depressed. I finish my beer, go inside the house, shut off the computer without responding to Eileen, turn off the lights and toddle off to bed. Tomorrow's another day.

Chapter Thirty Five

PASCAL

"WAKE UP, YOU lazy ass!"

I open my eyes to see full daylight streaming through the door. Greg and Rob are just coming in. It takes a few seconds after sitting up for me to realize that it's my day off and I slept right through breakfast.

"How was breakfast?" I ask, laying back down and stretching.

"Busy!" Greg says, walking by my bed and smacking me with a pillow.

"Hey! It's my day off. Don't be bitching at me. I deserve this!"

"Why? Because you've been so busy trying to get into Maria's pants?"

"Shut up!" I say, getting irritated.

"What's the problem lover boy? Don't want us talking about your *girlfriend* like that?" Rob pitches in.

"Are we tarnishing her honour?" Greg adds.

I realize I'm overreacting, and that any kind of real relationship with Maria is just not realistic; but I don't like to hear shit like that. "No. Just don't want you clowns screwing it up. I like hanging out with her, that's all."

"I'll bet. Don't think I didn't see you sucking her face last night," Greg says with a laugh.

I can't help smiling, despite feeling annoyed. "Shut up," I say half-heartedly before rolling over. I did spend most of the night with Maria. We sat and watched the band play with a couple of other staff. We sang along to some songs and at one point, she put her hand on my thigh. At the end of the night, before she had to leave, we sat by the fire for a while and when everyone else had turned in, we did do a bit of making out.

After a couple of minutes of lounging around in bed, I get up, grab a granola bar and an apple, and go sit outside. Some of the staff are sitting around the unlit fire pit.

"Anyone feel like going down to the lake?" I ask.

"Not me," Greg says. "I'm bagged."

"I gotta do the fucking inventory today," Blaine complains. "What time is it anyway?"

"Like, 11:00."

"Shit! I gotta go."

"I'll go to the beach!" says Stacey.

I'm a bit surprised by her saying yes; it's not too often that girls are volunteering to hang out with me.

"Alright," I say a bit nervously. "I'm just going to run in and get changed."

"Cool. I'll meet you back here in a minute," she says, as bubbly as always.

After going to the can and getting changed, I zip back outside. Stacey isn't back yet, so I sit down with Greg, Rob and Christine.

"Careful there lover boy," Greg starts, "might make Maria jealous."

"You're turning into a regular Casanova," Rob adds.

"I'm hurt Pascal," Christine says in a fake voice. "When am I going to get *my* shot?"

"You all suck."

"We're just joking," Christine says. "Personally, I think you and Maria are very cute." I can feel my face turning red, mainly from sheer embarrassment, but also with a bit of anger that Greg got all this started. We mostly get along, but he does sometimes treat me like a little brother. Christine continues; "These two are just jealous."

"Yeah hot stuff. We're totally jealous." Greg says. I actually think he regrets saying he didn't want to come to the beach. Had he known Stacey was going to say yes, he probably would have jumped at the chance to hang out with her. He's mentioned her a couple of times since she arrived yesterday.

Stacey comes out of the girl's cabin and starts walking towards us. To avoid any more embarrassment, I decide to walk over and meet her halfway.

"Ready?" I ask.

"Yup! I brought a Frisbee," she says, holding up a pretty nice disc; not a piece of crap, little one.

"Nice," I say, impressed. I bet she knows how to chuck it pretty well too. "Did you decide to stay at the Resort?"

"Not yet. I just decided to stay here for the whole day today. I'm keeping my stuff in the girl's cabin. Yesterday, my parents picked me up after breakfast and then brought me back at dinner. I kind of wanted to see what happens here during the day."

"Well, you picked a pretty good day to stay. There'll be lots of water skiing and tubing going on today."

"Don't people do that all the time?"

"Yeah, but today's the day both Resort boats take people out. They teach people how to ski, and take all the kids tubing. It costs like, ten bucks or something."

"That's cute. I bet the kids love it."

"And apparently, some of the guests are planning on trying to get as many people up behind one boat as possible. I guess last year, they got six."

"Super fun!" she says with genuine enthusiasm.

When we get to the beach, there are quite a few people there. After a cool day, and with only a couple of days left in the week, families want to make the most of nice weather. We grab a couple of chairs and set down our towels just as a little kid walks out of the water bawling his eyes out. It looks like he fell over while wading in the shallow water, and he's not too impressed with getting soaked.

"That was me as a kid. I used to hate putting my face under water," I tell Stacey.

"Really? I learned how to swim super early. I don't remember caring about dunking my head."

"Did you grow up around here?" I ask, to make conversation.

"Yup! My family owns a farm not far from here."

"Did you ever come here as a kid?"

"No way! I have six siblings. My parents would never have been able to bring us all here."

"Wow, six siblings? That's crazy."

"Never a dull moment; that's for sure. How about you?"

"Only child," I say.

"See, that seems weird to me. I can't imagine not having kids running around all over the place."

"I didn't mind it. I kind of like peace and quiet. Besides, my neighbourhood had quite a few kids. I had people to play with, but I could always go home if I ever wanted some space."

"I guess," she says. "How about some Frisbee?" she asks.

"For sure," I answer. She slips off her sandals and takes off her shirt, revealing a pink bikini top and a seriously toned body; most likely from living on a farm all her life. I catch myself checking her out as she unbuttons her shorts. I look away quickly, feeling like I'm doing something wrong. As I take off my own shirt, I suddenly feel majorly self-conscious about my skinny, white arms. This girl is hot, tanned, and could probably kick my ass!

"Ready?" she asks. I nod, trying hard to keep my eyes from wandering anywhere other than her eyes.

We wade into the water up to our knees; it's cold. If I go any farther, my balls will end up crawling up inside me for warmth. Her first throw is perfect; straight and right to me. Is it weird that I find a nice, clean Frisbee throw to be hot?

We chuck it back and forth for a few minutes. One of my tosses goes a bit off and she chases it down like a pro, high stepping through the shallow water and diving to catch it. The water is still cold, but it doesn't take too long to get used to it; the air is warm enough, and there isn't much wind.

"How about swimming to the dock?" she suggests.

"Ok, as long as you don't laugh at my swimming, or try to save me because I look like I'm drowning."

"But what if you are drowning? How will I know?"

"I guess if I go under for longer than five seconds and don't come back up."

She laughs and gives me a gently push on the arm. "You're funny. I bet you're a good swimmer."

What the heck is going on? I'm hanging out with a hot girl who just told me I'm funny. "We'll see," I say, walking slowly deeper. It's only about one hundred yards out to the dock. I do my best breast stroke, mainly because I look the most normal doing it. It does mean that I'm as slow as a snail though. Stacey politely matches my slow pace.

"See! You're a good swimmer."

"Thanks," I reply, "just as long as I don't have to get anywhere quickly."

"So you don't want to race?" she jokes.

"Not even a little bit."

We pull ourselves out of the water and sit on the dock, facing out to the lake. We both lean back on our arms, sit in silence, and let the sun dry us off.

After a minute, Stacey asks, "So what's up with this place?"

"How do you mean?"

"Well, there seems to be some weird vibe going on. It doesn't really seem like people get along all that well."

"This is only my third week here, but this one has been the strangest so far."

She looks at me for a couple of seconds without saying anything, then raises her eyebrows. "Are you going to tell me about it?"

"You want to hear the whole story?"

"Unless you have something better to do."

I'm glad she can't see the thoughts that rush through my mind at that moment; because for a split second, I think of lots of *way* better things I'd like to do, sitting on the dock with her; none of which are appropriate to tell her.

I tell her everything I can think of that has happened this week, starting with the tension between the waitresses, moving to Dave and his strange behaviour, and ending with the whole Ariel incident. I don't know if I should be telling her all this, but she's very easy to talk to, and she seems pretty cool.

"What about Christine?" she asks. "I met her with Courtney and she seemed different from what she was like today."

"Yeah. When Ariel was here, the three of them were kind of bitchy to everyone. They had the Mean Girls thing going on. But when Courtney's not around, Christine can be pretty cool.

But you're talking to the wrong person about girl drama. I don't understand any of it."

"I don't really either," she admits. "I don't see why people can't just say what they mean."

"Yeah," I say. It's weird but there's something about her that makes me feel very comfortable. I'm always nervous and jumpy around girls; it's just how I've always been. But after being with her for less than an hour, I feel very relaxed, just sitting and talking. There's no way in hell she has any interest in me, but I think she's looking for a friend here and nobody else has really tried to be nice to her.

We sit in silence again for a bit. There are more people at the beach now. We look over and see a few guests setting up some sticks in the shallow water.

"We should go and play sticks and cups!" Stacey says with excitement.

"What?"

"Sticks and cups! You try and knock the cups off the poles with the disc. It's super fun."

"How do you know that?"

"I told you I had six siblings right? I've played lots of games. It's a drinking game."

"Ok. But you've seen my throws; I can't promise I'll be good."

"That's Ok. I'm great at it!" She gives a big smile and dives into the water. Since I'm not much of a diver, I jump in and follow her to the shore.

Chapter Thirty Six

SARAH

"I'M NOT SURE this is a great idea."

"It's fine Sarah. We had six last year, no problem. We're going to get Telly up with us and we'll set a new Resort record."

Craig and Daniel had the plan last year to see how many people they could get up on skis behind dad's boat. They got all six people who wanted to be involved up on their skis; even Chris managed to stay up for about thirty seconds. The others were Terry and Craig, Michelle Watson and her husband Brad, and Emma Watson. This year, as is usually the case with the boys, they want to try to one-up themselves and go for seven.

Thursdays have always been water sports days at the Resort. Kids who have never had the chance to try waterskiing can learn, or the little ones can go for a ride in the tube. Both Resort boats are used, but for years we've taken people in ours too; usually the more experienced skiers.

"We'll have you in the boat as spotter," Craig explains. "Then Daniel will drive, and the seven of us will be in the water."

"That's a lot of people, and a lot can go wrong," I add. Sometimes, they are just too reckless.

"You'll make sure nothing goes wrong," Craig says with a grin.

The actual organization of something like this is a nightmare; too many people are involved and getting everyone in the same place, at the same time is almost impossible. Chris and Terry are playing a Frisbee game on the beach, Daniel is apparently off getting the boat ready, the Watsons are out on stand-up paddleboards, and I have no idea where Chantelle is. Craig can do all the legwork of organizing; I'll just wait. I decide to give it an hour and if it doesn't happen by then, I'll find a nice, quiet place to read my book; or maybe have a nap.

The beach at the Resort is by no means a luxurious, five-star beach; but it's perfect for what it is. There's a little arched, sandy area where people can sit in chairs while their kids wade in the shallow water or build sand castles. The dock was built to shelter the beach area, so it's usually calm. There's a little stretch off to the side of that main beach where the water is shallow for a fair distance. Along the shore, it's rockier, but the shallow water is great for games like beach volleyball. Right now, someone has set up the sticks for that drinking game with a Frisbee and some cups. Chris and Terry are playing against a couple of the staff; a skinny guy from the kitchen and that new waitress.

I like Terry; she's great for my brother, but I swear there's some spark between her and Chris. I know Chris said that he was going to live it up for the rest of the trip this year; but I'm not happy about him laughing, drinking, and high fiving with Terry. Craig doesn't seem concerned; he's managed to get the Watsons back to shore and is now texting someone, presumably Daniel or Telle.

I've only really known that I'm pregnant for a couple of days, although I suspected a bit before that; but I already feel tired and moody. I've completely cut out alcohol and caffeine over the last few days, and that's not helping either. It's not like I drink a ton, but I'm so used to certain things at the Resort, and drinking is a major one. I just have to make it through a couple more days of making excuses not to drink; tonight shouldn't be hard. I can use the excuse of wanting to stay sharp for the euchre tournament. Tomorrow night will be harder; the big final dinner, followed by karaoke, is always a big event. I could use the excuse that I'm taking anti-biotics, but then I'd have to explain some fake illness and where I got the anti-biotics. I think I'll have to resort to going up to the bar and getting a non-alcoholic drink that looks like it could be alcohol. That should work.

"You ready to go Sarah?" Craig calls over, snapping me out of my thoughts.

"Everyone here?" I ask.

"Just waiting on Telly. Apparently she's on her way."

"Have you talked to her since yesterday?"

"Just to text her about our big plans!" Craig responds. "I think she's fine. You know how she is; she has blow-ups like yesterday, but then she gets over it fast and it's like nothing happened."

"Yeah, but I'm worried about her. She walked out on Dimitri and her apartment before coming here; and she literally has no place to live."

"Really? That guy was a creep anyway though. It's for the best."

"Didn't you hear me? She moved out of her apartment and has nowhere to go!"

"Sarah, Chantelle has been on her own for years. She'll find somewhere to stay, with a friend or something, then she'll get a place of her own. She's very resourceful."

"That's what she said too," I say. Why am I so concerned if nobody else is?

"Here she comes now," Craig says, looking up towards the main lodge.

I turn around to see Telle walking down with Stanley.

"Don't tell her I told you about her moving out of her place," I tell Craig.

"For sure," he responds. "Be ready in five minutes!"

It looks like this is actually going to happen; so much for my quiet reading and a nap.

*

It still takes another half an hour to get everyone organized. Getting all the lines sorted out is actually a pretty big job. Daniel and I manage to get them all set out and a skier on the end of each one. A deep water start is really the only way to do this. He takes his seat behind the wheel and I look out back. All seven skiers give the thumbs up and we're ready to go. Daniel starts slowly to tighten the ropes, then gives it gas. He takes it a bit easy at first, not completely sure how much to accelerate, then gives it a bit too much gas. Before anyone has a chance to get up, a couple of people have the ropes ripped out of their hands. We circle around and spend another five minutes sorting everything out, ready to try again. This is going to take a while!

The next few attempts are more promising. Chris is by far the weakest skier of the bunch, so he takes a couple of spills. Our next attempt starts out great; Chris is able to hold on and stay up, but one of the Watson sisters loses control and falls before really getting up. The Resort boats are getting ready to take out anyone who wants to give it a go, and Stanley asked that we finish up before they start. Since we have their ropes, I guess we have to be back before they go out. He gives us the signal that we have one more chance for now.

We get everyone lined up and ready to go. After some

practice, Daniel has figured out how fast to accelerate; he gets all the lines tight, then he accelerates smoothly. There are a few wobbles, mainly from Chris, but all seven skiers are able to get up and stay up. There's a loud cheer from the shore as most of the Resort is watching us. We head out a little ways and make a slow turn to pass by the beach and give everyone a chance to cheer again. We're almost all the way around when Chris loses his concentration and veers to the side. He's third from the edge, so he ends up taking out Michelle and Brad, who were on his right. For a couple of seconds, it's a mess of skis and a splash, but everyone comes up fine. Daniel steers around and the other four skiers let go and coast towards the little dock in the water. We pick up Chris, Michelle and Brad and head back to the dock to collect the skis.

Craig and Daniel are a bit disappointed at not being able to make a more dramatic pass by the beach, but other than that, everyone is pleased with the performance. I can tell that Chris is a bit upset at being the one to screw it up, but everyone else has waterskied for most of their lives, and everyone reassures him it's all good.

Once we arrive back at the boathouse, I realize that Maman was out on the beach watching us. After docking the boat, we walk to the beach as people congratulate us all around. We make our way over to where Maman is sitting.

It's not often that we all just sit around on the beach anymore. When we were younger, Daniel, Craig and I would spend hours playing and swimming while our parents sat, drank and talked; sometimes to other parents, but just as often with each other. Chris and I sit next to Maman, then Craig and Terry sit too. Chantelle pulls up a chair, and Daniel's arrival makes me wonder when the last time was that we all just sat together. I can't even think of when that would have been, and yet it just kind of happens here without any planning or orchestrating. I can't help feel a bit sad that dad isn't here, but I also know that's a silly little girl idea. If he were here, it wouldn't be a nice moment of sitting together.

"What did you think mom?" Daniel askes as he sits down.

"Very impressive dear," Maman answers, without too much sense of being impressed.

"Even Chris managed to stay up for a few seconds," Terry jokes. Instant irritation flares up.

"I think he did great," I say, too harshly. I know I'm being unreasonable as I say it. "Considering he's never really skied before coming here."

Chris gives me the type of look that spouses recognize; that 'what the hell was that?' look. Terry looks away.

"I'm impressed with Chantelle," Chris says, deflecting the attention. He then turns to her. "You must not have done too much skiing recently; it's been a while since you've been here right?"

"It's like riding a bike," she shrugs.

"I think we had Telly out on skis when she was four," Craig says.

"She was a natural; determined as hell," Daniel adds.

"You've always been determined with everything," Maman says to her. "Determined and independent."

"Sometimes you have to be," Chantelle says in a far off kind of voice.

Nobody talks for a while. I wonder what Maman really feels about Chantelle. Obviously she loves her, but we all know she was an 'oops' baby; especially Chantelle. There are only six and a half years between Telle and Craig, but I'm pretty sure that Maman and dad never planned to start over with a new baby at thirty-five and forty years old. It wasn't long after her birth that they started to have problems, fighting more and more and talking less and less. By the time Chantelle was seven or eight, dad was sleeping in his own room. On top of everything, Chantelle was not an easy child. She got in fights at school, ran away from home at eleven, and left for good at sixteen.

"Well I'm glad you decided to come up, Telly," Craig says, getting up to give her a hug.

"Me too," Daniel adds, getting up to join the group hug from the other side.

"Get off me!" Chantelle says with a laugh, pushing the boys away.

For the next half an hour, we sit like a normal family and chat about nothing in particular. Maman tells us all about the gossip she's heard from the other ladies that sit around the lodge. Terry talks about the prospects of finding a teaching job. Daniel tells us all a story about a trip to Vegas he took with a client.

"What's up with you?" Daniel asks Telle.

"Not much," she responds automatically.

"Don't give me that bullshit," he says. Maman gives him a disapproving look. "What's going on? What made you decide to grace us with your presence?"

I look over at Telle. For all her talk about wanting to be honest and open as a family, I know she hates to talk about herself. I'm certain she isn't going to open up about what happened with Dimitri; certainly not to Daniel.

"Just needed a change," she answers vaguely.

"How are things in Toronto?" Craig asks.

"Always interesting," she answers, turning to look at me, raising her eyebrows a little. She looks back at the boys. "I love all the shit going on all the time."

"You working?" Terry asks.

"Funny you should ask that," Telle says. She pauses and

looks around at everyone. “I’m actually going to stay here for a while and work in the kitchen.”

“What?” I shriek. If I were in a movie, I would have spat out whatever I was drinking in shock.

“How did that happen?” Maman asks, clearly as shocked as I am.

“Well, I was talking to Dave, the cook, yesterday. He mentioned that they were busy this year. I half-jokingly said that I should apply, and we decided it wasn’t such a bad idea.”

“Are you *staying* here? On the Resort?” I ask.

“Yup,” is all she says.

“And Stanley’s cool with this?” Craig asks.

“Just ran it by him before we came down here.”

There are so many questions that I want to ask her. I know there’s something more to the story than that. But I’ll have to wait to be able to talk to her when we’re alone.

“So what’s the plan for euchre this evening?” Daniel asks.

Chapter Thirty Seven

MICHELLE

"I DIDN'T SEE YOU today at the beach," Stacey says as we're setting up for dinner.

"I don't usually hang around much during the day," I answer. Despite her annoying habit of talking constantly, Stacey isn't that bad. She hasn't fallen into the space vacated by Ariel; following Courtney around and laughing at everything she says.

"You live near here?" she continues.

"Yeah, not too far."

"You have kids?"

"I do," I answer, thinking of Scarlett. "My daughter's eight."

"Do you ever bring her here? I bet she'd love the tubing and skiing."

"No," I answer, not really knowing myself why I've never brought her here.

"Well those kids had a blast today. I went out on the boat to help out for a couple of trips. And just before that, some of the guests had seven skiers up for a minute or so. That was pretty cool."

"I'm glad you're enjoying yourself," I say. "If I could make a suggestion, stay away from Blaine." I've already seen Blaine looking at Stacey like she's a piece of meat. I swear I can see drool sometimes when he's eyeing his prey.

"Thanks, but I kind of figured that out myself about two minutes after I met him. Not really my type anyway," she says.

"Good to hear someone else has some sense," I say.

We continue to set up with her talking almost constantly. As much as I'm starting to like her, it won't be enough to counter her blabbing; too much of that will make me snap. I make a mental note to arrive with my music already on tomorrow at breakfast.

I make a trip to the kitchen to get some more dishes, and also to give my ears a break. Greg is standing at his stations, working away in silence. Pascal isn't around, so I assume it's his day off. Dave never says much as he does his shit off to the side, so the kitchen is pretty quiet when I walk in; the only sounds are knives chopping and food frying.

"Boys," I say. "Pretty quiet in here today. How's everyone doing?"

Greg looks up briefly, then looks back at his work. "Fine."

"Don't jinx the quiet, Michelle," Dave says. He has a light tone to his voice. "It's been peaceful and productive in here."

"Alright," I say. "But are you sure everything is alright there Greg?"

"Why would you ask that?" Dave complains. "Now he'll tell you about his little lover's spat with Pascal."

"It creates an unhealthy work place Dave." I'm never sure with Dave whether he's on the verge of getting mad, or whether he's half joking. I have a sense that I'm not pushing too far today; that he's in a pretty good state of mind. "I bet this is about a girl!"

"It's nothing," Greg says. "Just tired. Been a long week."

"Alright! Keep it all inside so it festers and bubbles away," I say as I turn to leave. I put my music on and walk to my tables, not making eye contact with Stacey, or anyone else.

*

As irritating as it can be to work here, there's an energy that makes it interesting. There's always something going on with the staff. The type of person that wants to work here is usually the type of person who also enjoys having fun. A bunch of fun-loving twenty year olds living together for the summer, working together, playing in the sun during the day, and staying up late at night is bound to result in all types of hookups. On top of that, each staff member has their own issues and their own agendas.

Then there's the guests. After seven years, I've caught a week-long glimpse into the lives of the people who come here. I've heard of marriages falling apart, kids growing up, and people passing on. When you've been working as a waitress for a few years in the same place, you get to know regulars and develop some relationships with them. But here, because you see people every day, at least twice a day, for a full week, you get a chance to learn a lot more about their lives. Then you don't see them again for fifty-one weeks.

As fucked up as it may sound, I kind of realize that this place is as much a home, with as much of a family, as I've got. I can't explain it, but I'm suddenly hit with a feeling of sadness; so much so that I have to stop what I'm doing and step out of the dining room.

I come to work here six days a week for the whole summer. I've known Stanley, Melissa, Dave and many of the guests for seven years. But I've never brought Scarlett here for longer than an hour or so. Then it hits me; I've never really accepted that this is what I am – a waitress at a family resort in the middle of nowhere.

I was twenty-one when I met Phil. After an extra year of high school, I needed time to do something other than school, so I found a job waiting on tables, another job as a nanny, and a third job on Sunday nights cleaning a bank. In six months, I saved up enough money to go on an adventure. I went out with a few girlfriends a few nights before I was supposed to start some travelling, as a kind of bon voyage celebration. As luck would have it, that night I met a smooth talking, gorgeous, bad-ass type named Phil. I decided to push my travel plans back a month to see where things were headed. It turns out they were headed full speed towards a hot and heavy, passionate year of sex, partying and fights.

What I wouldn't give to be able to go back and smack that stupid little, naive bitch right across the face and tell her to leave when we had planned. I've had this thought come into my mind a thousand times over the last few years, and each time, the next thought is of Scarlett. I can't imagine life without her now, and I'm filled with such guilt for being selfish that I hate myself more. At some point, the cycle has to stop. I have to accept where I am and make the best of everything … for her.

After a year, I knew that I had to get out of my relationship with Phil. I remember sitting on the floor of the bathroom in our tiny apartment. The white tiles were cold. The stuff between those tiles, once white I'm sure, was grey and dirty. We had just had a blow-up about him coming home late. He was drunk and yelling at me from the living room. I stared at the floor and listened to his drunken rant; and I decided for certain that I was going to leave. I'd thought about it before, but I remember clearly that instant where I really *knew* it.

In the morning, Phil apologized desperately. He seemed so sincere, as he always did. I still knew that I was destined to leave, but for the second time in a couple of years, I made the decision of a little girl; I put the leaving on hold. We had makeup sex and continued on with life. Three weeks later, I was pregnant. We gave it a go for the first couple of years of Scarlett's life, but it never had a chance. Scarlett and I left Phil on New Year's Day, when she was two and a half.

"You OK Michelle?" It's Stanley, standing just outside the dining room doors.

"Yeah," I answer quickly, wiping my eyes.

Stanley looks at me for a second, closes the dining room door and sits next to me on the little bench. I can tell he's so concerned. For some reason, I find that really funny and I laugh; which only confuses poor Stanley even more.

"What's going on?" he asks.

I know how concerned he is and how much he wants to help. But I also know how much he hates all this shit; having to talk to people about their problems. I guess the funny part is that I don't realize how lucky I am to have someone like Stanley or Melissa to care that much about me.

"It's all good Stanley. I'm just having a moment."

"Ok. Let me know if there's anything I can do."

"Just be you," I say, getting up and going back to work.

Chapter Thirty Eight

CRAIG

AFTER A GREAT day on the beach, Terry and I go back to our cabin to get ready for dinner. After our moderately successful waterskiing adventure, it was really nice to sit with everyone and chat, other than not having dad around. It's the first time we've all been together in a while. Mom made arrangements to have dinner with some of the other ladies, so we are going to eat with dad. I haven't seen too much of him this week; I think he's already kind of checked out and moved on.

Terry is still getting ready, so I grab a beer and sit outside while I wait. For me, getting ready involves having a five minute shower, brushing my teeth, and slapping on some deodorant. There are times when Terry will slip on some jeans, put her hair up, and be ready to go out. There are other times when she takes forever getting herself ready. I have a feeling this will be a long one.

Despite doing a pretty good job of relaxing so far, I have an antsy feeling. I don't really like sitting around. I never have.

Going on vacation for me is spending two days trying to settle down and relax, followed by a day or two of actually taking it easy, then a few more days of being bored of doing nothing. I know it's annoying as hell to anyone who is with me, but I'm just not good at doing nothing. Even sitting on the balcony for five minutes, waiting for Terry to get ready, makes me want to get up and do something. I grab my phone and check for messages. Other than the regular spam shit, there are a few messages from customers and parts distributors; nothing urgent. I pick a song to listen to while I wait, then run in to grab my knife and the piece of wood I've been working on, ambitiously trying to turn it into a bear.

When it comes to my phone, that's about all I do – text, check e-mail and listen to music. Terry always says that I'm like a fifty-year-old when it comes to technology; but I never really got into using my phone for anything else. Facebook to me seems like a nightmare.

A couple of years ago, I had a girlfriend who was completely obsessed with her Facebook and Instagram. Everything was documented with a duck face selfie. I remember the moment I knew it was over; we were sitting on the couch watching a movie and she was next to me checking the likes and comments from her thousand 'friends'. Every picture she showed me, of herself or any of her girlfriends, was basically the same. She would flick through countless images and judge them instantly, with some type of comment like, 'that's pretty' or 'ew, gross'. It seemed like such a waste of time to me, and yet it was such a major part of her life.

It has become very clear to me over the last few years that you don't really get to know most people that you spend time with, unless you spend time with them outside of work, or away from some structured social setting. We all have jobs and commitments that we have to do, and in those places, we meet lots of people. You can tell a lot about people's attitudes and true nature by seeing them at work, or at a dinner party, but you never *really* know who they are. I think we are all best described by what we choose to do with our free time. Isn't it those times where we reveal our true nature?

Assuming most people work for around eight hours, then sleep for another eight, this leaves eight hours of time in the day. Most of that time is eaten up with little tasks that need to be done, such as making food, doing chores, travelling to and from work, and a thousand other odds and ends. Whatever time is left is the time where we are free to do whatever we want. That's the time that defines us. There are people who will use that time to do stuff, and there are those who will spend every possible moment sitting and doing nothing. Watching the odd TV show or movie during your down time is fine, but so many people that I've met have no drive to do anything else. My weakness is not being able to put work aside. I choose to stay late when most guys in my business shut things down fifteen minutes early and coast to the final buzzer.

The funny thing to me is that people tend to think I'm strange for my constant need to be doing something. But is it really me who's strange because I want to get stuff done? I've been told to sit down and relax so many times I've thought about getting a t-shirt made with that as a slogan. I get called anti-social because I rarely go to parties and get-togethers; I find they usually turn into a bunch of people just sitting around together. Since I'm terrible at conversation, I'm actually a real bummer at parties. People who know me, understand that it's better I'm not there.

But if you give me a game to play, I'll go anywhere. The only bars I went to in college were the ones with a pool table that I could park myself at. As kids, when Daniel wasn't getting me in shit, we would be playing some kind of game. It's surprising that I still want to play games after years of getting beaten by Daniel and then having him rub my face in it. I guess I was destined to either give up and never play again, or constantly be trying to win games for the rest of my life. The cornhole victory on Tuesday was really satisfying.

I hear Daniel and my dad coming before they round the corner.

"There's old man LaPointe, whittling on his porch," Daniel jokes in some type of accent that's probably supposed to sound southern.

"Gentlemen," I say.

"How are you son?" my dad asks.

"Doing well, dad. How are you? Isn't Annette coming?"

"She is," he replies. "Just finishing up getting ready."

"Terry too."

"Why don't you join us?" my dad asks. "Let the ladies take their time."

"Sounds good," I answer. "Just let me pop in and let Terry know."

I finish off my beer and put everything inside. Terry is listening to music and straightening her hair when I open the bathroom door.

"I'm just going down to have a drink with Daniel and my dad," I say, peeking my head in.

"Ok, babe."

"You alright if Annette comes by here and you walk down with her?" I ask.

"For sure," she responds. "Maybe we'll sit and have a glass of wine ourselves before we grace you with our presence." She tosses her hair back and puckers her lips. I look her up and down, giving a little whistle, before closing the door. She has a way of being really hot right at the beginning of the evening so that I'm thinking about sex all night; and she knows that I'm thinking about it all night.

The men walk down to the dining room. As soon as we open the door, the murmur of conversation hits me. The dining room is about half full. It takes forever to get to our table when we walk in with dad; he stops to greet several people on the way. As we arrive at the table, Blaine walks up too, with a bottle of wine in his hand.

"How are we doing fellas?" he asks. "I brought over a bottle of the Pinot Blanc, Stéphane."

"Thank you Blaine. That'll be perfect." My dad slips a bill into Blaine's hand with the smoothness of a man who has eaten at some very fine restaurants. Most guests usually tip the wait staff, the bartender, and anyone else they think has done a good job, at the end of their trip. But my dad is old fashioned; he always has cash in his pocket to slip to someone who treats him well. As a result, most people treat him well.

"Haven't seen you much this week dad," I say, once we've settled in with a glass of wine. "Are you going to make it to euchre this evening?"

"Still not sure. How do you think your mother would react?" he asks.

For years, mom and dad used to play in the tournament as partners, winning the title three times. The year after they split was a tense, disaster of a vacation. But euchre night was when it really came to a head. Dad tried to play with Annette as his partner, and mom blew a gasket. Since then, dad has backed off and not played. I think he admits that first attempt to play was probably not a wise move.

"I think she could handle it," Daniel says. I don't share his confidence.

"I was talking with Carl, and he said he wouldn't mind playing,"

"That would probably be alright," I reassure him. "Who are you with this year?" I ask Daniel.

"Not too sure," he says casually. Despite getting to the finals last year with the girl he was seeing at the time, he's never really taken it too seriously.

"Courtney not really a euchre player?" I ask, noticing that she is making her way towards our table. It's clear there's something going on between the two of them this year, but Daniel doesn't really discuss it. He knows I'm not impressed by his sexual exploits, and dad has never been too keen on him boinking the staff here. He understood us hanging out with them when we were both a bit younger; but now that Daniel is almost thirty, I think dad believes he should have outgrown that.

"No idea," he answers briefly. As childish as it is, it brings me joy to make Daniel feel a bit uncomfortable, even for a few seconds.

"How is everyone doing?" Courtney asks casually. Whatever is going on with her and Daniel, he must have talked to her about keeping it hushed in certain places.

"Great," dad answers.

"Have you had a chance to think about what you want today?" Courtney asks, focussing her attention on my father while Daniel casually looks over the menu. Despite her interest in my brother, she knows who the big tipper is.

"I think we'll wait until everyone gets here," he responds. Turning to us, he asks, "Do you know if Chantelle is joining us?"

"Last I heard, she's coming. So are Sarah and Chris."

"So we'll be eight tonight, Courtney," my dad says. "Do you think we could slide over another table and a couple of chairs?"

"For sure. I'll get Blaine to look after that, and I'll be back in a few minutes."

"Thank you," my dad says, giving her his charming smile.

We chat for a few minutes before Terry and Annette come in. They have barely sat down when Sarah, Telly, and Chris join us. Knowing that mom is content with her dinner companions, the mood is relaxed for the meal. For the second time today, we are all able to sit together and talk; this time with my dad. The conversation doesn't ever get too deep, just casual small talk. As always, the food is good.

The plan for the evening is set. Terry and I are going to be partners, as are Chris and Sarah. Dad and Carl Harris are going to give it a go. Reluctantly, Chantelle agrees to play with mom.

Chapter Thirty Nine

CHRIS

"IT'S NINE FIFTEEN!" I call through the bathroom door.

"I know," is all Sarah responds. She's been a bit frosty today. I'm not sure if she thinks I did something wrong or if it's just a hormonal thing. Sarah has always been emotional; I have a feeling this pregnancy is going to make her behaviour even more erratic than normal.

"Should I text Craig and make sure he lets people know we're still coming?"

Sarah opens the bathroom door, looking very irritated. "Nothing starts on time here. We're fine. Go if you like, but don't rush me." She shuts the door. I tell myself to let it go and not push it. The last thing I need is a grumpy, pregnant wife for the last couple of days of the trip.

I text Craig anyway, just to let him know that we're running a bit late. He responds that things haven't even started yet. People are chatting and Zack is sorting out the decks of cards.

Euchre is the one event I really want to win. It's by far the most coveted competition of the Resort. Sarah and I have played together three times, and only gotten past the first round once. Sarah and Chantelle are the only members of Sarah's family not to have won the tournament; and Chantelle has never tried. This year, she's playing for the first time with Marion.

"You're right," I tell Sarah as she comes out of the bathroom. "Craig said they haven't started yet."

"I told you," she snaps.

"You OK?" I ask.

"Fine. Let's just go," she says without looking at me.

"Seriously," I push. "Would you like to let me in on what I did wrong?"

"Nothing."

I stand and look at her while she does up her shoes.

"Stop looking at me."

"Sarah, seriously. What's up?" I say as calmly as possible.

"Nothing. It just sucks that you're drinking and having fun and I can't; and I'm already starting to feel like crap."

"That sucks, sweetie. But there's nothing I can really do about it. You just want me to be miserable too?" I still try to sound calm and not like I'm challenging her, but I know being rational is just going to piss her off.

"You could at least try to understand," she says, raising her voice just a bit.

You know that moment when you know you have a choice to either be right and start an argument, or just let it go? Sometimes, when you're not really thinking, you automatically choose the first option, and then usually end up regretting it later. I know that I could push here and make my point that she's being selfish and I shouldn't have to stop having fun because she's pregnant. Luckily, at this moment, I'm aware enough to be able to see the futility of arguing right now.

"You're right, babe. I got caught up in a fun day, had a few drinks, and wasn't really thinking about you." I move over to her slowly, testing to see if she's going to either snap my head off, or soften.

"It's stupid. I know you didn't mean it," she says, softening slightly.

"I am completely focussed on you this evening," I say, wrapping my arms around her and giving her a kiss on the temple. "Let's go win us some euchre."

"Yeah, right," she says. "I'm cursed. I swear I get the worst cards when I play here; all nines and queens."

"This year will be different," I say confidently. "Little Chris junior will bring us luck." I give her stomach a little rub.

"Not happening."

"How about Ulysses, then?"

"Never! You are *not* naming our child."

Crisis averted. After a few years of marriage, I've gotten better at putting out fires before they get too big. A couple of years ago, I would have kept arguing, gotten into a bigger fight, and had a shitty evening. There are still times when I push things too far, but I've definitely learned when a little apology, even when not sincere, can make life easier. We walk together to the bar. I still fully intend on having a few drinks this evening. We'll see if I might have to apologize again tomorrow.

By the time we arrive, people are getting organized at tables set up around the room. Some games have already started. Zack is sitting at the bar with a clipboard showing the draw. Looking over the list, it looks like there are at least sixteen teams playing. We missed the drawing of matches, but Craig assures us it was all legit. Sarah and I face Gene and Maxine Bennett in the first round. Despite their sweet, helpful nature, they are cut throat when it comes to cards.

"Have you been having a nice week, dears?" Maxine asks

sweetly, as we sit at the table. I think that's their trick; they play the sweet, little old man and lady routine so perfectly that it's hard to get the desire to beat them. Not this year, granny.

"Very nice" I respond, grabbing the cards and giving them a shuffle. "First black jack deals?" I ask.

"Of course, dear," Maxine says.

"It's been very nice," Sarah says, giving me a bit of a dirty look. "How are your grandkids doing?"

"Growing so fast; aren't they Gene?"

"My word! Aren't they though?" Gene says with a smile.

Maxine gets the deal, so I slide her the cards. Despite hands that look as though they may have a touch of arthritis, she picks them up and shuffles them with ease.

The game starts slowly with a couple of single points. The conversation is steady; Maxine and Sarah go back and forth asking questions about the year's events. Gene pipes in every once in a while, adding some precision to a story Maxine is telling. I try to keep quiet and focus on the game.

Just as Maxine is updating us about her son's business struggles, I get dealt a clear lone hand in clubs. There's a spade turned up from Gene's deal. He's seated just to my right so I'm praying everyone passes. It comes around to Gene, who looks at his cards for what seems like an hour before flipping the king of Spades over.

"Clubs alone," I call. Because I have the lead, there's almost nothing that can stop me. I draw out all the trumps with my first three cards, then throw down my two aces. With my four points, we take an 8-5 lead.

"Nice job, babe," Sarah says with an air kiss.

The next few hands end with single points. It comes around to Gene's deal again and we're up 9-7. Double suited, I order him up and we just barely squeak out a point to win.

Since I didn't have time to grab a drink before playing, I get up after the game and go to the bar. Sarah and I made a plan that I would get her drinks that look like they could have booze in them, so I get her a rye and ginger without the rye, in a rocks glass.

Because we won our game fairly quickly, we get to stay at our table for the next game. Since our opponents haven't been decided yet, Gene and Maxine stay and chat some more. I immediately feel terrible for even suggesting to myself that they are anything other than really genuine, kind, old people. I wish they were my grandparents.

Looking around the room, I can see that Marion and Chantelle are still playing. They're seated over in one corner while Stéphane and his partner are across the room. They look to have won and are chatting with an older couple. As well as being on opposite sides of the physical space of the bar, Zack placed Stéphane and Marion on opposite sides of the draw too; the only way they could face each other would be in the finals. That would be awkward; but I kind of want to see it.

I grab a second beer and chat at the bar for a while. Euchre night is always nice because I actually have a chance to talk to people. Live music and dancing are great, but there's not much chance to make connections with other guests. It's nice to meet different people so I'm not always stuck with Sarah's family.

After about ten minutes, Sarah waves me back over to the table. I grab her a rum and coke without the rum. Our opponents in the second round are a couple named Carrie and Marc. They've been out a couple of times this week, and they usually make the most of it.

"Hey guys! How's it going?" Carrie asks.

"Great! How's your week going?" Sarah responds.

"Amazing! This place is a lot of fun."

"How are your little ones liking it?" Sarah continues. We

were introduced to the whole family on the beach a few days ago, but I can't remember the names of their two kids. I don't think Sarah remembers either; normally she would make a point of using the names. She thinks it's important to use people's names so they know you remember and care. I've always sucked at remembering people's names. Every year, a week or so before we come here, Sarah has to give me a refresher course on all the guests I've forgotten from the year before. Personally, I get by pretty well just never using anyone's name.

"They love it. Caleb's swimming has gotten so much better just since we've been here."

"Do you think you'll come back next year?" I ask.

"We'll see. We're thinking about it," Marc answers.

"What's the score here?" Zack asks, coming to our table as he makes a tour of the bar to see what's happening.

"Just getting started," Carrie says.

"Oh, ok," Zack says, a bit surprised. "Well, whoever wins here, your opponent is already waiting."

"Wow! Ok! Let's get going then," Carrie says, grabbing the cards and giving them a shuffle.

It's a brutal start to the game; they go up 5-0 after three hands. Sarah's curse kicks in fully; she has absolute shit cards. Annoyed that we aren't doing well, I take a chance the next hand, hoping she'll be able to win at least one trick, and call it hearts. It turns out to be a terrible call since Carrie has both bowers. We get euchred, and are suddenly down 7-0. Trying to break their luck, I excuse myself from the table and go to the bathroom.

When I get back, we manage to win a few hands. It's 8-4 when I get dealt an amazing hand in diamonds. I'm literally drooling at my cards when Marc flips over the ace of spades. My prayers of having him turn it down are crushed when he picks it up and flashes a confident smile. They win all five tricks, and just like that our tournament is over. We shake hands and wish them good luck.

"I told you I'm cursed!" Sarah complains. "Did you see the crap I was getting?"

"Yeah, that sucked. I had terrible cards too. Nothing you can do with that shit."

We check in to see how everyone else is doing. Craig and Terry are playing against the Watson sisters, and are tied at seven. Marion and Chantelle have won two games. Between games, they aren't sitting together. Marion is at a table talking to one of her friends while Chantelle sits at the bar. Stéphane and Carl lost their second game. They are chatting with Walter Watson.

"I don't think I want to hang around here until the end," Sarah says. "It looks like it's going to take a while."

I know she wants me to offer to go back with her, but I don't. "I think I'll stay for a bit if that's ok," I say in that way that isn't really a question, but seems to be asking anyway. "I kind of want to see how things go."

"Ok," she says, looking tired.

"Love you," I say, giving her a kiss.

I walk her to the door, stopping with her to say goodbye to several people. I give her another kiss before making my way back inside.

There are more people now who are not playing than there are people still in the tournament. A couple of people are just playing for fun off to the side; Stéphane is there with the Bennetts. Terry is sitting at a table by herself. It looks like Craig has gone to get a drink, but is caught up in a conversation with Chantelle.

"You guys still in it?" I ask as I sit down.

"Nope! Lost to the Watson sisters," she says.

"They're pretty good," I respond. "Was it close at least?"

"Yeah, it ended 10-8. How about you?"

"We got our asses kicked by Carrie and Marc over there," I answer, nodding my head in their direction.

"They're hilarious!" Terry laughs. "I met them the first night here and she was hammered."

"They were here on disco night. I think they were pretty pissed that night too."

"Good for them!" Terry says. "Even with a couple of young kids, they're still having fun together."

"Yeah," I add enthusiastically, raising my bottle. Terry lifts her beer and leans forward to clink glasses. We both have a drink.

"Sarah isn't much of a partier," I add, for no real reason.

"Neither is Craig," Terry admits. "He'll have a few drinks, but doesn't really ever tie one on."

"Funny," I add. "The other two LaPointe kids don't seem too shy about letting loose."

"Maybe too much," she says, then gives a cheeky look.

"Yeah," I agree. "I don't really know Chantelle that well, but she certainly doesn't seem too reserved. And I've definitely seen Daniel drinking hard."

"No shit!" Terry adds. "I try to avoid him when he gets drunk. He gets even touchier than normal." She gives a look of disgust.

Craig comes over to the table after finishing up his conversation with his sister. "Hey Chris. You and Sarah done?"

"Yeah. Heard you lost too. Not a stellar day for our clan."

"Mom and Telly are still in it, although I don't know how strong their partnership is."

"Why?" Terry asks.

"Tell was just talking about throwing the next game just to be done with it so she wouldn't have to play anymore. I think she's about ready to jump across the table and strangle my mom."

"That sucks," I add.

"I think I convinced her to stick it out. I think mom would really like to win."

"Would have been fun to have your parents squaring off in the finals," I joke.

"Fun like a dumpster fire, you mean?" he responds with a chuckle.

"Maybe it would have brought them together?" Terry suggests.

"In a sadistic way, it would have been pretty interesting to see that," Craig admits.

"Are you going to sit?" Terry asks. "And did you bring me a drink?"

"Shit, sorry. I got distracted. I'll go grab it, but I don't think I'm going to stay."

"Don't worry," Terry says. "I need to get up anyway." She turns to me as she gets up. "You staying for a while?"

"I think so."

"Alright," she says turning to Craig. "I think I'll stay here for a bit then, babe."

"Ok," he says, giving her a kiss. "See you later, Chris."

"Later."

Terry walks over to the bar to grab a drink. I can see that Chantelle and Marion have started their game against the Watson sisters. It's the semi-final. In the other match, Carrie and Marc are up against Walter Watson's brother, Gerry, and Michelle's husband, Brad.

When Terry comes back, she has a couple of shots of something and two beers.

"What's all this?"

"There are only a couple of days left, so I think we need to live it up."

As I take the drinks, I'm struck with several thoughts. I think back to Sarah getting pissed at me earlier. If me having a couple of drinks this afternoon ticked her off, I'm assuming me taking shots now would be frowned upon. I also get a flashback of Terry and Craig standing red handed when I went over to drop off her phone. Immediately after, I get an image of the dream I had a few days ago. As a result of all of this, I feel a sense of guilt. I'm hanging out and taking shots with, basically my wife's sister in law, remembering a sex dream involving her, while my pregnant wife is at home sleeping. That makes me sound like a real slime bag.

"Bottom's up!" Terry says, raising her shot glass.

"Cheers!" I say, and knock it back. "Yeesh! What was that?"

"Four Horsemen!" she answers.

"Smooth," I add, still wincing.

After a few seconds, Terry asks, "How is Sarah doing with your dad's news?"

"She's alright. I think she's most concerned about it being a kind of first domino that starts a chain reaction of people not coming."

"Craig basically said the same thing."

"Does *he* want to keep coming?"

"Yeah. I can't see him not wanting to come."

"Sarah too," I add. "She just wants *everyone* to be here."

"I don't think Craig is as concerned about that. I think he'd be OK with just your mom, you guys, and Chantelle every once in a while."

"Sounds fine with me," I say, raising my glass. She does the same and we drink. I'm definitely feeling good now; the shot, along with a couple of gin and tonics and a few beers are giving me a nice buzz. Terry is good company; we chat a while and laugh lots. When there's a lull in the conversation, I suggest we check out the score in Marion and Chantelle's game.

As we approach the table, I can tell that Chantelle is

miserable. She looks irritated and bored; however, they are winning 9-7. I guess she decided not to throw the game.

"How are we doing here?" I ask, probably a bit too loudly.

"Great," Chantelle says very unenthusiastically.

"We're doing well, Chris dear, but we really have to focus now," Marion adds.

Chantelle looks at us and gives an eye roll. Terry and I turn and look at each other at exactly the same time.

"How about a game of pool?" she asks, smirking.

"Sounds good," I say.

At the back of the bar, there are a couple of areas for pool. They are separated from the main part, but still very open; not really rooms themselves. The doorways are large and open, and where one wall would be, there are simply shelves separating the space from the main part of the bar. There are two small, bar-sized tables that are old and slightly warped. One table is free, so after grabbing a couple more drinks, Terry and I get set up.

"Now, are you going to get upset when I beat you?" Terry brags as she rolls a couple of bent cues on the warped table.

"Probably," I answer, racking up the balls. "But that won't happen, so it's alright."

I accept the shitty cue that she gives me and step back from the table. Terry takes off the button-down shirt she's been wearing. I can't help notice that she fills out the tank top she's got underneath very well, and that her jeans are hugging her hips quite nicely. She places the ball on the table, leans over and breaks with some serious power. It's just about the hottest thing I've ever seen. I pray that she gets something in and that I don't have to get up and shoot with a big, fat hard-on.

I give my head a shake and look away. I try to pull up one of the many classic images I've used over the years to get rid of a boner. For whatever reason, the image that my brain decides to show is one from when I was around thirteen. Our Phys Ed teacher was Mrs. Ellerbe; she was a butchy, hairy woman who smelled like a mixture of sweat and ass. I'm instantly repulsed, but also amused by this thought. I give a chuckle and look back at the table.

"You're up," Terry says, walking over to the little table in the corner where we had set our drinks, "and you're stripes."

I'm pissed enough now that I'm probably past the point of being really good, and I'm entering the stage of being absolute shit. I manage to sink one ball; however, the next shot is awful. I stumble over to the table and sit on the stool. After surveying her options, Terry decides to shoot a ball just in front of where I'm sitting.

I love Sarah a lot and I'm really happy that we're starting a family together. She's beautiful, smart, and funny. But right now, as she bends over the table and takes a shot in front of me, I realize that Terry is *hot.* I look at her ass as much as I can without seeming like it. Or at least I hope I'm not making it too obvious.

After making a couple of shots, Terry accidentally sinks the eight ball.

"Fuck!"

"Told ya I'd win," I say.

"That was cheap."

"But it counts," I say with a smirk.

"How about a game of doubles?" Carrie asks loudly from the doorway. She and Marc just lost their semi-final. It looks as though they have been drinking quite a bit themselves. As Terry sets up the table, I go grab myself a glass of water. If I have any more drinks, I'm going to end up getting myself in trouble.

Having Carrie and Marc playing is just what I need to stop focussing on Terry bending over the table. The two of them are loud and drunk. The game is sloppy and takes forever, but it's fun. After Terry and I beat them, we hear that the final game is about to start. Marion and Chantelle have made it to the finals to face Brad and Gerry.

"Wanna watch?" Terry asks.

"I bet you five bucks Chantelle and Marion have a big blow-up before the game ends," I suggest.

"No," she says, "you don't think that, do you? They wouldn't."

"It wouldn't really be *that* surprising would it?"

"I guess not, but I'll take the bet," she says, holding out her hand.

By this point, there are about ten people left in the bar. Most of the Watson clan has stayed to cheer on Brad and Gerry. We sit at a table next to the big game, where we have a clear enough view. It's quiet as Brad deals the first hand; there's actual tension in the air. Looking from Marion to Chantelle, their body language could not be more different; determined mother, trying to win a card tournament that she has played more than twenty times, and disinterested daughter who couldn't give a shit about the tradition.

It's actually awkward for the first couple of hands. Gerry tries his best to lighten the mood with a few comments about the hands he's getting, but the ladies remain silent and serious. Instinctively, I want to say something that will try to break the tension, but I fight the urge. It would inevitably be something stupid. It's tied at two when Chantelle gets the deal. She picks up the cards and shuffles them as she looks around the table.

"Wanna hear a joke?' she asks nobody in particular.

"I sure do!" Terry pipes in. Nobody else speaks for a moment.

"Maybe now isn't the time, dear," Marion says sternly.

"I think it's *exactly* the time," she says firmly, and with a sarcastic smile. She shuffles the cards once more. "This guy and girl meet in the elevator. The man strikes up a conversation by asking, 'where are you headed today?' The woman answers, 'to give blood'. He asks her, 'how much do you get paid for that?' The woman answers, 'twenty buck.' The guy says, 'Really? Wow. I'm going to the sperm bank and they pay me seventy-five bucks.' The woman looks pissed as she gets off the elevator."

At this point, Chantelle starts dealing the cards. "A couple of days later, they meet again in the elevator. The guy says, 'Hey! You again. Off to give more blood?' The woman looks at him and shakes her head."

After dealing all the cards, Chantelle pauses to take a sip of her drink. With beer still in the bottom of her mouth, she says, "Not today. Sperm bank," and points to her mouth.

There's at least two seconds of silence before Terry lets out a laugh. There are only a couple of people that have hung around now; most left because of the awkward vibe. The Watson sisters look at each other with their mouths agape and laugh. Gerry and Brad aren't too sure how to react, but after some laughs fill the room, they give in and chuckle. Chantelle stays stone faced and looks at Marion.

"Funny mom?" she asks.

"Yes dear," is all she says. She looks at her cards, then at Brad, who picks up his cards, looks at the queen of spades that Chantelle turned over, and passes.

Chantelle's joke does the job of breaking the tension in the room a bit. There's some light conversation between the players, and amongst the spectators. But the cards seem to take a turn in Gerry and Brad's favour. They end up winning the game 10-5.

After the game, Marion is gracious, but clearly upset. She congratulates the winners before frostily thanking Chantelle for playing. She's out the door within minutes of the game being over.

"Well that was a fun evening," Chantelle says to Terry and me after everyone else has drifted away. "Who's up for a drink?"

"I'll stay for one more," Terry answers.

"I think I'll turn in," I say. "Congrats on getting to the finals."

"Thanks."

"See you Chris. It was fun," Terry says, getting up to give me a hug. "I think you owe me five bucks," she adds quietly in my ear.

On the dark walk back to our cabin, I wonder if I'll be able to wake Sarah up for some sex. I somehow doubt it.

Chapter Forty

DAVE

I SHOULD HAVE KNOWN there was no way I'd be able to get to sleep tonight. I lay in bed and tried to read for a while, but I couldn't focus. As I was laying there, staring and the ceiling, the lyrics to a Peter Gabriel classic came to mind.

Got to get some sleep
I'm so nervous in the night
I don't know how to stop
No, I don't know how to stop

I told myself yesterday that I was going to give myself a break from any substances for a couple of days, but I was kidding myself; the beach barbecue made that impossible. There was no way I was going to make it through that without a little help; but I didn't have to spend the rest of the night the way I did.

There's no fucking way I'm going to make it until morning without doing something either.

After everyone had eaten, I talked for a bit with Chantelle LaPointe while everything was being cleaned up. It always takes a while to transport things back to the kitchen and put shit away. Chantelle actually ended up helping out, and it turns out she knows her way around a kitchen pretty well. We smoked a joint on the way back to the kitchen, then had a couple of drinks as we were doing the cleanup. I jokingly suggested she get a job here and it turns out she didn't think it wasn't such a crazy idea.

By the time we had everything put away, the rest of the staff was long gone. We sat in the kitchen and talked for hours, drinking and smoking. I ended up getting so fucked up, I think I passed out; because I have no memory of lying down, nor of Chantelle leaving. It can't really be called sleep, but I was out cold, lying on a couple of boxes in the back room for about two hours before I woke up just before breakfast. I managed to drag my ass upstairs and have a two minute shower before having to get started this morning.

Why I didn't just grab her and fuck her right there in the kitchen, I don't know.

The day didn't get much better; I tried to have a nap between breakfast and dinner, but my head was pounding and I felt like vomiting. I was determined not to do anything stronger than pot, so I went for a drive and ran a few errands to kill time and get my mind off things. About two kilometers from the Resort, I came within a couple of inches of hitting a woman who was running on the side of the road. I have no fucking clue what I was thinking about, but I did not see her until I was right next to her. The look of fear on her face as I passed snapped me back to reality pretty quickly.

Dinner was not fun. I told everyone to leave me alone and I didn't speak another word the whole evening. Everyone tiptoed around like I was an open bag of tarantulas. I love cooking. I always have; but sometimes, when my head hurts, and my stomach feels like I just swallowed a pint of raw sewage, and

I'm jumping between chills and sweats, cooking is tough. After dinner, fighting the urge to pop a couple of pills, or do a line, I came upstairs and smoked about fifteen cigarettes, completely unable to sleep.

Maybe I'll crush up all the pills in the bag, mix it with the rest of the coke and snort myself right the fuck to the Promised Land.

As shit as I feel right now, I know I'm alive. I'm sure the day will come when I just decide to remain constantly high; but for now, I need these sober times to keep me grounded.

I read a story once of a painter. He lived the classic starving artist life for many years until all of a sudden; his work was being praised by the richest art critics around. He became extravagantly wealthy in a matter of months. He spent a year living a life of luxury; and during that time, he couldn't paint a thing. Every urge to create had disappeared. One day, he ate something that made his body so sick that he was spewing out liquids from almost every hole in his body at once. He was violently ill for three days.

While he was sick, he experienced a pain and suffering that he had not felt in a long time. He didn't go out, spend any money, drink any booze, do any drugs, or even eat any food; none of the stuff that he had lived for the past year. In that suffering, he finally felt like he was alive again; as he was during his life of poverty. For three days, he crawled from the toilet to a canvas, where he painted what would become his greatest masterpiece. The only person who ever saw it before he died was a whore he spent a couple of nights with a year later. He never sold it or showed it in public.

After that illness, he gave everything he had to the poor. He spent the next three years of his life living day to day, trying to make himself suffer in order to feel alive again. He purposely ate foods that were spoiled. He broke his own leg and didn't get it looked at for weeks. The thing that killed him in the end was an infection in a self-inflicted wound that hadn't been treated. In his tiny, little apartment, they found his decaying body, along with over thirty works from the previous three years, including that very first one.

Long before teens started cutting themselves, this guy was doing self-harm. He didn't keep much of a journal, but he did scribble some sentences here and there during his days of suffering. He wrote about pain being a penance he needed to experience to prevent himself from getting too wrapped up in his success. He felt that the more he indulged in luxury, the less alive he would be; and that in the end, allowing himself to live off his success would actually kill him as an artist, and as a person. So he caused himself pain and suffering because that was the only thing that made him feel alive. The irony of it all, of course, was that the suffering that he was causing himself was also destroying his body.

So here I am doing my penance, up at 2:30 in the morning, smoking a cigarette I don't want, unable to sleep, and wishing I were high, or dead.

But I'm alive.

The thing I'm starting to doubt is my ability to separate my thoughts from actions. My whole life has been filled with dark thoughts; but I've always been able to separate them from reality. Will there ever be a day that I decide to do whatever that fucked up part of my brain is telling me?

Today at dinner, I had the cleaver in my hand, chopping cabbage. There have been a hundred times when I've thought about doing something with that knife, usually throwing it across the room at someone's skull. Today, however, I had the strongest urge I've ever had to place my hand on that cutting board and remove a finger in one chop. I heard the sound of ligaments snapping and bone crunching. I felt the pain fire up my arm. I saw the blood shoot out in a line across the board. I put down the knife, calm as can be, and walked outside for a smoke.

Still far from sleep now, I throw on my jacket, grab the joint that I rolled two hours ago and placed on the table in front of me, and I leave my room. The Resort is calm and quiet apart from some faint laughing coming from the staff cabins in the distance. I take my usual route, making a lap of the Resort; it takes about ten minutes to do the full loop.

At this time of night, the Resort is quiet. The half-moon is high in the sky, and there are hardly any clouds. Some cabins keep their porch lights on, so you can't see as many stars as you would expect this far away from rural areas. For most of these late night walks, I stick to the little alleys and paths that lead around the Resort. Today, as I've done a couple of times, I cut in behind the first cabin.

Tonight will be the big one.

It's quiet as I walk slowly up to the window. The little curtains are mostly closed. I stand and listen for a minute, then keep walking; nothing much to see in a quiet room. The second cabin is a bit bigger; probably a three bedroom. All the lights are off, and the curtains are fully closed.

My little hide-and-seek walks started a couple of years ago. I've only done it maybe ten times in total. I doubt I ever would have started if I hadn't heard some moaning coming from an open window one night when I was just out walking. I'd always imagined what was going on in cabins as I walked around in the middle of the night; but I never really seriously considered creeping up and looking inside. But that night, I couldn't help myself; I think most people would have gone and had a peek. It turned out to be a couple of guests having some late night, drunken sex after a night out. It was sloppy and amateur, but it was hot in a way I can't fully explain.

Since then, I've only ever caught one more couple in the act. I watched tons of porn in my life, but there's something about watching real people fucking, when they don't know you're watching, that takes it to a new level.

After passing by a few of the outer cabins, I stick to the path as I come around to the beach. There aren't as many trees in this area and it would be far easier for someone to see me lurking around here. Sometimes, at this time of night, there are people still sitting on porches, having one last drink before turning in; but today, the Resort is silent. I grab a seat on a beach chair, look out at the lake, and smoke my joint.

Hardly anyone locks their doors around here. Maybe next cabin, I'll walk right in and get some real action.

Sitting and staring out at the lake for ten minutes, enjoying the effects of the bud, does the job of relaxing me. Instead of finishing my loop around the perimeter of the Resort, I head straight back to the main lodge. I grab my Kierkegaard anthology and lie down. It's not long before I'm able to drift off into a dreamless sleep. I'll get about four hours before breakfast prep.

Chapter Forty One

PASCAL

YESTERDAY WAS THE perfect day off. I slept late, hung out with Stacey on the beach in the afternoon, had a nap, and then went to see a movie with Maria in the evening. We had to get a ride there with her parents; which was kind of awkward, but it was still nice to get off the Resort and hang out with her. She didn't come back here for the night, so her parents dropped me off. She walked me to the cabins so we could have a little make out before she left, and then I sat and had a couple of drinks with some staff.

I know there are way harder jobs out there that people have to do, so I don't want to sound whiney; but working six days a week here is hard. The last two weeks, I didn't make use of my day off. I ended up just lounging around and wasting it. If I'm going to make it through the summer, I have to use that day to recharge for the week. And maybe tone it down on the drinking. I don't know if Maria feels the same, but if there's something starting up between us, maybe we can spend more nights just hanging out together instead of going out dancing and stuff.

I lie in bed for an extra couple of minutes while I wake up. All I really have to do before leaving for breakfast is brush my teeth.

"Let's go, lazy!" Greg says as he passes by my bunk and gives it a kick. "You actually have to *work* today princess."

Greg was super snippy yesterday. I don't know if it's because I had a day off and he had to work; but that would be stupid because he's had his own day off. If it's because I was hanging out with Stacey and he's interested in her, that would be stupid too because he had his chance to join us. Instead of starting off with a stupid fight, I choose to ignore it.

Slapping on some deodorant and brushing my teeth takes about two minutes. After getting changed quickly, I'm ready to go. I stop by the fridge and grab a bottle of water before heading out the door.

"Hang on," Greg calls from his bunk. He's just putting on some socks. "I'll walk over with you."

I guess whatever had him irritated yesterday has mostly warn off. On the way over to the kitchen, we discuss the night before. He wasn't around when I got back from my date with Maria. He tells me how tense dinner was with Dave in the kitchen. I guess he was in one of his 'don't you dare talk to me' moods. After cleaning up dinner, and getting stuff ready for this morning, Greg came back to the cabins so tired he sat around for half an hour, then he went to bed.

"I wonder what the mood is going to be like today," I say.

"Yesterday morning, he was like a zombie!"

"Yeah, I've noticed he's been like that in the mornings." I think back to when I saw Dave take that bag of pills from the very sketchy looking dude.

"What do you think he does at night?" Greg asks. "I don't ever see him out at the shit that's going on around here.

I've always been really bad at keeping secrets and holding on to gossip.

"I saw him take a big bag of pills from a guy a couple of days ago."

"You sure it was a bag of *pills*?" Greg asks.

"Pretty sure. He took it from the guy, then shoved it pretty quickly in his pocket; but it sure looked like pills."

"Wonder what it was?"

"Something like Oxy?" I suggest.

"Could be," Greg nods. "But I don't think taking some Oxy would make him act like that."

"Maybe he ran out, and he's suffering withdrawal."

"But you saw him buy a bag, like two days ago. That would be a lot of Oxy to take in a couple of days."

"True," I admit.

We reach the door of the kitchen and both stop at the same time.

"I think you should go first," Greg says with a little smile.

"And why is that?"

"He likes you better. You're the sweet, innocent type. He probably won't snap and stab *you* with a paring knife."

"Probably?" I ask, opening the door and peeking inside. "That's comforting."

When we walk in, Dave is at his station making a Hollandaise sauce. It's one of the things that he hasn't taught us how to make yet. I don't know what he does to it, but it's really good. He's pretty secretive about it.

Greg and I walk in without talking, but making enough noise for Dave to know we're there. I turn to Greg and mouth, 'say something!'

'No way,' he answers silently.

We decide to get started on our prep work. We have lists for each day's meals at our stations. Dave has every detail explained and colour coded on laminated pages. Now that we've done each day's meals a couple of times, I mostly know what to do anyway. There's no real need to ask Dave anything; but with only the sounds of utensils, pots, and pans, a kitchen can be a quiet place.

It's about half an hour before anyone else shows up. Michelle is first to come into the kitchen.

"Morning boys," she greets.

"How's it going, Michelle?" I ask.

"Not too bad," she answers cheerily. She's another one where you never know what kind of mood she's going to be in. "It's a bit quiet in here again though."

Greg and I both shrug our shoulders.

"Dave!" Michelle calls, walking over to the back, where he has his station. "How are you doing?"

"Fine," he responds, not looking up.

"You sure? Because the tension in here is sitting in the air like a bad fart."

Dave stops what he's doing and looks up at her for the first time; it's actually the first time he's really looked up at all, as far as I've seen. He's not looking fabulous.

"Just trying to get work done," he answers.

"I know. But it might be nice if you boys communicated a little in here, you know?" she says, looking and gesturing back at us. "Maybe talk a little about what you all did last night; or maybe some casual sports talk or something."

"Listen," Dave starts, setting his knife down and facing us all. "I never said anything about talking. You two can chat all you like; just don't be loud and obnoxious." He then looks at

Michelle. "I'm tired. I'm going to get my shit done. If I don't want to talk in my own kitchen, then I won't."

"Fair enough, Dave," she says calmly. "But you've been moody lately and I care about how you're doing. If you keep it up, eventually, I'm going to sit you down and have a good, long talk about what's going on; we can get all mushy and emotional."

Dave gives a sarcastic grin and says, "Great! I look forward to that."

Just then, Courtney walks in and goes to grab some plates. The way we all turn and look at her must make her feel like we were talking about her.

"What?" she says, with serious attitude. She turns and storms out without giving us a chance to say anything.

"You think *I'm* moody?" Dave says, totally straight faced. After about a second, he shows a faint smile. The three of us crack up. Without another word, he turns and gets back to work.

Once again, the mood is lightened enough for us to loosen up. Stacey's arrival in the kitchen livens things up even more; she has a way of adding a little sunshine into a room. She tells us of the birthday celebrations her family had for her brother's birthday the night before. There were over thirty family members there!

The rest of breakfast prep is fairly uneventful. Dave doesn't exactly open up; he stays pretty quiet the whole time. As I'm making a trip to the fridge to grab some strawberries, I stop and look over at him as he's wiping down his work area. He wipes the same cutting board over and over, and his lips are moving. His skin is pale and he's got dark circles under his eyes. I must stare at him for a while, because Greg gives me a smack on the arm as he passes me. I snap out of it, but I can't help thinking back to what Greg said about the paring knife.

Chapter Forty Two

SARAH

"THOSE EGGS ARE just not sitting well," Chris says as we walk back from breakfast.

"Maybe you shouldn't have drank so much yesterday," I answer.

"I didn't really drink *that* much," he responds. "I wasn't even all that late. There were still people out when I left."

"Trust me," I tell him, "you'd had enough."

He had come back to the cabin all liquored up and horny. There's not much that's less of a turn on than a drunken husband stumbling into bed in the middle of the night, reeking like booze and looking for sex.

"Nothing a good nap won't fix," he says with a yawn.

"Probably a good idea; we have dinner with my mom tonight. I'll probably have to spend the day getting the rest of the family organized."

"Or you could just let it all work out on its own."

"What's that supposed to mean? You know nothing will happen unless I put it all together."

"No, actually I don't know that. You never give it a chance to just happen."

"Great. You too."

"Me too, what?" Chris asks.

"The least you could do is support me. Nobody else ever does. If I don't make the plan, then Daniel will find some excuse not to be there. And who knows with Telle?"

"She did not look pleased last night after the final game."

"That's what I mean. I bet I'm going to spend half the day having to convince her to come to dinner."

"Why not let Craig do all that? Just tell him you're not feeling great, then spend the day in bed with me," he says with a smile, putting his arm around my waist.

"I'm really not in the mood, Chris," I answer, trying to be perfectly clear that it's not happening.

"Anything I can do to change that?" he asks.

"No."

"Ok then," he says, getting the message pretty clearly. "I'm still planning on having a nap. If I'm not up by 3:00, wake me up. I wouldn't mind getting out on a kayak if it's not too choppy."

"You're going to sleep until 3:00? That's four and a half hours!"

"So what? It's VACATION, Sarah. Plus, I'll probably read a bit first."

As we reach the cabin, he goes straight inside. I take a seat on the deck and look out at the lake. Some families have already gotten set up on the beach. It takes a while for the sun to hit it full on, so at this time of day, it's usually pretty cool down there. Some kids are putting on life jackets, but most of the adults are still wearing some kind of long sleeved shirt.

Maybe Chris is right; I should just not worry about dinner tonight. If Maman wants to make sure that all the kids are there, then she can get started with the organization. And if it doesn't happen, then it doesn't happen. Why stress myself out about it?

I manage to sit for about a minute before I grab my phone and text Craig. He's the easiest of the bunch to get a hold of and to get on board with the plan.

U and T will be there for dinner with Mom right?

Daniel almost never returns my texts unless there's something in it for him, so I don't expect much. But I send him a message anyway.

Dinner with Mom today, K? Important to her.

To my surprise, he responds immediately.

Dad's last dinner

I hadn't really thought about it until reading Daniel's text, but this really is probably Dad's last dinner here. I suddenly don't know what to do. Several times, Maman has insisted that we all spend the last dinner with her this year. She was pissed last year that the boys ate with dad on the last night. I literally heard about it all year. I don't know how he feels about it, but I'm sure dad would like to have us with him for his last dinner. Shit.

I get a message from Craig.

OK. Have you talked to anyone else yet? Wonder what dad's plans are.

Texts from Craig are funny; he communicates in full sentences, with correct punctuation, and with very few emoji's. He texts like an old man.

D just reminded me it's dad's last dinner. Don't know what to do.

You talk to the ladies and I'll talk to the boys. How about meeting for lunch and seeing what's up then?

K

How long can I sit and postpone going over to see Maman? I pop inside and make a tea. Chris is reading in the bedroom. I'm not usually an herbal tea drinker, but I'm trying to avoid caffeine. The first few cups were alright, but I really fancy a black tea right now. I guess I have to settle for camomile. Taking it back out to the porch, I sit with my book. I'm almost certain I'm not going to get any reading done, but it's worth a shot.

The book sits on the table as I sit and look out at the water. Despite this being a vacation spot, with kids running around and constant activity in most areas, there's still a calm feel to the Resort for me. Growing up here, I've learned to tune out all the people and just appreciate the beauty. I've seen this lake for almost my whole life, but it never gets boring to sit and look at it. I've seen misty mornings, glorious sunsets, choppy storms, and water that's as still as the stars. Soaking in the nostalgia and the cool air, I finish my tea and summon up the courage to go next door.

When I knock on the screen door and look in, I see that Maman is in the little kitchen area of the main room.

"Come in dear," Maman says.

"Are you packing already?" I ask.

"Just getting a few things organized that I won't be needing anymore."

"Is Telle here?"

"She either got up early this morning, or she never came back last night," she says, pretending not to be bothered by it.

"Did you text her to see where she was?" I ask, feeling concerned.

"She wouldn't have answered, Sarah. You know that."

"But you should have texted me!" I explain.

"I had no idea she wasn't here until recently, dear. I was up early, and left for breakfast. Her door was closed, and I was not going to wake her. When I got back, I checked in and she wasn't there."

I take out my phone and text her immediately.

Where R U?

"Aren't you worried?" I ask.

She stops what's she's doing and turns to face me. In the most parental way, she crosses her hands and tilts her head just slightly.

"Sarah, dear," she starts. "Chantelle has always been this way. There have been so many nights where I've worried about her, and she was in far worse places than here."

There's a look of acceptance in her face, but I still see a hint of sadness in her eyes. I know that for a long time, Maman felt guilty about how Chantelle was raised. After it had sunken in that Chantelle had moved out for good a few years ago, she felt such guilt that she hadn't really been there for her youngest daughter. At the same time, the fact that Telle was her youngest, and that she'd left so young, meant that Maman was left alone so much earlier than she had ever planned to be.

"I guess it is pretty safe here," I admit, feeling calmer.

"Did you come to help me pack dear?" she asks with a smile.

"No thanks," I say. "I have plenty of packing of my own." I take a breath before asking her about what her plans are for dinner. For just a second, I hear Chris' voice in my ear telling me not to say anything and let it all figure itself out.

"Do you need something, Sarah?" she asks.

"Just wondering about what you were thinking for dinner." Like a cartoon, Chris' talking head in my mind makes a face and pops like a balloon.

"This has already been discussed, Sarah. You and your brothers are going to sit with me this year. As for your sister, I have no aspirations, but it would be nice."

The certainty with which she says this makes my stomach drop. I was fully on board with her this morning, but now I'm not sure any outcome will work out. I'll end up with an ulcer no matter what happens. My concern must show clearly on my face.

"Is there a problem, Sarah?"

I hadn't really thought about it until now, but I really don't want to be the one to tell Maman about Dad buying a place on the lake. There's a chance she knows already, but I can't be sure. I'm not ready to be that messenger.

"I'm sure it will be fine, but you know how the boys are."

"Well I have faith in you Sarah," she says with a smile, and then turns back to pack some more.

"I'll talk to you later then," I say with some sarcasm. Just as I'm coming down the stairs out of her cabin, I see Telle walking from the main lodge.

"Hey sis!" she says. It's a complete déja vu from the night after she had first arrived. I can't stop asking the exact same thing I did then.

"Where were you?" I'm hoping I sound a bit less confrontational than I did the last time.

"The room I'm going to use while I stay here opened up, so Stanley said that I could move in whenever I wanted. Since I was out kind of late, I decided to sleep there last night." She pauses and looks at me. I know what I want to say. '*Why didn't you text someone to let them know where you were?*' But I also know we've been down that road before and it's a dead end.

“Is it nice?” I ask.

She looks at me and smiles, gives a little nod, then answers. “No. It’s a little shit hole.”

“Well that’s nice!” I say with a laugh.

“How’s mom doing?” she asks.

“Fine, I think. I’m just trying to figure out dinner tonight. Please tell me you’ll be eating with Maman.”

“Don’t think so,” she says. “I’ll be in the kitchen helping out and learning what they want me to do.”

“Really?” I ask, unable to hide my disappointment.

“Dave said he wants me to start for real on Saturday for the first dinner of the new week, so I have to get used to the place tonight.”

Maman comes out of the cabin with Bijou. I don’t know if she heard us talking and is trying to look casual, or she genuinely didn’t know we were out here, but she doesn’t acknowledge us until she’s reached the bottom of the stairs. She looks up and sees Chantelle.

“Well, hello Chantelle,” she says icily.

“Mom,” Telle replies with similar frostiness.

I should say something. I could bring up something completely unrelated to throw them both off. I could talk about Daniel; he’s always a good distraction. I could tell them both I’m pregnant! That would do the trick.

“You didn’t come back last night?” Maman asks. I missed my chance to speak.

“I did not,” Chantelle replies very dryly.

“It might have been considerate to let someone know where you were.”

“Plenty of people knew where I was.”

“Just not your family,” mom adds in that tone filled with disappointment.

"Knock it off mom," Chantelle says. Her own tone and body language are clearly sending the message that she's getting serious now. "Stanley let me know last night that my room was free. I wasn't intending on staying there, but then you were so fucking unpleasant to be around during the stupid euchre tournament that I didn't feel like being here. By the time I went there, you were long asleep and it wouldn't have mattered."

Maman starts to speak, but Telle just gets louder. "And I think it's best if you drop the whole concerned parent shit. I don't have to report to you. I'm here to grab my stuff." With that, she walks into the cabin and lets the screen door slam shut.

Maman looks down at Bijou, gives a little tug on the leash and walks off, not looking in my direction. Once again, I'm left with nothing really to say.

If I follow my mom, I don't know what to say to her. I can't really promise her that the boys will be there for dinner. I have no idea what to say about Telle because I kind of agree with her for once. If I go and talk to Chantelle, I have no idea what I'm going to get. She's clearly pissed now, and when she gets like that, I usually end up making it worse. I feel like going and curling up under a blanket and sleeping until morning.

I decide to talk to Telle. Maybe I can calm her a little. When I go inside, she's stuffed most of her clothes into her duffle bag, and has moved into the bathroom.

"Do you think you'll work here all summer?" I ask, just trying to make some conversation.

"Why? Don't you think I can make it through the summer?" she snaps.

"No. I was actually just asking," I answer, trying not to sound confrontational.

She turns from the counter where she's packing things into her makeup bag. Our eyes meet. I imagine my expression reveals that I have no clue what to say, and that I'm walking on eggshells. She looks down and says, "Sorry." Then she turns back to packing. "I know you didn't mean anything by it. She just makes me very mad sometimes."

I'm completely floored. This is a bit of maturity that I haven't often seen from her. "It's alright," I say. There's a moment of silence between us that I just can't help but try to fill.

"Are you excited a bit? Could be fun working here. I know I always wanted to."

"Why didn't you? I thought you planned to work here with Lisa when you were both nineteen."

"Yeah, that was always the plan, but plans don't always work out, right? She got a boyfriend and spent that summer in Europe. And dad got me that job as an intern with one of his friends."

"Now I'm living your dream!" she jokes.

"Are you excited?" I ask again.

"I don't know if *excited* is the right word," she says, stopping to give it some thought. "It'll be nice to be away from everything for a while. I actually doubt I'll make it through the whole summer. I can see myself getting cabin fever pretty quickly."

"You have your car though. You can come and go whenever."

"Yeah," she shrugs.

"And you're not with the rest of the staff. That's nice. How did you swing that anyway?"

"Dave suggested I ask Stanley about a room. He has one up there too, and he says they're rarely full. This week being so busy is not the norm. Stanley didn't seem to mind."

"I can't imagine you staying with all the rest of the waitresses and chamber maids," I say with a chuckle.

"Oh, I'd fucking kill someone!" she laughs. She grabs her bags and takes a look around. Without any sense of sadness, she's ready to go.

"Any chance of you being able to sneak out and come and sit for a few minutes for dinner?" I ask. I know it's probably too soon to be asking, but I want to plant the seed in her head.

"Doubt it," she says pretty confidently. "But I'm sure I'll be out for Karaoke afterwards. Let's have a drink."

"For sure," I answer.

She turns and walks off towards the main lodge. She's always been quick with goodbyes.

My phone buzzes.

How's it going there? Had a talk with dad and Daniel. Meet you at 1:00 at your place?

Not going too great here. 1:00 is fine.

Chapter Forty Three

STANLEY

"HOW'S ALL THE setup going Blaine?" I ask as I look around the dining room.

"Fabulous," he answers. "What do we do again if one of the family guests is 18 years old? Kid's glass or wine glass?"

Since it's our 75th anniversary, I ordered some souvenir glasses for all the guests. One of Melissa's nieces designed a logo with our name and the year; it's really professional looking. We decided on beer mugs for the men, wine glasses for the women, and some cool kid's mugs for the little ones. I know some people might think that's sexist, but tough beans. If they don't like it, they don't have to take the glass!

"Go with the kid's cup for now. If they want to change it, we can do that after dinner."

"I certainly hope the staff will be receiving one of these bad boys at the end of the summer, Stanley. This might be worth something someday," Blaine jokes as he holds up one of the beer mugs.

"We'll see about that. Melissa and I might have something planned."

We're actually getting these really nice beach towels made up for the staff. We'll make sure there are enough mugs left over for them too.

"This is looking nicer each week, Stanley," Michelle says, coming over to put her arm around my shoulders. "The guests are going to love it."

"Well our guests keep us in business. We gotta butter our bread on the right side."

All the staff is here a little early tonight. We have some decorations to hang up, and everyone has decided to dress up extra nice for tonight's dinner. I asked Blaine, Zack, and Michelle to say a few words on behalf of the staff. They did a great job the last two weeks. I asked Dave to come out and say something, but he said he preferred to stay in the kitchen. I never actually expected him to come out, but it was worth a spin.

This week is one of the special weeks for me; so many of the guests have been coming here for such a long time that they really are like family. Every week kind of has its own vibe to it. Some weeks, the guests keep mostly to themselves. Other weeks, everyone has just bonded and it's like one, big party. We're spending a little extra time decorating this week.

"You wearing a dress tonight, there Stacey?" Blaine asks as he's unpacking boxes of glassware.

"The only dress I own," she answers. "I'm not much of a dress girl, as you've obviously noticed, but I do have one that I wear to weddings, and to church on Christmas and Easter. It's not even a hand-me-down either! My parents bought it for me when I was sixteen. Before that, I had to wear my sister's old dress for my grade eight graduation."

"I wish I'd know," Michelle says. "I have a couple of dresses I could have brought in that would fit you."

"That's super sweet. I might take you up on that for *next* week's final dinner!"

"Sounds good," Michelle says.

Stacey has been a nice addition to the staff. I hate to see anything bad happen to Ariel obviously, but having Stacey here has almost calmed things down a bit. She has such a positive energy about her that it's hard to be negative for too long. I think Michelle has even started to take a liking to her. Michelle rarely likes the other waitresses.

"You've had the same *one* dress for two years?" Courtney asks, stopping what she's doing at her table nearby.

"Wow," Christine adds. I don't think she means it in a mean way.

"As I said, I'm not really a dress person," Stacey admits. "I was actually pretty disappointed when I opened the dress. I was hoping for a dirt bike."

From behind the bar, Blaine gives a laugh. "That's awesome."

Stacey shrugs her shoulders and smiles. Courtney looks like she's just heard Stacey say something truly shocking; like she has a tail, or her parents are aliens. Courtney walks into the kitchen, looking at Christine and rolling her eyes on the way by. I'm starting to see a bit more of what Michelle has mentioned over the course of this week. This is Courtney's third year here and she is definitely acting like she's more comfortable in her position.

The wait staff has a good handle on the setup, so I move into the kitchen to see how Dave and the boys are doing. When I walk in, the first person I see is Chantelle LaPointe. She and Dave came to me yesterday and asked if she could work in the kitchen. There wasn't much I could say; we really could use another person in there, and if Dave is alright with it, considering how picky he is about his kitchen, then she's got the job.

"Hi Stanley," she says, carrying a box from the walk-in.

"Hi Chantelle. I didn't realize you were starting today. Nice to see you."

"Dave wanted me to have a day where I could 'get used to things' before I start in tomorrow. Guess he thinks I don't know what I'm doing."

"Not true," Dave calls from the back. "You're already better than these two," he says, gesturing with his head towards Pascal and Greg.

"Oh, see! Now why you gotta be like that old man," Greg jokes.

"What can I say," Chantelle boasts, jokingly. "Guess you boys had better step up your game."

"Oh, we will," Pascal chimes in. He turns and flips the spatula he's holding a full rotation, catches it by the handle and gives a wink.

"That's great. How long do you practice that at home on Friday nights?" Chantelle says.

"Ohhh! BURN!" Greg exclaims.

Everyone, including Dave, has a laugh. I walk out of the kitchen and give my head a scratch. A couple of days ago, the staff was fighting; and walking through the kitchen was like crossing a mine field. Now, everyone is laughing and joking around. If there's one thing about people that I've learned after doing this for twenty-seven years, it's that you never know what's going to happen and that you have to enjoy the highs when they are here, because there will be lows.

Since everything seems to be running smoothly, I decide to pop outside and get some work done before Melissa makes me have a shower and get all dressed up.

The early afternoon sun is shining down and people are out

enjoying it. It's almost always a nice day on Fridays; the Resort gods like to give the guests one last day to soak up the sunshine.

I like to spend a couple of hours cleaning the place up on Fridays because most guests, being all dressed up, decide to take pictures after dinner. I take all the best flower pots to set them up around back, and I usually give the back lawn a cut.

By the time I'm done, almost everyone is out enjoying the beach. There's a volleyball game happening. Kids are out on paddle boats. Even the group of ladies that usually sit inside are out on the big back patio.

If it were up to me, I'd cancel the Friday dinner and let people stay outside all day. I hate speaking in front of people, and it's become a tradition for me to make a speech at the final dinner. I usually use the same one, with a couple of tweaks, but I feel the pressure to make it special this year. My first two speeches this year have been alright, but I want to step it up a bit this week. I've written a few things down, but I still have to put it together. Melissa promised she'd help me. I don't think I can put it off any longer, so I make my way home.

Chapter Forty Four

BLAINE

DINNER IS FINALLY set up; at least my part. I fucking hate Fridays! It's by far my busiest day. Everyone is ordering all kinds of wine and shit for dinner, so I'm running around smiling and schmoozing with all the guests. It's like the voting for a league MVP in the NBA or the NFL. People remember the end of the season far more than the beginning. This dinner is my chance to remind everyone how much they love me so that they'll up the tip money tomorrow morning. Some guests tip me tonight, so that extra little effort to make them feel special might persuade them throw in an extra twenty.

On top of that, this year we have to waste time putting up a bunch of decorations. Stanley is really pumped up about this 75th anniversary. Hopefully his speech this week will be better than the last couple. He is **so** not a public speaker. Plus he asked a couple of staff to speak too. Listening to Michelle and Zack speak to everyone is like listening to my grade twelve English teacher lecturing about the meaning of whatever Shakespeare play I didn't read. Thank God the guests get at least one normal speaker when I take my turn.

And then Stanley goes and has the brilliant idea of making our order a day early. I had to be up way too early this morning to restock the bars and unpack all the shit. If I want to be on my game, I'm going to have to have a little nap.

"Alright people! If everything is ready to go here, I'm going to get a little beauty sleep before I have to be beautiful."

"Shit! That could take a while. See you in August," Rob says.

"Funny! I guess I set myself up for that one."

I cut through the kitchen to see what's up in there. For once, there's music playing and it doesn't feel like the usual morgue. *Sultans of Swing* seems like a strange choice, but the kitchen crew are kind of weird cats.

"Smells good in here, boys," I say as I walk in. There's some kind of sauce simmering on the stove that smells really good. I notice Chantelle is there. "And girl," I add, flashing her a smile. She looks down and starts chopping something.

Since our night of passion, she hasn't really given any signs of wanting to hook up again. She did tap me on the ass in front of her family a couple of days later, which was really awkward, but any efforts on my part to hit on her have been completely ignored.

"What's cookin'?" I ask, looking directly at Chantelle.

"Red wine sauce," she answers without looking up.

On my way over to where she's standing, I pass by the pot on the stove to give it a whiff. Just as I'm about to lift the lid, Dave calls over from his station. "Don't touch that lid."

"You didn't even look up from what you were doing," I call. "Are you some kind of kitchen ninja?"

"Sauce needs to simmer without being disturbed," he explains, very briefly.

"Well it smells fantastic, buddy."

I walk over to where Chantelle is working.

"So we're going to have you around for a while," I say quiet enough for only her to hear. "That's great."

"It is."

"I was thinking about going to have a little nap. Care to join me?"

"No thanks," she answers, not looking up. "No time to 'nap'." With the last word, she looks up. Once again, she has me thinking. Her face is expressionless, but I swear I see that slight playfulness in her eyes.

"Well if you change your mind, the offer doesn't expire."

"Good to know," she says flatly, and gets back to work.

"Dave," I call out on my way to the door. "I'm having whatever is in that pot this evening."

*

On my way back to the cabin, I see Daniel talking to Courtney by his car. They seem in a pretty intense conversation, so I keep walking, looking down at my phone. It's been a bit weird seeing Daniel after our afternoon adventure with Gabriella up the road. He was right about her; she's a freak. She was not at all shy about me being there. In fact, she fucking loved it; it was like Daniel had brought her a diamond necklace or something.

The whole business of doing *my* business with another dude's junk swinging all around sure was different at first, but it didn't take long to forget about it all and have some fun. We had a little debrief the next day, but there's not much more to say, so now we both just kind of act normal; which feels kind of abnormal if you know what I mean.

It struck me yesterday that I've had a sexual encounter with two members of the Lapointe family this week. Maybe I can persuade older sister Sarah to give me a blow job or something, so that I can have the Lapointe hat trick. Judging by the way she looks at me, especially since I fucked her little sister, I doubt that's going to happen. And it's looking more and more like it won't happen with Chantelle again either. Time to focus back on Christine.

The cabins are quiet when I get back. The kitchen boys are working away and won't be back before dinner. Zack is around somewhere. That guy is perfect for his job; he's constantly talking to someone or organizing something.

I close the blinds, set my alarm, and get into bed. I'm hoping to get an hour or so before I have to have a quick shower and get my game face on.

Chapter Forty Five

CRAIG

"HAS SARAH CALMED down a bit?" Terry asks.

"Pretty much. Daniel's driving her crazy though. He's not committing to anything for dinner."

"Why does he *do* that?"

"I think it's just a control thing. He doesn't want to say anything for certain so that he can change his mind at any time. You know how he's always fifteen minutes late for everything. He likes to walk in and be in charge."

"Is that why you're usually ready fifteen minutes early for everything? To balance things?" Terry jokes.

"Probably," I admit. I actually hate being late when there's a set time we're supposed to be somewhere. I have a feeling tonight's dinner is going to be another occasion where Terry takes forever to get ready.

"Well, I'm going to have a nice, long shower," she says, as if reading my mind.

With time to kill, I decide to go for a walk. I turned in pretty early last night then had a nice sleep in this morning.

We had a boat ride and spent time on the beach this afternoon. All in all, it was a nice, relaxing day; it's put me in the mood to take a few pictures. Every year, I take out my camera and see if I can come up with some creative shots. I've got quite a few saved that I plan on making into a book one day. I like walking around with the camera in my hands; and not some little phone camera, but my Nikon. I find it changes my perspective. Most of the time, as I'm sure we all do, I just kind of walk through life looking at things through the lens of how they relate to me. But with a camera in my hands, I find myself looking at people and objects interacting completely separate from myself.

As I step out onto the balcony, the first thing I notice is Terry's bikini draped over the rail of the porch. Next to it is a bottle of suntan lotion. In the distance, through the trees, you can just see the lake glistening as the late afternoon sun hits the water. I position the shot so the bikini and lotion are in the bottom left, framing the view of the lake. The beauty of digital photography is that I can take twenty-five shots, slightly different in angle and exposure, in a few seconds. Looking them over, I think I may have just taken the cover of my book.

I walk up the little alley that leads from our cabin to the main road. On the left are five or six cabins. They're much more secluded than the ones by the main lodge. Both sides of the road, particularly the right side, have tons of trees that shade the whole area. On that forest side, there's a little ravine that runs just next to the alley. I stop at a small clump of rocks that's making the water bubble and change course. Up close, it looks like rapids in a river. I try to get a shot, but the lack of light makes it tough. Someone more advanced with a camera could probably get the shot I want.

The next half an hour is spent trying to get some creative photos, but none are as good as that first one. I'm on my way back home from the other side of the Resort, cutting across the lawn, when I see Carrie and Marc, the Toronto couple, hanging out on the beach with their kids. The kids are playing in the sand at the feet of two loungers where Carrie and Marc are lying, holding hands between the two chairs. They're both wearing hats. From a fair distance, I take a shot from behind the chairs. Their forms are mostly silhouetted against the bright sky. It's a beautiful picture that could be an ad for some tropical vacation. When I walk over and show it to them, they like it enough that they pass on their e-mail for me to send it to them.

I love taking candid photos of people, but I always make a point of showing them after I take them. I don't want to be known as the creepy guy who's always taking pictures of people.

*

When I get back to the cabin, Terry is showered, dressed, and is putting on her make up. She's wearing a summer dress that goes just above her knees. It's a light, flowy material that hugs her form perfectly.

"Hey, babe," she turns from the mirror and says. "Did you get some nice pictures?"

"I think so," I answer, walking over to her. I put my hands on her hips and lean down to kiss her. She's still holding some kind of makeup brush, but she returns my kiss with her hands by her side.

"Someone's frisky," she says with a smile.

"How about we have a little play time before dinner?" I suggest.

"I've spent an hour getting ready!" she protests. "I'm not getting all dirty again now. You'll just have to wait."

"But I like you dirty!"

"I know you do," she says with a sexy look.

"You know you always do this to me," I tell her.

"Do what?" she asks innocently.

"I get all turned on before we go out, then I'm thinking about sex all night."

"That's a good thing!" she says. "Anticipation is exciting."

"So's a quicky before dinner."

She laughs, kisses me again, then goes back to her makeup.

After a fairly quick shower, I put on the best clothes I brought; a pair of dress pants and a short sleeved button down. I completely forgot to pack nice shoes, so it'll have to be my black converse. That will drive Sarah and my mom crazy. We have a couple of minutes so Terry and I decide to have a quick drink before going to dinner. The final plan is that Terry and I will eat with Sarah, Chris, Mom, and possibly Daniel. Dad and Anette are going to sit with Stanley and Melissa tonight. It actually works out perfectly that mom will be able to have us all there.

After our drink, we stroll down to the dining room. Sarah and Chris are already there with mom. As we approach the table, I can tell there's a bit of tension.

"Hey all," I greet them.

"Hey Craig," Chris answers.

"Hello, dears," mom says. We both go over and give her a hug.

"How are you doing Sarah?" I ask as we sit down. She doesn't look too pleased.

"Fine. Just a bit tired."

"Did everyone have a nice day?" Terry asks, making conversation. There's a moment of silence before Chris answers.

"I had a very nice nap."

"I think once you get longer than three hours, it's not a nap anymore," Sarah says, clearly irritated.

"Well whatever it was, it was nice."

"How about you mom? You have a nice day?" I ask.

"Yes, very nice dear," she answers in an offhand way.

"Although it would be nice to be able to have a family dinner with *everyone* here at once." She shoots a glance and a forced smile in Sarah's direction. I know exactly what's coming.

"Are you implying that I should have done something more to get everyone here?" Sarah challenges. "Because you could have gotten on the phone and talked to Daniel yourself you know."

"I don't think that's what your mom was saying, Sarah," Chris chimes in. The look Sarah gives him shuts him right up. With one little question, I know now that I've opened up a whole can of worms.

"Last I heard, Daniel is coming," I say, hoping to cool things down a bit.

"Great. We'll all wait with bated breath," Sarah says.

"Although it sucks she can't be here now, it's kind of exciting that Chantelle is working in the kitchen," Terry says.

"I don't know if *exciting* is the word," mom says.

"You don't like her working here?" Terry asks.

"Oh no, I'm sure it will be fine."

"Maman doesn't think Chantelle will stick it out for long. Isn't that right?" Sarah says, directing her question directly at mom.

"It would not be out of character for her to get bored and leave, dear," mom answers in a patronizing way. "I would just hate for her to leave poor Stanley in the lurch."

"Maybe she'll surprise you and make it work," Sarah snaps.

Blaine approaches the table at a good time. "Hey gang," he says. "Hard to believe the week is almost over."

"It's been interesting," Chris says.

"For sure," Blaine responds. "What can I get for you?" He directs his question to mom.

"Shall we get a bottle?" I ask nobody in particular.

"I think I'll just have a Perrier for now," mom answers.

"That sounds like a good idea," Sarah adds.

Chris looks at me and shrugs. "I'll have a glass or two."

"Alright, how about a bottle of the Shiraz?" I ask.

"Sounds good," Blaine says. "Should be great with the steak this evening. I walked in the kitchen earlier and they were working on a wine sauce that smelled like Heaven. I think Chantelle was working away on it actually."

His reference to Telly doesn't get the reaction he expects. Mom looks down at the menu. Sarah gives a forced, little smile.

"Can you put that on *our* bill, Blaine?" Chris says. "We're in Blue Jay."

"You don't have to do that," I protest.

"I know. You treated us the other day to that fancy bottle. Let us get this one."

"Shiraz with three glasses, then?" he asks Terry.

"Sure," she responds.

"And a couple of Perriers?" he turns to Sarah and mom.

"Thank you Blaine," Mom says, looking up briefly.

When he leaves, there's an awkward silence that hangs over the table. It's that silence when a family has spent some time together and there are little tensions that have flared up. Most small talk topics have been discussed. Nobody really wants to get into any of the shit that's festering, so there's not much to say. As always, Terry speaks up. There are many things that I love about her, and her ability to talk and put people at ease is one of them. I suck at it, but she's a natural.

"Does anyone know if there have been any bears around this year?" she asks.

"I don't think so," Chris answers.

"I think I heard something rustling around our cabin last night. I peeked out the window, and I swear I saw a shape that looked like a bear."

"Really?" Sarah asks. "That's scary."

"Did you mention it to Stanley?" mom asks. "I know he likes to know about any sightings."

"Well, I can't be sure it was a *sighting*," she says. "I'd had a few drinks and I was half asleep." She looks at Chris and smiles when she says that she had a few drinks last night. Once again, Sarah shoots him a glare that he seems to purposely avoid seeing. For a second, there's a strange vibe. I think the tension between Sarah and Chris somehow involves Terry.

"Yeah, I think we can chalk that one up to the booze," I say jokingly. Terry had come back pretty pissed last night. I wouldn't trust anything she saw.

"Could be, but I definitely saw a shadow or something."

"Could it have been a raccoon, or a deer or some other animal?" Chris asks.

"I guess," Terry admits. "It could even have been someone walking."

Across the room, I see Daniel, dad, and Annette arriving with Stanley and Melissa. Daniel says good bye to them all and makes his way over to our table.

"Folks," he says, sitting down next to Terry.

"Nice of you to show," Sarah says with contempt.

"Who's in for a bottle of wine?" Daniel asks, completely ignoring Sarah's comments. "My treat."

"We have one on the way," I say.

"Excellent. I'll get the second one. How are you mom?"

"I'm fine dear. It's nice to have everyone here now."

Once again, the look on Sarah's face shows exactly what she's thinking. Daniel's arrival puts mom in a good mood. He's always been able to do that. I know all parents say that they love their children equally, and I'm sure mom tells herself that; but in truth, Daniel has always been her special boy. When Sarah was born, mom didn't really know what she was doing. Sarah was apparently a very difficult baby. When Daniel was born, Sarah was two and a half, and starting to be a sweet little lady. Both my parents describe Daniel as being the easiest baby ever. Mom bonded much more with him; and his birth coincided with a time of joy in her relationship with dad. By the time I came along, the first cracks in their relationship started to appear. And poor Telly didn't stand a chance.

"Yup, everything's great *now*," Sarah says sarcastically.

Blaine's arrival at the table makes it that Sarah's dig fades off without comment. He presents the bottle to Chris and pours him a taste. After Chris has taken a sip, Blaine pours a glass for the rest of us, including an extra glass he brought for Daniel.

After we've given our orders to Michelle, we settle into a kind of superficial, tense conversation; sharing events from the past couple of days. We're still waiting for our food when Stanley and Zack start setting up a microphone to the dining room sound system. It's definitely not a state of the art set up; whoever is using it ends up sounding muffled and far away.

The wait staff continues to dart around as Stanley starts in on the speeches.

Testing. Whoa, down a bit Zack! Sorry about that folks. One of these years, we'll get ourselves a new stereo in here. I think it's probably seventieth on the to-do list (laughs). Well, here we are again. It's been so nice to catch up with all of you this week. Hard to believe the week is almost over (groans). As you all know, this is our 75th year in business (claps). For any newcomers who don't know our story, my grandfather, Bill, bought this piece of land in 1940. My dad then ran the place for twenty years. Then I took over (light cheers and whistles). Sorry to those of you who have heard this all many times (We love you Stanley!). One thing that many of you might not realize is that while this year is a big one for the Resort, the next couple of years will be special for us too. Next year will mark the twenty-eighth year Melissa and I have been in charge, which will mean that I will have run this place longer than either my dad or pops did (clapping). To think we've been doing this now for twenty-seven years is amazing. Over those years, we've come to meet so many special people. I'm sure you'll think I say this every week, but I don't; this week is very special to me for all the friends we've made (We love you Stanley!). I love you all too (Pause). Part of running this place is seeing faces coming back, but also some that leave for whatever reason. Hopefully we'll continue to see all of you for years to come. Stéphane, I hope you'll be sure to come by and visit any time.

With the last sentence, Stanley turns to dad and raises his glass. My dad and Annette both smile and do the same. I look over at my mom. Without looking away from Stanley, her face hardens. She is absolutely fuming and confused at the same time. Nobody has told her that my dad bought a place and won't be coming back.

So I hope you all have enjoyed your week. We had some nice weather for early in the summer (claps and cheers). What with this being a big anniversary year, I asked some of our staff to say a few words. So enough of me. I don't want to turn this show off the road. I'll hand you over to Zack.

As the microphone is being passed over, with static and feedback, mom turns to Sarah and asks in a voice which is both a whisper and a scream.

"What did Stanley mean by that?"

"Why do you look at me?" Sarah says, a bit too loudly. "Why don't you ask Daniel?"

This time, Daniel turns and looks at Sarah. He can't ignore that one. Trying not to be rude to Zack, who's starting his speech, he leans in to speak softly. "Dad was saying that he's probably not going to be coming back for the week next year. He was saying that it's more and more difficult to find the time."

With that, he picks up his glass of wine, leans back, and looks at Zack making his speech. It's mostly the truth, but he hasn't told her about the place dad's buying. Sarah and I exchange a glance. I'm not going to be the one to add information.

When Michelle arrives from the kitchen with our food, Chantelle is helping her carry things out to us.

"Look at you Telly," I say. "How's your first day?"

"Good. I haven't really done much." She sets down a plate in front of mom, who doesn't even look up at her. "I'm just getting used to how things are run."

After passing everything out, she zips off to the kitchen again. Michelle makes sure everyone has what they need.

"Bon Appétit!" Daniel says, digging into his steak.

Mom doesn't touch anything. Instead, she's looking over at Stanley's table. When dad excuses himself from the table, she stands up, walks over to him as he walks towards the washrooms, and says something in his ear. He turns and answers her; nothing too long, just a couple of words. She glares at him a moment, raises her finger and says something to him. Without waiting for an answer, she turns and walks out. Dad stands for a minute, watching her go; he glances back towards Annette and Stanley, and then continues to the washrooms.

Everyone at the table watches the interaction except Daniel, who is busy scooping some hot mustard onto his plate.

"What do you think she said?" I ask Sarah.

"I don't know!" she snaps.

"Relax," I mistakenly say.

"Relax?" she says loudly. "That's easy for the two of you." She gestures towards Daniel. "You never have to deal with any of this."

"What's the problem?" Daniel asks.

"Why didn't you tell her?" Sarah asks Daniel.

"Tell her what? I said dad wasn't coming back."

"So who's going to have to talk to her about the rest of it? Me!"

It's Michelle's turn to take the mic.

I'm not much for making speeches, so I'll keep it short. I've been here for seven years now (claps and cheers). Thank you. I'm so grateful to Stanley for giving me the chance to be a part of all this. I get a chance to see all the behind the scenes stuff that Stanley does to make this place special (Stanley!). He also makes it a very special place to work. So from all the wait staff, I want to say thank you to Stanley for all he does, and we hope you all had an amazing week. I hope to see you all again next year. (Applause)

"I think you're being a bit dramatic, Sarah," Daniel says.

"Don't you dare tell me I'm being dramatic," Sarah snaps.

"Whoa, easy Sarah," Chris says, gently putting his hand on her arm.

"Don't!" she says, pushing his arm away and standing up. She stands for a moment with tears forming in her eyes before storming off.

"Boy! I sure am glad I chose this table to eat at," Daniel says with a laugh.

"I should probably go and talk to her," Chris says, standing up and setting his napkin on his chair. He gestures towards his food. "Don't let them take this just yet. I'm hoping to be back for it."

After Chris leaves, I look over at Daniel.

"What?" he says. "That was not my fault!" He puts both hands in the air.

"You didn't exactly help things," I say.

"What am I supposed to do? Start a whole big explanation, with all the details, right in the middle of Zack talking?"

"Whatever," I say.

Blaine steps up to the microphone.

Hello everyone. I hope you're all enjoying your meals.

Daniel puts his hands to his mouth and shouts, "Blaino!"

Thank you! (points at Daniel). Well, it truly has been a pleasure this week …

Chapter Forty Six

MICHELLE

IT FEELS GOOD to get my speech out of the way. I hate public speaking, so I keep it short and sweet. Afterwards, I pop over to where Stanley is seated and give him a hug.

"That was lovely Michelle," Melissa compliments me from the table.

"Oh yes, very nice," says the other woman at the table, Annette. She's the second wife of Stéphane LaPointe, considerably younger than he is; but I guess that's usually the way it goes. I never really got to know her, mostly because in the dining room, I've always been responsible for Marion's table since the split. Without knowing her very well, I just don't really like her.

"Thanks," I answer politely.

As I'm leaving the table, Stacey comes up behind me.

"That was really good Michelle!" she says, putting her hand on my back.

"Thanks. I hate that shit though."

"No! You did great."

Blaine starts talking as I do a scan of my tables. Everyone

has their food; the Miller family looks to be done and waiting for some desert. Looking over to the side of the dining room, against the big bay windows, I notice several people have left Marion LaPointe's table; only her sons are left with Craig's girlfriend. After grabbing some dishes from the Millers, I pass by to see if there's a problem. There are three plates that haven't been touched.

"Everything alright here?" I ask, gesturing towards the food.

"Yeah, just some family drama," Craig answers.

"Would you like me to pack anything up?" I ask.

"We'll give it a couple of minutes, then maybe."

"Alright. Let me know if there's anything you need.

As I'm turning away, Chris comes back to the table.

"You're not taking my food are you?" he asks.

"No, no. Just checking in."

"Anyone else coming back?" Craig asks Chris.

"Don't think so. She was *not* interested in talking to me."

"Maybe I should go and try," Daniel says with a laugh. Craig shoots him a dirty look. I feel a bit like I'm intruding on some family stuff.

"Should I leave these two then?" I ask, pointing at the other two plates.

"I think you can take them," Chris says, taking a bite of steak.

"I'll pack it up for them."

I'm not too sure what happened, but clearly the LaPointe ladies are pissed about something. You never know what to expect with them.

Blaine is still going as I pass by on my way to the kitchen. He's recounting some event that happened at the bar this week, which is right on the cusp of being inappropriate for young children. As much as I hate having to speak in front of all the guests, Blaine seems to love it more.

The kitchen is buzzing when I come in to deal with the dishes.

"How's everyone doing?" I call out.

"Busy as shit," Greg answers.

"Really?" I ask, looking around. "Don't you have extra hands in here today?"

"Yeah, but these crème brûlée things take forever," says Pascal. "And with the speeches happening, everyone is finishing dinner and ordering desert at the same time."

"Actually, if we didn't have Chantelle here, we'd be fucked," Greg adds.

"Thanks, champ," Chantelle says.

"Quite a day to start, I guess," I say as I pack up some food and scrape my dishes before putting them in the washer. It's a small thing to do, and it takes some time, but helping out the kitchen crew is so important. When the people in the back don't like you, waitressing can be brutal.

"I prefer to be busy. Beats standing around," Chantelle says.

"Not sure what happened at your mom's table after we dropped off the food, but when I went over there, her and Sarah had left without touching anything."

"Not surprising," she shrugs. "My family is special."

"Well, I've always liked being in charge of your family table. You're all very nice."

"Yeah, but I guess it's the same with everyone. There's only so much of your own family that you can take. You get to see all the behind the scenes shit; kind of ruins the movie."

"Oh, it's like when I saw that show about how they made Monsters Inc. Totally ruined my dream of having a cool monster come out of my closet."

"Yeah, Pascal. It's *exactly* like that," Chantelle says.

"Everyone thinks their family is fucked up," Dave says from the back. "Which makes everyone's family fucked up!"

"That's deep Dave," Greg jokes.

"It's true though! Think about what most families are. You have parents who are trying to keep their own shit in order; paying bills, working, trying to find time for their own relationship. Then you throw in kids who are really only half-people."

"Half-people? That sounds harsh," Pascal says.

"Think about it. Kids can't do what they really want. They don't have a say. They're constantly told to do this or not to do that. Inevitably, they end up trying to distance themselves from their parents. The reality of parent-child relationships is that you're producing little humans who probably want to be the complete opposite of you. How much do most kids and parents have in common really? Family is connected by genetics; in most cases, that's about it. Then kids get married and new people enter the family. And what do *they* have in common with any other family members? They're just there because they're fucking one of the family."

"I guess that's one way of looking at it," I say.

"Don't get me wrong. It is what it is and it has to be. If it weren't that way, then we may as well just clone ourselves. Families are a hot mess of people, who probably wouldn't choose to be together otherwise, and who take each other for granted more than they do with people they don't know. But hopefully they also support each other more than they do other people. Family is always there because they have to be. You don't choose your family."

"So if every family is screwed up, then having a screwed up family is normal?" Pascal asks.

"Now *that's* deep!" Greg says.

"Some families really are pretty normal though," I add.

"Yeah, but don't those families always seem weird?" Pascal

says. I can't help but laugh. Even Chantelle, who always seems to be pretty serious, chuckles.

"Family is great in all its awkwardness. But the best family is the one you choose; the people you decide to surround yourself with; to joke with, argue with, and be around because you *want* to be around them. That's real family. If they happen to be the same as your blood family, then that's great. If not, they're still family."

Nobody says anything for a moment. He's right. I hope Scarlett will never feel she *has* to spend time with me because I'm her mom; and I hope I always want to be around her. But I know the rest of my family is seriously fucked up. I need to surround myself with people who matter.

Courtney comes into the kitchen with dishes of her own. She plops them down on the counter and looks at all of us. It's kind of funny that this is about the third time in the last couple of days where she has walked in right when there's a pause in some random conversation. She must think we're talking about her.

"Are my deserts ready yet?" she asks Greg, who is closest to her.

"Just about." He takes the tray he's been placing his deserts on and walks over to me.

"Here you go Michelle," he says as he hands me the tray with a little bow. He then walks back to his station and starts preparing the next tray. Courtney gives a frustrated grunt and walks out. As I'm on my way out, Greg gives me a wink.

Chapter Forty Seven

CHRIS

"I'M NOT TAKING anyone's side, Sarah. I just said that maybe things weren't as bad as you made them out to be."

I've been trying to talk sense to Sarah for about half an hour now. She's absolutely furious at the world, and when that happens, I am usually her punching bag.

"Oh, really?" she yells. "And that's not taking *everyone* else's side? How about for once, you just support *me*."

"Sarah, I support you. I just think that maybe you might have overreacted a bit. You got pissed at me for napping, you snapped at your mother several times, and you yelled at Daniel; although *he* probably deserved it."

"Just leave me alone," she says, turning to walk off towards the lodge. There's no point in going after her. Once she has a chance to cool off, I'll talk to her.

As I watch her walk away, I notice Stéphane and Annette walking across the lawn towards their cabin. They must have stayed at dinner quite a while. I ended up scarfing down my food and then going to find Sarah. I probably should have just taken my time.

Stéphane is walking a bit slowly; Annette has to wait for him a couple of times. It's probably that old hockey injury that he likes to talk about. He hurt his knee at the start of the first period of a big game. He went in the dressing room, took a shot of whiskey, taped it up and went on to score two goals. It was only afterwards that he learned he'd torn his ACL.

Just at the top of the little hill on the way to their cabin, Stéphane stops and puts one hand on his knee. Then as if in slow motion, he just kind of sits down on the grass. Annette turns and watches him. Before realizing there's a problem, I'm thinking what a strange place it is for him to have a seat. I see Annette waving her hands before the sound of her screaming gets to me.

"HELP! HELP!"

Not having reached the lodge yet, Sarah turns to look. She looks at me and we both run towards her dad.

"HELP! He collapsed," Annette calls as we approach.

"What happened?" I ask, slightly out of breath.

"I don't know. He was breathing a bit heavily, and then he just collapsed."

"Dad?" Sarah says, kneeling down to him. "What's the matter?"

"I don't know," he says in a pained voice. He's breathing heavily and wincing.

I take out my phone and call the police. I have no idea how long it takes to get an ambulance here. As I'm talking to the operator, Stanley comes tearing down the hill from the main lodge. For an older guy, he can really move. He goes straight to Stéphane.

"What happened?" he asks. Annette is looking terrified, covering her mouth, with tears starting to roll down her cheeks.

"He collapsed as they were walking back to their cabin. I saw from over there. I just called an ambulance."

"Forget it," Stanley says. "It's faster if I drive him. Ambulance will take at least twenty minutes just to get here. I can get him to Mercy in ten. It's small, but good."

Everyone looks a bit worried, but Stanley seems sure. Some other staff come down with the stretcher from the pool. Stéphane's breathing is still laboured, but softer. They load him into Stanley's van, with Annette and Zack joining him in the back. They're on the road within minutes.

A crowd is starting to gather outside now; many guests could see from the large windows of the dining room. We text Craig and Terry, who come out quickly.

"What happened?" Terry asks.

"Dad collapsed walking back to his cabin. I think it's a heart attack," Sarah says.

"We don't know that," I add.

"Did the ambulance get here *that* quickly?" Craig asks.

"Stanley took him."

"Do you know where he took him?"

"He said Mercy."

"You're going to have to drive, Sarah. I had a few glasses of wine," Craig says.

"No problem."

"We'll meet you out front in five minutes," I tell him.

"You don't have to come," Sarah says. "We could be a while."

"You sure? I think I should come."

"It's alright," Craig says. "Daniel and Telly will want to come. You two stay here," he adds, meaning Terry and me.

"Maybe we can come up later," Terry suggests.

"I'll go talk to Telle. You find Daniel," Sarah says.

"Got it."

The next ten minutes are spent running around. Sarah talks to Chantelle, who says she'll drive up herself in about half an hour. I help Sarah pack a little bag with some snacks, a couple of water bottles, and a book. She's running around like crazy, probably more as a way of avoiding thinking about her dad than actual necessity. She throws her bag over her shoulder and looks around. I walk up to her and wrap my arms around her. At first, she's rigid.

"He'll be OK."

"You don't know that," she says sadly. Her shoulders drop a bit as she relaxes and allows herself to be held.

"He's strong, Sarah; really strong."

"He looked so scared," she says as tears start to fall. "I've never seen him like that."

"You don't know what it is. It could be bad heartburn for all we know," I try to suggest, not really believing it myself.

"You know that's not true," she says quietly.

After a minute of allowing herself to cry, she gets herself together, wipes her eyes, and walks to meet Craig and Daniel.

I'm left alone in the cabin. I sit at the little table where Sarah and I eat lunch some days. This is the last thing she needs right now. Sarah is always tense during our week here; but this week, she's been exceptionally edgy. I hope the stress of all this doesn't affect the pregnancy. A close friend of hers had a miscarriage last year. Sarah talks about how she's still struggling with it. I know that Sarah would be completely devastated if that happened to her. The main reason she didn't want to work towards becoming a partner at her dad's firm was that she wanted to be able to start a family. As nervous as she is about the whole idea of becoming a mom, she wants it more than anything.

My thoughts are interrupted by a knock at the door. Since

most people just knock and then poke their heads in, I stand there looking at the door without saying anything; but nobody appears.

"Come in," I call.

When the door opens, it's Terry.

"Hey," she says, stepping inside.

"Hey."

"What are you up to?"

"Nothing really. Just sitting and thinking."

"Yeah, I was too. Then I didn't really want to sit and think alone."

"Good call," I say.

There's a weird, awkward silence for a couple of seconds. I have no idea what she's thinking, but I know that I'm feeling a bit guilty about some of the thoughts I've had about Terry this week. I doubt she has any similar thoughts, and I hope she hasn't picked up on anything. I don't really know Terry that well. Sarah and I don't get much of a chance to see her and Craig during the year, other than at special occasions, like Christmas or birthdays. I've had fun hanging out with her this week, and I'm pretty sure she's had a good time too. But Stéphane's health worries have put us together in circumstances that are a bit more serious. We've never really interacted this way.

"Guess you haven't heard anything," she says.

"Nope. I was thinking of texting Sarah, but I figured it might be more bugging her than helpful."

"I got that feeling too," she admits. "Kind of like I'd just be in the way if I went along."

"Yeah," I agree.

Another moment of silence.

"Are you going to go meet them?" she asks.

"I don't know. Does it make me an awful person if I say I don't really want to go?"

"Not if I'm not an awful person for agreeing."

"Are we both awful?" I ask.

"No," she says after thinking for a moment. "If Craig wanted me there, I'd go immediately."

"Me too," I agree.

"They're all there; plus Stanley and Annette."

"That's right."

"What would we do there? Get in the way."

"Absolutely!"

"Plus, I really don't like hospitals."

"No kidding," I agree again. "Hate 'em."

Moment of silence.

"I am going to text though; just to see what's up," she says, taking out her phone.

"Me too." I grab my phone and send Sarah a text.

How's everything? Let me know what's up when you get a chance. Love you.

Brief silence.

"Shall we sit outside?" I ask.

"Sure. Think we could have a beer?"

"Sounds good."

Chapter Forty Eight

PASCAL

THERE'S A DEFINITE downer mood around tonight. One of the older guests, Chantelle's dad, had a heart attack earlier and had to be rushed to the hospital. Stanley insisted on taking him in his van instead of waiting for an ambulance to come. I had to help carry the stretcher to the van. That was creepy; the guy looked in serious trouble. His face was white and he was struggling to get a breath. I guess he's still alive, but someone said that he has to have emergency surgery.

Friday night is supposed to be karaoke night; but I don't know if people are going to want to get drunk and sing after that. I guess he's pretty well known around here; they've been coming for years. It's weird because we were just talking about family with Chantelle in the kitchen. She was obviously concerned about her dad, but she wasn't like freaking out or anything. If my dad had a heart attack, I'd go mental.

I really don't feel like just sitting around tonight, so I'm out for karaoke. I texted Maria to see if she was going to be able to make it out. She had something to do with her family, but said she'd hopefully come after.

"Ok, skinny. You gonna be the first to sing something?" Blaine asks me.

"Holy crap, no!"

"Come on," he says, coming out from behind the bar. "I'll introduce you."

He starts to walk towards where the microphone and screen have been set up in the corner. There aren't many people in the bar, but there's no way I'm getting up and singing something.

"No way," I say, getting up and moving towards the door. "I will run out of here."

Christine and Rob, who are also sitting up at the bar, burst out laughing. It's funny, but I'm not joking. I will bolt out of here if he says I'm going to sing.

"Relax buddy," Blaine says with a laugh. "I wouldn't do that to you … yet. Maybe after a drink or two."

"Not much of a performer?" Christine asks.

"You could say that."

"Did you have some childhood trauma in a school play or something?" Rob asks.

"Did you piss yourself on stage?" Blaine pipes in.

"No, I didn't piss myself. I just don't really like being in front of lots of people."

"There are, like nine people here right now," Christine adds, scanning the room.

"Nine too many for me to get up and sing anything."

"So you're more an 'alone-in-the-shower' type of singer?"

"Oh, I'm a rock star in the shower."

"Maybe we should just set up a shower and have you in your birthday suit in front of everyone singing then," Blaine jokes.

"I think I've had that nightmare before, actually."

We all have a laugh. Blaine turns and walks up to the microphone. Just in case he decides to call me out, I stay standing and ready to run.

"Good evening everyone," Blaine starts. "Welcome. Zack isn't here at the moment, but he asked me to get things set up. I know those of you who know Stéphane LaPointe are concerned about him. I don't really have news other than he's at the hospital and they are looking after him. Hopefully we'll get an update soon, but I know his family is with him and he's getting good care. That being said, the equipment's all set up and ready to go if someone feels like getting things started for us this evening. No pressure, if we're not up to it right away; but we will turn on some tunes, and if you feel up to picking a song to sing, please do so."

There is some polite applause as he puts the microphone on the stand and walks off. He turns up the music that's playing so that people will hopefully get a bit more energy. Nobody gets up right away though. A few more guests show up over the next half an hour or so, and the mood starts to liven. I have a drink and check my phone; no message from Maria yet.

Eventually, a couple of guests get up and look over the song list. I've seen them out a few times; they usually get pretty drunk. I think their names are Darryl and Charlie. After looking for a couple of minutes, they seem excited to find something. It only takes a few notes for me to recognize the Spirit of the West classic, *Home for a Rest.* Charlie takes the slow intro lines before they both start singing. It's the perfect type of song to get things started; light but rowdy. By the end of the song, most of the bar is singing the chorus.

> *You'll have to excuse me, I'm not at my best*
> *I've been gone for a month, I've been drunk since I left…*

At the end of the song, while the music plays out, Charlie

and Darryl do a little square dance on the stage and everyone gives a cheer. The performance loosens people up a bit. Another guest gets up and sings a Mariah Carey song that she has no business trying to sing. I don't know if it's the singing that attracts people, or just the fact that it's the last night, but people start to filter into the bar. After the third song, the place is pretty full. Blaine is pouring drinks at a steady rate. I'm happy that he doesn't have time to think about embarrassing me.

I've had a couple of drinks already when Maria shows up. Without really thinking about what I'm doing, I get up and give her a kiss. She's clearly surprised, but doesn't pull away or anything. We've never really had any public displays of affection yet. I can feel my face going red as soon as I do it.

"Hey," I say lamely. "You look great."

"Thanks," she answers. "Sorry I took so long."

"No problem. I'm happy you came."

From next to us, Christine and Greg start making loud kissing sounds. My face goes a deeper shade of red.

"Do you want a drink?" I ask her, trying to hide my sudden nervousness.

"Yeah," she answers, slipping her hand around my waist and stepping up to the bar. She orders some kind of fruity cooler. There's no table free, so we sit up at the bar. Greg and Rob leave to play some pool. When Courtney comes in, she pulls Christine aside and they talk at a stand-up table across the bar. I don't think Christine really wanted to leave, but she did. Over the second half of the week, since Ariel left, the two of them seem to have been hanging out less and less. I think it might be because when Stacey arrived, she showed no interest in putting up with any of Courtney's crap. I think Christine saw this and realized maybe being Courtney's second wasn't very fun.

After watching karaoke for the last couple of weeks, I've

decided there's three groups of people. Some people pick classic songs that everyone knows; like *Single Ladies*, or *Sweet Caroline*. These people usually think they are good singers; and sometimes they are. An older man steps up and sings a really great *Mack the Knife*; it's corny but actually sounds pretty good. Another highlight is a version of *Up Where We Belong*; a pretty classic duet.

There's a second group of people who pick some pump up songs to get everyone hyped up. These people are usually a bit drunker and they want to be cheered, laughed at, and have people sing along. Usually they aren't very good, but they don't give a shit. Charlie and Darryl step back up again and thrill everyone with some *Tubthumping*; it's brutal, but they don't seem fazed.

I like to think that if I ever decided to sing a song, I'd be part of the third group; the people who pick a kind of obscure song that not everyone knows, but who do it well. The trick is to pick amazing song writers who don't have amazing voices. Not like Bob Dylan, because his voice is too unique; but someone like Paul Simon. I think if I had to sing right now, I'd go with *Late in the Evening*.

Sitting a bit back from the stage gives me and Maria a chance to talk while we have a couple of drinks and listen to the singers. I'm trying to have just enough to drink so that I feel good, but not so much that I'm going to end up puking on my shoes later. The music's still kind of loud; but as we're talking, I get to lean in and smell Maria's hair. It's stupid, but whatever shampoo she uses is really nice. I hope I smell alright.

"Are your parents coming to get you later, or are you staying here?" I ask. She doesn't usually stay on the Resort overnight.

"Nope. I'm staying here," she says with a smile.

"Cool."

"Are you trying to get rid of me?" she asks.

"NO. no. I was just wondering," I answer in a panic. It's not until she laughs that I realize she's joking. "You're mean. I almost had a heart attack."

"Sorry," she says, still laughing. "It's sweet that you're that concerned about me being offended though."

"Because you know it's the complete opposite of that. I was hoping you'd be staying."

"Yeah? Why?"

If I were at all smooth, I'd be able to think of something perfect to say here that would impress her; something sexy enough, but not crossing over into creepy. Something that shows I'm interested while also not sounding needy. My slightly drunk brain tries its best to scan through hundreds of movies to find a line that would be perfect. When that doesn't lead to anything, I try to remember something that I've witnessed some guy say to a girl over the years, in a bar or at a party. But somewhere in my head, the wiring that lets me do those things sparks and fizzles out. I got nothing.

"I really like hanging out with you and I hate it when you get picked up and we have to say goodnight at the end of a night."

Immediately after it leaves my mouth, I have no memory of what I just said. Maria looks at me for a second before smiling.

"Well, maybe we shouldn't have to say goodnight tonight."

I'm such an idiot that I don't even realize the meaning of what she's suggesting. My face must show the confusion that I'm feeling because she tilts her head, raises her eyebrows and smiles.

"I think that sounds nice," I say, still not entirely sure I know what she's saying. "If only we had somewhere to go."

"Well," she says shyly. She pauses for a second, looks at her drink, then back at me. "I know that the people that were in Sandpiper, the little cabin tucked away on the hill, checked out a day early and the next guests aren't coming until Saturday. I just cleaned it today."

My heart is suddenly beating ten times faster than normal. I feel like I've just climbed up a hundred flights of stairs. Trying to control myself, I ask, "Are you saying what I think you're saying?"

Once again, she raises her eyebrows just a little and smiles. In the same instant, I feel like I'm about to pass out, throw up, and explode.

"Are you sure nobody will be there?"

She smiles and nods.

"Can we go now?" I ask.

She laughs, and then nods.

Chapter Forty Nine

DAVE

IT'S THE FOURTH night in a row that I've stayed at the Resort. That might be a record. I've avoided going out because I don't want to see any of the people I usually get fucked up with. But all the people I know are people I usually get fucked up with. My attempt to get off all substances has failed miserably; I've taken something each day until today. I'm not counting the joint I smoked at two this morning. But not going out has at least stopped me from getting completely blitzed.

So I'm back on my porch, doing my penance. The temptation to take some pills before dinner was almost too much to handle; I ended up walking about half an hour away, sitting under a tree, looking out at the lake, and reading some Kante. With my brain feeling like a swarm of tsetse flies, it was brutal trying to focus. I didn't read half as much as I should have. But it distracted me from the feeling of needing to get high. Had I stayed in my room and tried to sleep, I wouldn't have been able to, so I would have ended up doing something.

Fucking pussy!

I light my tenth smoke. Each one is just an appetizer for the joint that's sitting on the counter in the bathroom. Its time is coming; there's no point in denying that.

My phone buzzes from the small, wicker table next to me. I'm pretty sure I can guess what the text is about.

Kickers?

It's G, letting me know he's got some Oxy. There's no need to respond. He'll be in touch again. And again. And again…

It's taken me a while to realize that I've surrounded myself with people who either want something from me, or want to get high with me. I've burned a lot of good bridges along the way. The conversation in the kitchen earlier made me see that I don't really give good people a chance. I'm moody, antisocial, stubborn, grumpy, and just generally a joy to be around.

I'm a piece of shit; a waste product, not deemed fit for anything useful.

How many 'relationships' have I sabotaged over the years? There hasn't even really been one for three or four years, since Monique. The reality of that was that she was more fucked up than I was. Finding out that she was fucking our dealer was just about the perfect ending. Since then, there's only been stoned, meaningless sex.

Worthless piece of shit couldn't even satisfy that crazy bitch.

I know why I'm thinking all this now. Ever since I saw Chantelle, I haven't been able to stop thinking about her. For fuck's sake, I'm obsessing over a nineteen-year-old girl. I've officially crossed into the dirty old man phase; there's no way she sees anything other than that. But she's not your typical nineteen-year-old who comes to work here. She's got attitude. She's lived her life; not with mommy and daddy, but out in the world. She's a survivor. I could use someone like that in my life.

The only chance of getting with her is to slip something in her drink.

It happens though. After a certain age, what the fuck does it really matter? How many women marry guys ten, fifteen, even twenty years older? That's the story, isn't it? Young, impressionable, naïve girl falls for experienced, charismatic, predatory older guy. The only problems are that she's not naïve and I'm not charismatic.

When I was seventeen, having my first sex with Laura MacPherson in her parent's basement, Chantelle was being born. She was probably potty-training when I was getting on a bus to go and live on my own. That's fucked up. But I swear there's a connection of some kind there.

I butt out my smoke and look out at the forest. Just below me, I see two people walking up a hill towards the cabins at the back of the Resort; they're hand in hand. I can't make out what they're saying, but I can hear them talking. As they pass closer to the light of one of the cabins, I see that it's Pascal and his little girlfriend. They aren't heading towards the staff cabins, and their pace doesn't look like they're just out for a stroll; so I assume they're heading for a little privacy in the woods.

"Huh, looks like Skinny's getting some action," I say to myself.

I watch them walk up the little alley where they disappear behind a cabin. They reappear again going up a little, rocky path. When they circle around another cabin, they don't come out the other side. After a few seconds, a light goes on in the cabin. I think it's Sandpiper that they're in. Little Pascal has found himself a place to take a girl. I never would have imagined it!

I have to go there.

There's a bizarre feeling of being proud that Pascal's getting himself some action. I give the guys in the kitchen a pretty hard time, but he's a good kid; kind of feels like a little brother. But the reality is that I'm old enough that he could just as well be my kid. That feeling of pride is mixed with curiosity that's nagging at my brain.

I could probably go and watch a couple of virgins try to fuck.

There's no devil on one shoulder, nor is there an angel on the other; but the voices talking to me now are very real; and they're getting louder. *It's wrong. Leave them alone. It wouldn't hurt anyone. Who gives a fuck? Record it. Go and break it up. Don't be an idiot. Everyone would go and watch; it's like free, live, virgin-porn. They want you there.*

Go up there, bust down the door, fuck them both, and show them what it's all really about.

I get up and walk inside. My hand grabs my phone. I put my key in my pocket. I stand staring at the door. A minute goes by. Two minutes. My phone buzzes in my hand. It's probably G again, seeing if I want to buy some Oxy; or maybe something else to fuck myself up. Maybe it's Shawna; she'll be fucked up and looking to get laid. I could drive over there, do a couple lines of coke and have some sloppy sex with that wasted skank.

I look at the screen. It's Chantelle.

If you're up, how about smoking a joint and talking some philosophy? Been a long day.

I look up at the door again.

sounds good when?

kitchen door in 10?

k

Chapter Fifty

SARAH

THE AMBULANCE PULLS away and leaves us standing outside in the cool, early summer, night air. Dad is on a half hour ride to a bigger hospital where they'll be deciding about the need for a bypass surgery. The doctors assured us he's stable and he'll be fine, but I'm still nervous. What if something happens in the ambulance?

"There's nothing we can do now, Sarah. It's best to head back and get some rest," Craig tells me. He must be able to read my face. I've never been very good at hiding my emotions.

"I know."

I suddenly feel completely exhausted. It's just before one. When we got to the hospital, dad was already being examined; Stanley must have been flying when he brought him here. The four or five hours since have been both torturously long, and have flown by at the same time.

"How about I drive back?" Craig suggests, putting his arm around my shoulder.

"Sure."

"How about you Telly? You OK to drive back?" Craig asks.

"Yeah, I'm good," she answers. I don't know how, but Telle has stayed calm throughout this whole thing. She was the one to call Maman and fill her in on what was happening. She brought us all coffee when she showed up. I barely know my own name at this point. Daniel was pretty calm too; he's following the ambulance to make sure everything's alright once dad gets there.

The drive back to the Resort is eerily quiet along some dark roads. After leaving the hospital and getting on the highway, we probably see two cars the whole way back. I fight the urge to shut my eyes, because I know I'll fall asleep and then I'll have to wake up again and won't be able to get back to sleep.

By the time we pull in to the Resort, I can barely drag myself back to our cabin. I notice there are a few empties on the deck as I walk up. I open the door as quietly as possible. I would like nothing more than to have a long, hot shower right now, but I'm too tired. I settle for washing my face and brushing my teeth.

"How are you doing?" Chris asks from the door of the bathroom.

"Sorry, I didn't mean to wake you."

"I wasn't really asleep. Terry and I sat and talked for a long time. I only just got into bed. Are you alright?"

"No, not really," I answer.

"He's doing OK though, right?"

"I think so. They gave him some drugs to get his blood flowing better. Then he was transferred to see about what they're planning on doing next."

At the hospital, talking to everyone, I was able to hold it together. But when Chris hugs me, and I put my head on his chest, I can't hold it in. I let the tears flow. He holds me without saying anything for a couple of minutes.

"Let's get you in bed. You need to rest. Can I get you anything?"

"I don't think so. I'm so tired, but I don't know if I can sleep."

"Well, lie down at least. I'm sure it won't take long."

"What about packing? I haven't even done anything." I haven't really had time to think about the fact that we're leaving tomorrow.

"Sarah," he says, taking my hand. "It'll get done. We have tons of time in the morning. We'll pack up after breakfast. When we leave, we'll go to the hospital and see what's up."

I'm too tired to argue about anything. I let him lead me to the bedroom. We lie down and Chris starts to play with my hair, which always relaxes me.

"How's everyone else doing?" he asks.

"Fine. Annette was a mess, but Craig, Daniel and Chantelle all seemed so calm."

"People deal with things in different ways."

"I guess. My way is just to freak out though."

"That's not true, babe. You just wear your heart on your sleeve."

"I'm sorry about earlier, I…"

"Forget it. It's nothing. You need to just rest."

A few hours ago, I was furious with Chris. It all seems so stupid now.

"What did you and Terry talk about?" I ask, starting to feel more relaxed.

"Nothing really; just kind of passing the time. We checked in on your mom to see how she was doing."

"Really?" I ask, surprised. "That was sweet. How was she?"

"I'm not too sure. To be honest, it was kind of awkward. She seemed concerned, but not panicked or anything. Terry was convinced she was just putting on a front."

"It's so weird."

"What is?"

"Just life, I guess. You can just move along and get all wrapped up in the little things of life that seem important at the time; and then, before you really know it, everything is changing."

"This sure is a year of change."

"It's scary."

"I guess you just have to focus on the stuff you can control and hope the rest of it works itself out."

"I'm not very good at that," I admit.

"You'll get better at it; we both will." He puts his hand on my stomach. "I imagine Junior will teach us both patience."

We lie like that for a while. As crazy as it sounds, with all the focus on my dad, I almost forgot I was pregnant. It feels good to lie together, with Chris's hand on my stomach, knowing that our baby is growing in there. I just want to always keep him or her that way, but I know I won't be able to. As we lie together, our breathing becoming one, I feel myself drifting off to sleep.

"This place is never going to be the same, is it?" I ask sleepily.

"No. But that isn't necessarily a bad thing. Without your dad on the Resort, your mom will be more relaxed. Your dad will be a short drive away; we can visit a couple of times in the week. And we get to create a whole new set of memories with *our* family. I bet it won't be long before Terry and Craig get married. Then they'll have some kids of their own. We'll be sitting on that beach watching them play and talking about how we can't imagine life without the kids."

As Chris paints a beautiful picture of our future lives, I drift off to sleep.

Chapter Fifty One

STANLEY

I POUR MY SECOND cup of coffee and step out onto the balcony. I should probably already be making the rounds and checking out what everyone is doing; but the peace and quiet of our balcony is too tempting this morning. It's been a real doozy of a week. After driving Stéphane to the hospital yesterday, I couldn't just leave; so I ended up staying for quite a while. Before I knew it, it was past midnight. When I left, he was about to get transferred. I think he's going to be alright, but that was quite a scare.

I've known Stéphane for twenty-five years. We're pretty close in age. He's always been fit and healthy. For goodness sake, he's married to a woman who is probably half his age; I never asked how old she was, but she's definitely young. He's been keeping up with her for five years or so; he must be in pretty good shape.

The whole darn mess has got me thinking about what Melissa said earlier this week. That could just as well have been me. It was only a couple hundred feet from where dad had his heart attack.

The screen door opens and Melissa comes out with a cup of tea.

"This is a nice surprise!" she says, sitting down next to me. "On turnaround day, you're usually running around like a mother hen by now."

"I just can't get over Stéphane. When Chris said they'd called an ambulance, I just thought of dad and that endless wait when he'd had his heart attack. There's no way I was going to watch that again."

"Yes," she answers. I'm expecting more, but I guess there isn't much to say. After a minute, she adds, "He is older than you, Stanley. And we don't really know anything about his life-style; his diet, exercise habits, or family history."

"Family history," I say, not really to her. That's at least one strike against me.

"Your life is very different from your father, Stanley; and certainly different from your grandfather. Warren told you you're in good health when you saw him in January."

Our doctor, Warren, is a friend of mine from school. It's great having a doctor who's a close friend; we can get in to see him whenever we want. It was a bit weird when I went in for my check up a few years ago. At somewhere around 50, doctors start wanting to stick their fingers up your backsides to check your prostate. That certainly took our friendship to a different place.

"I know, but how much can he really know?"

"He's very good, and you're in good health," she says in a kind way. "But maybe this should make you think of slowing down a bit. Have you given any more thought about the offer?"

"No," I answer immediately.

"Stanley, I know you read the message from Eileen."

Melissa has always been right on top of everything. There's

no point hiding anything from her; she knows what's going on faster than a rocket full of monkeys. I've spoken to some men about them cheating on their wives, and I've never really understood how they manage it. Besides thinking that's just wrong, there's no way I could ever get away with it.

"I just don't know what I'd do, Mel. And I just don't trust that man."

"It doesn't have to be him. Didn't Walter mention he might know some people you could talk to?"

As always, she knows everything.

"I don't know how serious he was. That might have been just talking."

"It doesn't seem to me that Walter Watson is the type to say something he doesn't mean," she says calmly. There's another moment of silence.

It's a cool morning, but the lake is still and the air is calm. Some guests will already be at breakfast. We get things going a little earlier today because some people like to get an early start on their travels. In truth, it helps us when people get moving quickly. There's lots to do before next week's guests start showing up this afternoon.

"If you want to talk to him, today is the perfect day," she suggests.

Melissa saying that makes me think that I've known it all along; and the reason I'm still sitting here is that once I go and say my goodbyes, I'll be faced with the chance to chat with Walter before he leaves. If I don't talk to him today, I'll have a good excuse not to talk to him for a whole year; he won't be here.

"If I do say something to him, then I'll have to meet with people and that takes time; time I don't have during the summer."

"I understand, Stanley."

I know she's got more to say, but I don't want to hear it. We sit in silence again while I finish my coffee.

"We're just getting into the swing of the summer, Mel. I don't know if I want all that distraction," I add. Despite wanting badly for the conversation to be over, I can't stop talking. "This week already made me feel exhausted. And I'm behind on lots of things; my list is so long, my pen ran out of ink."

"Why don't you hire another maintenance boy? If someone could take over some of the grass cutting and sand raking, that could free up some time. There'd still be lots for you to do; and maybe you could focus on the jobs you enjoy more."

She's so reasonable. It's very frustrating.

"Let's just say I find the time and talk to some people about selling. What would we do? I don't think I could handle doing nothing."

"Stanley, I don't want to do *nothing*. That would send us both to an early grave."

I look over at her. She's sitting back in one of our fancy chairs. The gray in her hair is becoming more prominent every year. For a long time, she coloured it; sometimes at the salon and sometimes with the cheap boxed stuff. I think she always felt a bit guilty about spending money on getting her hair done professionally. I hope I never once made her feel that way though. Now her hair is more gray than brown. She has no makeup on and she's still the most beautiful woman in the world to me. I realize that I haven't really looked at things from her point of view; I never let myself get that far. That was pretty crummy.

"What is something you'd like to do?" I ask.

She looks over at me. I know she doesn't want to push too hard with the whole selling thing. But I also now realise how much she has thought about it.

"I'd like to do a bit of travelling; nothing touristy though. I would like to spend some time and see real life in some other countries."

I nod.

"And I was thinking we could open a business. You've always been good with carpentry, Stanley. And everyone knows you can fix anything."

I smile.

"I have a bit of an idea I'd like to make something; maybe some jams. Maybe we could have a little berry farm. That would keep us both nice and busy, but not too busy. We could see how it goes. With the money that they've offered for this place, we could spend years finding out what we wanted to do without having to worry about just scraping by."

Hearing her put the words to things I've thought myself actually helps to ease my mind a bit. I'm not ready to decide anything now, but I feel better about thinking about it.

"Thank you for talking with me, darling," I say, getting up, leaning over and kissing her on the cheek.

"Thank you for listening, Stanley; and for talking with me. You know there's no rush for anything. I'm just happy you're open to thinking about it. I hope you know how much this place means to me too."

She takes my hand and kisses it. I leave her sitting on the balcony, enjoying some quiet time with her cup of tea.

When I get outside, the air is crisp and clean. After straightening the chairs on the front deck, I turn to walk towards the main lodge. My friend the deer is at the edge of the trees, motionless as a statue and looking at me. We exchange a look in the still morning air. Her ears flap away some bugs. She tilts her head to the side, with an almost questioning look. One thing you can't put a price on is a connection to something deeper. I've not always been a religious man, but there's something that surrounds me here at the Resort that speaks to me in a way I can't explain. If I didn't know better, I'd swear the forest was asking me what I was going to do. The deer turns slowly and walks into the forest, not turning around once.

Walking towards the main lodge, it's not long before the smell of breakfast hits me. People are coming and going; some are moving quickly to get things done before having to leave, others are strolling along, soaking in the last few moments of peace before returning to their work lives. I recognize the laugh before seeing who it is. Looking to my right, I see Beryl and Hugo Weber working their way up the little hill that leads to the lodge. She's laughing away at something Hugo said. As always, they're arm in arm.

Another one strolling along towards the dining room is Walter Watson with his family. I stop for a moment and look at the main lodge. It's looking a bit old from the outside; the wood paneling could use a coat for paint. Walter looks up from his conversation with his wife and waves. I wave back and start walking towards them.

Lightning Source UK Ltd.
Milton Keynes UK
UKHW01f0626290518
323380UK00001B/227/P